HEART'S SONG

A Modern-Day Rock Romance

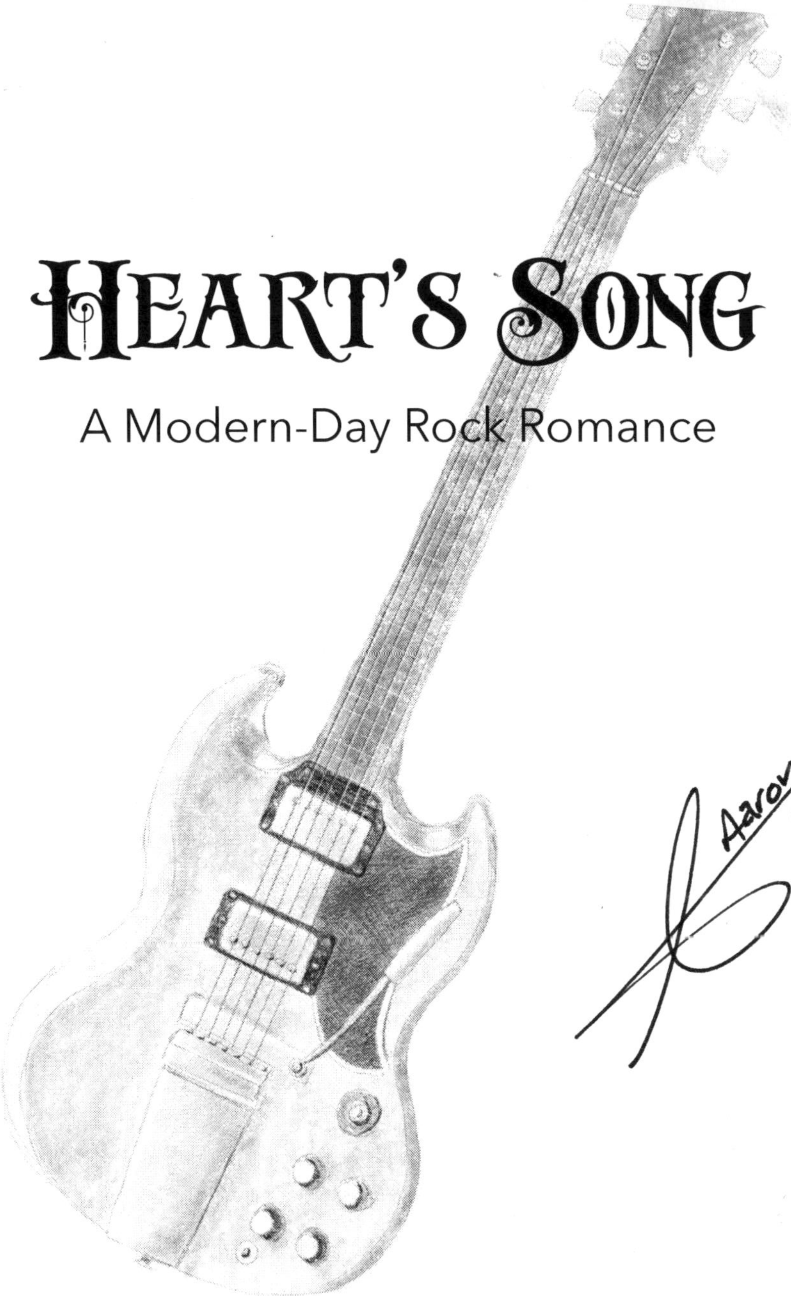

Heart's Song Endorsements:

Superbly Unique! The adage says, "The course of true love never runs smooth." This romance tale is a testament to those whose love runs a tough course. Well written, and a fast read that keeps you turning the pages!
—**Linda Wood Rondeau**, author of *Miracle on Maple Street* and *The Fifteenth Article*

Aaron Gansky and Kaye Morrison are both gifted writers. Blend their talents and you've got a recipe for some kind of wonderful! Together they've created in *Heart's Song* a world so hauntingly real and characters so achingly human, you'll forget this is fiction. I wanted to go onto Facebook—where Geoff and Emily reconnected—and friend them myself so I could go on following their lives and cheering them on.
—**Ann Tatlock**, novelist, editor, and children's book author

Wow! Just Wow! Aaron and Kaye swept me right into the middle of *Heart's Song*. It was love letters in the modern age via email, text, and video chat with some live action in between. Rock and Roll meets conservative grace. A mix of wonderfully crafted words and deep layers of real life truths. Geoff and Emily will live in the reader's heart long after they read the last line.
—**Cindy Ervin Huff**, blogger, reviewer and author of *Secrets and Charades*.

If a romance could be categorized as hard-hitting, *Heart's Song* qualifies. The story, written in the form of back and forth messages of emails and texts, shows up-and-coming rock star Geoff developing a relationship with Emily. Both come to the relationship as wounded people who want to find love on their own terms. Full of beautiful poetry and rough rock lyrics, *Heart's Song* plunges the reader into what life on the road is like as two wounded people stumble their way into love and forgiveness. For those who love an edgy romance full of brutal honesty, *Heart's Song* is at the top of the charts.
—**Carol Grace Stratton**, author of *Lake Surrender*

Heart's Song begins with a bang—and with all the resulting collateral damage. In the first few sentences, I found myself gripped, empathizing with

Emily's plight and with Geoff's frustration over not being able to "fix" things. Life is far too messy for that. The letters written back and forth between the characters gives the story a sense of reality and an immersive experience for the reader that is almost eerie. These characters became people I cared about very quickly. I have read five books by Aaron Gansky. He is a versatile author and a master in the craft of storytelling. *Heart's Song* is just the latest in a series of great stories. Please, Mr. Gansky, keep them coming.
—**Mike Apodaca**, author of *Godsend*

I haven't read a novel, let alone an epistolary novel, this good in years. After the first email from Emily to rock star Geoff, readers won't be able to tear themselves away. The two people in this romance are seemingly opposites: one comes from a stable home, the other from a dysfunctional one; one is a visionary, the other more practical; one is a believer in a caring God, the other is not. Both have been broken by the modern-day culture—Emily has been abused by a boyfriend suffering from PTSD, with physical and emotional scars to prove it; Geoff is gaining fame in his rock music world. Yet this novel breaks stereotypes: there are kindnesses and beautiful friendships in Geoff's world and loneliness and betrayal in Emily's. Both struggle to communicate with each other in this raw, honest book and fail again and again, yet persevere. And although Geoff initially rescues Emily, she is a strong woman who teaches Geoff about "blank paper," a beautiful metaphor of forgiveness and a new start. Kudos toco-authors, Aaron Gansky and Kaye Morrison.
—**Mary Langer Thompson**, *Poems in Water* (Green Fuse Poetic Arts, 2014) *How the Blue-Tongued Skink got his Blue Tongue*, (Another Think Coming Press, 2016).

Rock and roll romance is more than a subtitle: it's the perfect metaphor for *Heart's Song*, a story about the great love two people can find when they start to actually listen to each other's dreams. Rollicking us through the ups and downs of a garage band on the rise and the personal struggles of Emily and Geoff, *Heart's Song* is told through their modern-day letters to one another. These epistles are the heart of this story--a true, honest look at how love develops and perseveres through the hardest times. Once again, Gansky gives us raw emotions wrapped in beautiful language, propelling this romance into a work of literary art." –**Lindsey Brackett**, author of *Still Waters*

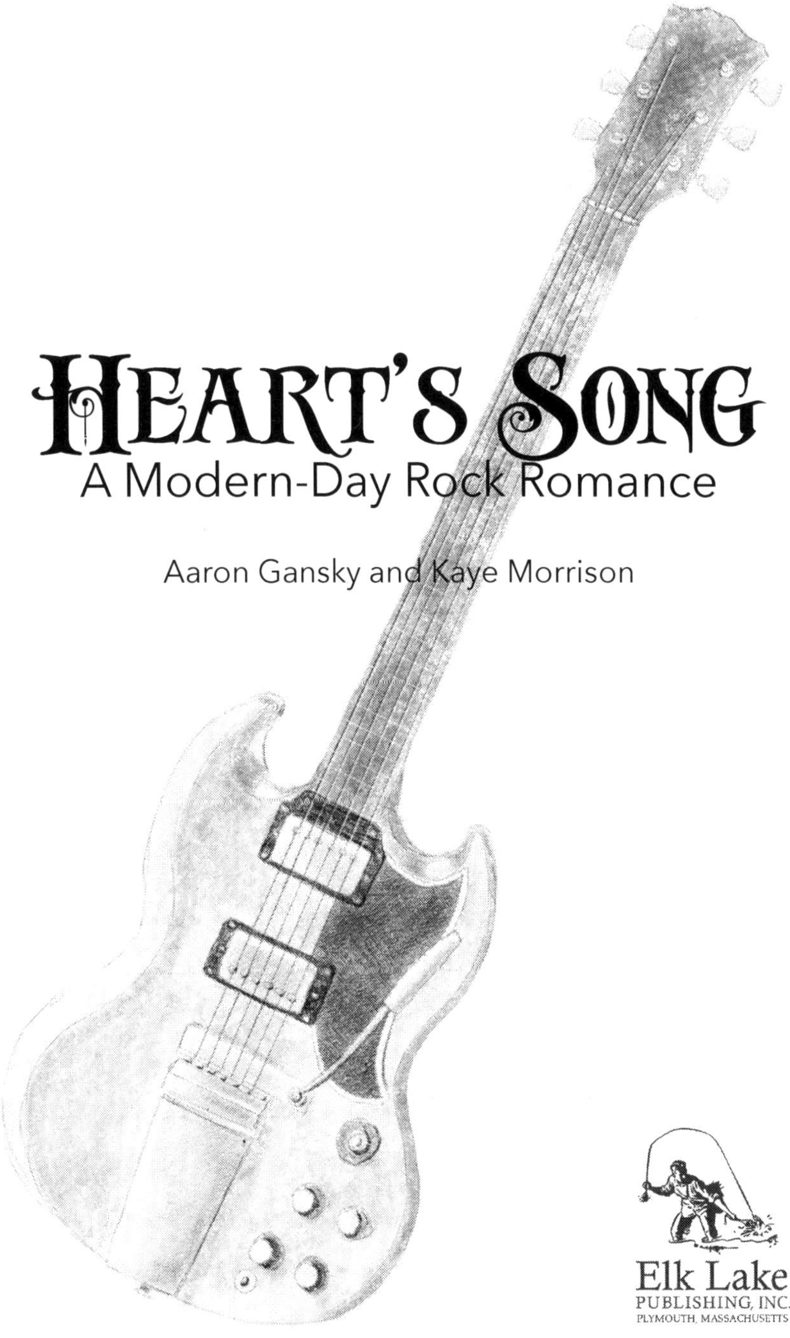

Heart's Song

A Modern-Day Rock Romance

Aaron Gansky and Kaye Morrison

Elk Lake
PUBLISHING, INC.
PLYMOUTH, MASSACHUSETTS

Cover Design: Jeff Gifford

Interior Design: Cheryl L. Childers

Editors: René Holt, Deb Haggerty

PUBLISHED BY: Elk Lake Publishing, Inc., 35 Dogwood Dr., Plymouth, MA 02360

Library Cataloging Data

Names: Gansky, Aaron and Morrison, Kaye (Aaron Gansky and Kaye Morrison)
Heart's Song/ Aaron Gansky and Kaye Morrison

372 p. 23cm × 15cm (9in × 6 in.)

Description: Elk Lake Publishing, Inc. digital eBook edition | Elk Lake Publishing, Inc. POD paperback edition | Elk Lake Publishing, Inc. Trade paperback | Elk Lake Publishing, Inc. 2017.

Identifiers: ISBN-13: 978-1-946638-24-3 (ebk.) | 978-1-946638-25-0 (POD) | 978-1-946638-26-7 (trade)

Key Words: Email, Social Media, Rock 'n' Roll, Abuse, Bands, Friendship, Romance

LCCN 2017949005 Fiction

Dedication

To all the bands I've loved before. I'd list them all, but #notenoughpaper

ACKNOWLEDGMENTS

This book has taken a very long road to publication. It began as a curious desire I had at Antioch while working on my Master of Fine Arts to write an epistolary novel. I figured a romance would be a good fit for that, an idea that was further supported after reading *Which Brings Me to You*, an epistolary post-modern romance novel written by Steve Almond and Julianna Baggott. But there was a problem: I didn't know anything about writing romance, and it became super clear that I would need a co-writer. I began the book with long-time friend Jennifer Golden, but she was not able to continue the project, so I pitched the idea to Kaye Morrison, a friend I'd met at a writer's conference some years ago. Though she was roughly the age of my mother, she knew how to write romance. Graciously, she accepted. Thanks to both of you for helping me see this through to the end. And I'd be remiss if I didn't mention my love for rock and roll. Geoff's passion in this novel is my passion, too, though I didn't sing (at least not on key). My friends Josh Fell, Matt Bodell, Kevin Felt, and Harvey Gamble all started a band called Sunblush, and they were good. I was their number one fan and followed them to all their gigs. Eventually, Joey Anderson joined the band as their drummer. I decided I wanted to be in a band too, and I tapped Matt Bodell on the shoulder to play bass for me, found a drummer in Mike Vennes, and set out to play a few gigs. We called ourselves The Sideshow Token (a name I thought, at the time, was incredibly cool). The thing holding us back? I still thought I was the singer. Once I learned my talents were not in my voice, I moved on from The Sideshow Token to a band called Knome, a band Mike Vennes had started long ago with his brother Marty and singer Justin Moen. We played quite a few shows for a number of years, but life eventually found us headed in different directions.

And then there was Gainsae: Justin Moen and I found Josh Sharp to play bass, Andy Herrick to play drums, and Bryce Odom to play guitars for us. Eventually, Josh left for normal band reasons, and my wife's cousin, Jarrod Worlitz, joined to fill in on bass. This was our core band for several years, and we weren't terrible. We were pretty good, in fact. And we're all still friends, though we don't actively jam anymore. All of this to simply say thank you to all my friends and musicians who poured into my life and fed my love of music. And especially to Justin, who keeps pushing me to pick up the old guitar again. Who knows. Maybe I will.

Book One

Cut the cord and the cornea
Everything's a perfectly clear blur
From where I bleed
This is our hate breed
—Sideshow, "Hate Breed"

Emily Amherst's Journal

Monday, January 2, 2012, 8:38 a.m.

A week of emails has brought me to this: Geoff's number in my phone and me too scared to push "send."

I never figured I'd be one to fall for another man while I was with someone else, but Barry's changed. He's not the handsome, gentle giant anymore. His time in the service, the PTSD—it's all been too much for him.

And then Geoff comes along again, a digital voice from an analog past. I was flattered he remembered me at all, but his emails this last week have awakened something in me: a desire to be cared about. Appreciated. Treated with more affection than a slap on my backside.

Barry will find out. Even if I don't save the number in my contacts, he'll look through my call history, search up the number and find Geoff's name. He won't care our relationship is based on an old friendship, or that I hadn't talked to Geoff in years until last week. He won't ask questions. He'll assume the worst.

But maybe this is what I need. Maybe it's the final straw. Maybe I shouldn't be with Barry. I've only stayed with him this long because I keep thinking he'll get better.

Swallowing, I press "send."

"This is Geoff. Leave me a message."

I pull the phone from my ear and rest my feet on the glass coffee table. Why give me his number if he isn't going to answer?

Until now, Geoff's been words on a screen—a very enjoyable, nostalgic trip. Hearing his voice made him real again, almost tangible. I want to reach through the phone and touch him, to be transported to his world of fast-living and smooth talking. I want to be anywhere away from Barry.

I didn't know him well in high school. As a senior my sophomore year, Geoff climbed high on the popularity ladder, a ladder I never climbed. I was the quiet one, content to hold the rails. I hadn't imagined he had such depth, such character, such charm.

But then, he might be faking it. Pretty easy on the internet. But we go back. He's got no reason to play the heart-hurt rock star. If he wanted to impress me, he'd shed his humility, I'm sure—play up his successes, not his failures.

I take a few steps from my couch to the kitchen. I microwave water for tea and lean against the counter.

Someone kicks my door.

My heart double-pumps. I press my hand to my chest and steady my breathing.

"Let me in, Emily." Barry. Not even nine and he's already sloshed or riding last night's bender. He kicks the door again.

I kneel and crawl to the bedroom, hoping Barry won't see me through the front window.

"Open up, Emily."

Did he drive here? The thought terrifies me.

For a moment, I consider slipping out the balcony. I might be able to climb down without Barry finding out. My downstairs neighbors would understand.

"Your car's in the lot, Emily. I know you're here."

Maybe I can wait him out. I'll be quiet. He'll get bored and go away. Maybe he'll forget why he came. Maybe he'll pass out. I could call the police.

I reach for my phone and feel my face flush. I left it on the coffee table. If I try to make my way back, Barry's sure to see me.

"Stupid girl!" He slams a meaty hand against the door. It grows quiet, and I feel the familiar tremors of someone going down the outside stairs.

I close my eyes, exhale slowly, crawl back to the living room. Still on my knees, I crack the blinds and peer out the window. Nothing. I inch to the coffee table, eyes pinned to the window. I grab my phone and stick it in my back pocket. It's still quiet outside. He must have left.

My nerves steady. I grab my purse and keys for work, taking my time. I want to be sure he's had time to leave. I might be late to work, but Frankie will understand. I send him a quick text. "*Barry's outside. Waiting for him to leave.*"

A few minutes later, he texts me back. "*Be safe.*"

Ten minutes later, I gather enough courage to crack open the door.

Barry's fist smashes the door open. It hits me in the face. "Playing possum?"

I grab my nose. Blood drips. I rush to the sink. "Get out before I call the cops."

He grabs my face hard and squeezes. "You're lucky you're pretty," he slurs. "Touch your phone and that'll change." His face pales; his eyes swell.

This is more than drunk. This is high. He's mixing his pills, or he's taking something from the street. Terror chokes me. This is how every horror story begins.

He drops his hands and races to the bathroom.

I don't wait. I snatch my purse and sprint for the door.

Barry's too fast. He grabs my hair as I pass by the bathroom and pulls me back. Vomit streaks the sink and floor. He stares at me, and his breath reeks of alcohol. "I never said you could leave." He sounds suddenly sober and scary.

"I'm going to work," I say, hoping my voice will stay calm, easing his agitated nerves. I wipe the blood off my nose and grab his wrist, try to stand up straight. Barry pulls my hair hard. I stagger back. His breath stinks of vodka and vomit.

My stomach knots, and I worry I might puke. "You're hurting me."

"You don't work Sundays."

Tears pool in my eyes, and Barry tightens his grip, bends me back. I reach out for something to steady myself. My legs burn, my back aches, my ankles twist. "It's Monday, honey."

"Don't lie to me, you stupid tramp."

My phone rings, and Barry snatches it from my pocket.

Please be Frankie.

"Morris?" he says. "I told you not to talk to him." He yanks my hair and my legs give. I fall back, but he catches me by the throat. I grab his wrist, hoping to stay up, hoping to breathe.

"You're going to LA, aren't you?"

I whisper like a mother to a child, hope my tone soothes him enough to turn me loose. "No. Geoff keeps me posted on Mark. Mark's in the hospital, remember?"

"Shut up. You made up that whole Mark story so you could chat with your little rock star, didn't you?" He presses his forehead to mine, as if he's going to kiss me or smack me. His breath is thick with bile.

In one fast motion, he slams me against the wall, his hand still clamped around my neck. Spots swirl. I can't breathe. This is it, I think. This is how I die.

Barry drops the phone and smashes it under the heel of his boot. He lifts me off the floor with both hands. My lungs burn for air.

He pulls me from the wall, swinging me around. I gasp. My lungs fill with sweet oxygen, and I realize I'm in the air. I hear the crash, feel the pain of the glass coffee table shatter into my skin, stabbing my back. His fist rushes toward me. I try to cover my face, but my arms don't move. Pain blackens my vision.

To: Geoff Morris
Emily Amherst
Tuesday, January 3, 2012, 2:23 p.m.

I was hoping I'd open my door this morning and you'd be standing there. Hope I don't sound like a whiner.

I called into work today, asked for a sabbatical. Is that possible in retail? I told Frankie, "I've worked seven years and never taken a vacation. You owe me. I've had some family issues come up, and I need a couple of weeks to recuperate."

He was quiet on the phone for a few minutes, then came back with a counter offer. Two weeks paid leave if I promise to come back. I'm such a mess right now. I need the time, so I accepted his offer.

I've tried to make small talk, convince myself I don't need help. But I do. This won't be easy to write, but here goes.

Barry beat the crap out of me yesterday. He's been angry before, but never violent toward me. He's lost his mind. He's been watching me closely since we started talking again. I knew it made him jealous, but I wasn't about to stop talking to you. You cared about me, and I needed that.

I hadn't seen Barry since he left me at the party, but he showed up sloshed yesterday morning, pounding on my door. I tried to be quiet, to lay low, hoping he'd leave. I waited and waited until I was sure he'd left. But when I opened the door to go to work, he smashed it in. I tried to calm him down, but he was drunk and high on some sort of drug. He didn't even know what day it was. He saw you had called and flipped out. He slammed me against the wall, choked me, and threw me backward onto my glass coffee table.

Things got pretty foggy. I'm not sure when he left, but I remember Olivia, my building super, holding me in her arms. She'd called the police, she said. I woke up a little later at the ER. The police insisted I press charges. I didn't … too afraid, but Olivia made sure they drew up a restraining order.

Olivia hired some folks to clean up the mess and set me up in her spare room for now.

I'm terrified. I'm a wreck. I can't stay with Olivia forever, but I have nowhere else to go. Barry doesn't like me having friends. The only one around is Daddy, and if I told him what happened, he'd kill Barry. That's not an expression. I mean murder.

Olivia said she'd get a locksmith to change the locks and install a deadbolt, but I'm not sure that will make me feel any safer.

I can't lift my arms to pull my shirt off. There's blood everywhere. You can't imagine how many stitches I have. I look like a rag doll stitched together. Sutures up my back, across my shoulder, around my jaw and forehead. Not much to look at right now.

I'd say Jennifer didn't know how good she had it. I'm sure with you, she never reeked of dry blood and broken ribs. She's an idiot for walking out on you.

I used to wonder why women who got the crap beat out of them never seemed to leave the relationship. Now I understand. Fear. Embarrassment. Humiliation. I feel so stupid.

I'm not one to beg or play the victim, but I need help. It takes a lot for me to ask. I hope you'll still take me to Seattle, get me away from here.

Please? Where are you? Are you close to Ralley? I can pay my way. I've got money in savings. If you're in town, my address is 377 Crestwood, Apartment 2.

If you can't come, I understand. I know you're busy. Probably playing another gig. I shouldn't have even asked.

I understand if you don't want to get involved. But a girl can hope, can't she?

Hoping for a knight in shining armor.
Emily

To: Emily Amherst
Geoff Morris
Tuesday, January 3, 2012, 3:18 p.m.

Please believe I'd pick you up in a heartbeat, but I can't. I'm six hours away in Los Angeles, getting things ready for our trip up to Seattle. I'm working crazy hours at Killer App to get them self-sufficient for a few weeks. But I can do something.

The important thing is getting you out of Ralley. Barry's dangerous. He won't care about new locks. You're not safe there. I want you as far away from him as possible.

I bought you a train ticket. I called Olivia at her office. She'll get you a ride to the station. Go to Amtrack to redeem your ticket. The password is Sideshow. The train leaves at 5:30. It'll take you to Union Station in Los Angeles. I'll be there to pick you up. Pack light. Yaz and I will get whatever you need once you get down here.

We've got a gig tonight, but we'll be done early. Maybe 11. Your train comes in at midnight. You can stay with me. I've got a sleeper couch with sheets from the 70s. You can have my bed. It's only a twin, and the mattress is older than me, but it'll work. If you prefer, you can stay with Yaz and his family. They've got this sweet little guest room. Queen-sized bed, new mattress, sheets with about a million-thread count. Floral down comforter, matching drapes. It's all very rock star. You get the idea.

I thought about coming up to get you, but Yaz talked me down. He knows if I drove up there, I'd hunt Barry down before finding you. And, if Barry and I ever meet, they'll be taking one of us to prison and the other to the morgue. I wouldn't be much help to you in jail.

Stop reading now. Print this message out, pack whatever you

can't live without, and have Olivia drive you down to the station. She's waiting. Finish reading this letter on the train.

By now, you should be on the train. I'll change the subject to something happier now.

Here's the story about Jennifer: I maintain everyone has an "ex." Don't get me wrong. I know people in general have more than one ex-girlfriend/boyfriend/husband/wife, whatever. Still, there's one who will forever be known as "ex." That's Jennifer for me. She's the one I'll compare every woman to until I'm dead. She's the standard, the one I loved like I didn't know it was possible to love.

We met freshman year at UCLA. Hailey was still in high school and dating someone, though I can't remember who. I'd made up my mind to move on, to give up my childish fascination with her and find myself a mature woman. I took Intermediate Poetry with a narcissistic, tactless professor. She was a poetry major. I was filling units. I figured it'd be easy (I'd been writing sonnets and sestinas since junior high), and I could pick up some chicks. So, it comes time for us to read our poems, and mine, like a lovesick puppy, was about her. And, surprisingly, hers was about me. We started talking after that—online, emails, text messages, whatever. A year later, we were engaged. Found an apartment on Anaheim Road. She moves her stuff in, and I do too.

Cue the voice from VH1's "Behind the Music." And then, tragedy struck.

I walked out for class one morning after we'd had breakfast, realized I forgot my keys, walked back in, and she was in the bathroom throwing up. Not "I'm-so-sick" throwing up, but finger-down-the-throat throwing up. It was a loud ordeal, all messy and smelly, and when she saw me come in, she screamed. Called me some pretty unladylike names, like I'd done something wrong. I let her shout and scream and hit me and cry until she finally sat on the floor and cried like an eight-year-old. I skipped class, sat with her, held her. Finally, I told her she needed help. I wanted her to see a counselor or check in someplace where they could help, you know? She disagreed.

It's a common story. Boy gets Girl. Boy catches Girl forcing herself to throw up. Boy asks Girl to get help. Girl goes crazy and leaves Boy. I'm waiting for the end of Act III where Boy gets Girl back. I can dream, right? Admittedly, my dreams have changed since Mark got sick, since I started talking with you again.

I told you the story was long. I never said it was exciting.

When you see me, you should know I've put on a few pounds since college. Not much, but enough to be a little insecure. I'll say it this way—I take my shirt off at our shows, the crowd digs it; I get some cat calls. But most nights you'll find me doing some push-ups and sit-ups, jogging through parks I probably shouldn't jog through. Seedy places, but I'm never scared. Yaz runs with me, and he's got his black belt in Kenpo Karate. He's essentially a ninja. Kenpo's ruthless. I carry non-lethal defense. The two of us make a pretty mean Batman. He's all the moves; I'm all the gadgets.

And don't feel stupid, my heart. Only stupid thing you did was hook up with Barry.

I'll see you in a few hours. I'll feel better once you're safe in my arms.

Get some rest on the train.

Love,

Geoff

To: Geoff Morris
Emily Amherst
Tuesday, January 3, 2012, 4:31 p.m.

Really? You can't wait until I'm in your arms? You hardly know me. It's been years. Don't get me wrong, I appreciate the sentiment. Nice to have someone looking out for me.

I can't believe I begged like a dog for you to help me. Can't believe I'm agreeing to this, but I am. I may be dumb, but I ain't stupid. I'll tell Daddy I'm vacationing. He hasn't been well lately, and I don't want to upset him with the truth right now. The time away will give me a chance to heal before he sees me again.

You'll know me when I get off the train. I'll be the one with the swollen jaw, busted lip, and sutures. Look for the Bride of Frankenstein, but thinner. Not the junior plenty I was in school.

Olivia helped me change and get cleaned up. She's putting a few things in a backpack for me. Insisted you told her "only what I must have." She's rifling through the mess now.

Turns out, while I was unconscious, Barry tore my phone out of the wall. The apartment's trashed. I think he was looking for my computer, but I had that tucked away in a kitchen drawer (don't ask). Then, he took off in my car. It was a junker anyway.

Doctor pulled seventeen chunks of glass from my back, mostly from my shoulder blades. Pulled each shard out with forceps. Couldn't figure out why I didn't flinch. I thought it would hurt, but it didn't. Guess I'm numb. After four hours in the ER, I walked out with 178 sutures, a broken rib, a cracked jaw, and a face fit for a Halloween mask. She gave me some pain meds, nothing narcotic, but the pills are huge.

I appreciate your offer to stay with you, but I think I'd feel better with Yaz and his wife. I can't reach my bandages, so I'll need someone to help me change them. Maybe she can help? Sweet of them to offer me the spare room, but I don't expect to stay free. I've got some money saved up, and I want to pay them rent for the time I'm there.

And I'll pay you back too for the ticket. Not sure how I'll ever be able to say thank you for your kindness and support. I'm honored you made arrangements for me.

I'll write more from the train. Hope you read this before we meet.

Thanks again.

Em

To: Geoff Morris
Emily Amherst
Tuesday, January 3, 2012, 7:31 p.m.

I'm on the train now. Can't say the seats are comfortable, but not much would be now. I stand more than I sit, pace more than I stand.

I'm still stunned Barry flipped out. Did I miss the warning signs? The red flags? He's not a violent man, even with the PTSD. He had it under control, I thought. Weekly counseling did wonders for him. But he switched doctors a few weeks back. He stopped talking as much, took to drinking. I called him on it, but he insisted his doctor said it was fine. Either he lied, or he got a terrible doctor.

But I thought I was in love, thought I could change him. How cliché, right? I'd made up my mind to fix him, but I couldn't. I can't blame Barry for what he did. I should have left sooner. It's my fault.

And then you came along. Your messages gave me something to look forward to, like I was living a fantasy. Here you were, someone special, someone going somewhere, and you were interested in me, in my boring life, my boring job, my boring everything.

I dreamed of us, wondered what it'd be like to snuggle up with you, spend a quiet evening watching TV or partying while you rocked out on stage. You weren't presumptuous; I was. Now you're riding to my rescue. I'd imagined you as a knight in shining armor; instead, you're coming with valor and chivalry as a guardian angel. Forgive my presumptuousness, please? I never wanted to be pushy.

You tried to save Jennifer too, and she broke your heart, but I won't let you down. I'm not too proud to ask for help or to take it. I may not as beautiful as her, but I know how to say thank-you.

I don't expect anything more from you. You've done enough. I don't want you to think you're obligated to take care of me. I'm not looking to nail you into a sick sort of guilt relationship. I'll get back on my feet and pay you back, if that's what you want. But "thank you" doesn't feel right. It's not enough. Instead, I'll say "I love you."

I should try to get some rest. I'll see you in a few hours.

Indebted. — Em

From the Journal of: Geoff Morris

Wednesday, January 4, 2012, 1:11 a.m.

I check my watch again and bury my hands in the pockets of my jacket. She should have been here by now.

"Settle down," Yaz says. His tattoos dance as he speaks. The woman at the information booth hasn't taken her eyes off us since we came in. Either she recognizes us or Yaz's shaved head and face tattoos frighten her. Must be new to LA. "She'll be here soon."

"One o'clock, the website said."

"Trains are like planes, man, except they don't fly."

"Thank you, Confucius."

The overhead lights glare off the beige flooring, making the whole lobby look gold.

I sink into a plush chair and put my feet up. At this hour, Yaz and I are about the only ones in the station, aside from a couple kids scattered throughout, playing on their phones.

A voice announces her train. I shoot up and stride toward the ramps.

"Man, you gotta relax," Yaz says.

"Still hyped up from the show."

He pulls the loop of his earlobe, stretched out with half-inch black plugs. "She's going to be pretty beat up, man. You gotta be ready for that. She's not going to look like she does on Facebook."

On Facebook, she's a dream, with her strawberry blonde hair and milk light skin. She's got no trace of the over-produced LA beauty. Hers is all natural, springing from her heart. "I'm ready," I say.

"Not acting like it."

People spill into the lobby, and we move through them, past the ramps, and toward the platform. The crowd parts for us—a benefit of hanging with Yaz: People leave you alone.

Emily stands near the train; her backpack sways near her knees. She can't wear it, not with what Barry's done to her.

I clench my fists.

Her eye is swelled nearly shut, her jaw crooked beneath her nose. She carries the weight of the backpack with her elbow, not her shoulder. She drags her left leg behind her a bit. She stares at the floor.

She needs a word now, some encouragement, but what do you say?

"Wow," Yaz says. He rubs his hand over his mouth.

My heart clenches like a fist. I make my way to her. Her hair falls loose around her neck and shoulders, probably to hide whatever scars she has back there. "Em?"

She smiles, but it comes out like a grimace. "My knight in shining armor." Tears strangle her voice.

Yaz takes her bag.

"Don't talk," I say. I take her arm, making sure I'm gentle and slow. I've seen this face, but not like this. I've heard this voice, but not like this. We're friends, her and me, and her pain shreds my soul. I swallow down my anger, the urge to pick her up and hold her. She doesn't need affection; she needs strength.

We walk slow, behind the crowd. I want to say something, but can't think of what, so I say, "Em, Yaz. Yaz, Em."

"I guessed," she whispered.

Yaz tosses her backpack over his shoulder. "Car should be warm. Got here twenty minutes ago."

We walk to the car through the murmur of soft conversations between travel-weary passengers and bleary-eyed friends. In the parking lot, our footsteps echo under the dim Los Angeles night.

The air's thick with smog, and I want to be back in Ralley, to drive up to Sycamore Lake and count the stars, to see my breath in the cold night air. I want to find Barry and return his favor.

I slide into the back of Yaz's car next to Emily. She rests her head on my shoulder and closes her eyes. "Let's get her set up at your place," I say. "She'll be more comfortable there, and Steph can help take care of her."

In the rearview mirror, Yaz grins. "Steph would never let her stay with you anyway."

"Chivalry, Yaz. You must be rubbing off on me."

"Mommas, lock up your daughters. Rock star's got a good streak."

I take Emily's hand and press it against my lips. "Shut up and drive. I've got work tomorrow."

To: Emily Amherst
Geoff Morris
Wednesday, January 4, 2012, 2:33 a.m.

By now you're settled into the guestroom at Yaz's. I've gotta get up in a few hours to get into work. Not used to morning shifts. I'll be sleep-drunk after tonight. Show went well. When I close my eyes, I see the lights, you know? I miss the crowds at the gigs, the speakers throbbing fatty guitar solos, and melodic bass lines laid over tribal drum beats. It's in me, music. It heals.

I was going to tell you that when we picked you up. Had my whole monolog planned out, then I saw you hobble off the train. I blanked. Anger, rage, right? I saw you, and I wanted to hurt Barry, wanted to inflict the same injuries, wound by wound, stripe by stripe. You didn't want to hear it then; I could see it in your eyes. Probably don't want to hear it now. You're like that. You're good, even when you shouldn't be. I mean that as a compliment.

You didn't blink when you saw Yaz. Even in LA, he gets looks. It's the shaved head, the tattooed scalp and face. Already, he's got plans for the little un-inked skin he's got left. But you ignored the distended earlobes, the face piercings, ignored the sideshow gaze most people give, and looked at him with innocent eyes.

Yaz isn't the only one like that in LA. Not even the only one in the band. I've got the fewest tattoos out of Sideshow (six). Los Angeles isn't Ralley, but you get that. Might be a bit of a culture shock. Was for me. Not sure I've completely adjusted to LA living. Not sure I want to. Everybody thinks they're somebody. This city breeds a culture of self-importance. But there's something exhilarating about it. You don't like it, but you want it, you need it. You catch yourself saying absurd things like, "What do you mean you don't have gluten-free soy lattes?!"

Long story short, I can't sleep. I'm sitting here, guitar in lap, and I can't get your face out of my head. Here's the crazy thing, your face, the one I'm remembering, isn't from tonight. It's the one a few years back, my senior year in college. I made it back up to Ralley and bumped into you at Frankie's. You were checking groceries then, so I guess it was before you finished up your schooling and took over the office portion of the store. There you were at the front, rolling melons across a scanner, and the light from the front window got tangled up in your hair, like sunlight swimming through amber ale. I'm sad I was too caught up in my life to take the time to get to know yours.

What is it about your innocence that drives me crazy? Even now, sunk deep under the bruising, you still have an appealing purity. Don't see much of it here in LA. Don't lose it. When people criticize you for it, or try to take advantage of you (they will, you invite it with those Bambi eyes), keep your chin up and send them to me.

I'll call Hailey after work tomorrow, solidify plans about the trip, see how Mark's doing. Then, I'll stop by Yaz's. We bowl Wednesday nights. It's a thing with us. Not sure if you're up to it in your condition, but you're more than welcome to come along.

Love,

Geoff

PHONE TRANSCRIPT

Wednesday, January 4, 2012, 6:00 a.m.

EMILY AMHERST: I'm sure you're sleeping, but I couldn't get you out of my head. Not sure why.

EMILY AMHERST: Little girls dream of meeting their hero. This wasn't what I'd dreamed. But you and Yaz are the two most handsome men I've laid eyes on, tats and all. The outside's not important to me. You two have gentle hearts and touches. Thank you.

To: Geoff Morris
Emily Amherst
Wednesday, January 4, 2012, 1:00 p.m.

Please save me some embarrassment and tell me Yaz's wife's name. You guys call her "girl." She's a goddess, but I'm betting that's not her name.

She's taken me under her wing and become quite the caregiver. She swooped right into nurse mode when I arrived. I laughed when she shut you guys out of the bedroom. The look on your faces when the door slammed: priceless.

She started the shower and cut my shirt off with scissors. It was old anyway, and I doubt I could get the blood off. She pulled a giant trash bag over my head and neck to keep the water off the sutures. She scrubbed the dried blood off my arms and wept. I did too.

Fluffy bed or not, I didn't sleep well. It's hard to lie down. I'd give odds the "goddess" made a hundred trips downstairs to peek in on me. She couldn't have slept much herself. Yaz and the Mrs. are awesome. I see why you love them.

I woke up about 3:00 to find a small lump at the foot of my bed. Sometime during the night, their son, Tripp, crawled under the covers next to me. When his mom came in to get him, he told her he wanted to make sure the hurt lady was okay. Sweet. I probably scared the poor kid to death.

This family makes me miss mine. When Mom died, Dad sank into a deep depression. He was empty without Mom. His heart started giving him problems. I worry about him. I don't know what it'd do to him if he saw me like this. I miss the security of family.

The goddess brought me breakfast in bed this morning. There's no expression for the agony of moving. I didn't expect to hurt this bad a day later.

Yaz's wife wanted to toss my shirt from yesterday, but I hung on to it. Silly as it seems, I can smell your cologne on it. Helps me feel a bit of that family security. Guess you think I'm weird. Too bad.

Guess Seattle's out of the question. When I mentioned it last night, Yaz's wife said, "Over my dead *$#*@! body." Yaz added his thoughts, which I shouldn't repeat. Filthy mouths, stainless hearts. She insisted I stay with her so she could help me heal. Can't expect you to watch over me while you're gigging.

Seeing you again last night, I remembered your chiseled face and huge green eyes. I remembered the tan skin and bulky arms. But your smile when we got in the car made me hurt a little less, melted that innocence you like so much. I can see why you've got women throwing themselves at you.

Can't decide if I'm flattered or embarrassed about the thought of me keeping you up. I hope it's because you're excited to see me, but I'm afraid you're repulsed by me. I wanted our reunion to be something better than this. When I'm better, can we have another chance? Reunite again for the first time? A fresh start?

In a week of email, you've given me six years of happiness. I'm trying not to fall for you, but my heart turns to you no matter how hard I twirl the wheel the other way. Is it because you're a star? Because you're devilishly handsome? Because you're a tender and gentle soul?

Olivia overnighted me a new phone. Told me I didn't have to pay her back so long as I called her first and kept her posted on how I'm doing.

Don't think I'm up for bowling. I can hardly get out of bed. But maybe we can bowl on the Wii over here? I'd kill for some Wii bowling, a Coke Zero, and a Hershey Almond Bar.

I got in touch with Hailey today, finally. No news on Mark,

but she says he wants you to play "Time Passin' Man." I'm guessing there's a story there. I didn't tell her about this mess. No need right now. It's not about me. Told her I'd had some surgery (which I kinda did), and I couldn't really travel. Maybe you and her can have a nice night together up there. Buy her dinner. Take her mind off Mark. I'll try not to be jealous.

I've written a novella. I should hush so you can work. Don't wanna get you fired.

Thank you again for all you have done.

Waiting to hear from you.

Em

P.S. 483-401-0978—That's my number.

PHONE TRANSCRIPT

Wednesday, January 4, 2012, 2:19 p.m.

EMILY AMHERST: Hello?

GEOFF MORRIS: Hey. It's Geoff.

EMILY AMHERST: I know. Recognized the voice. You called.

GEOFF MORRIS: Had a break here at work. Going to be a long day. Hoping to be back in time to bowl. How you feeling?

EMILY AMHERST: It hurts from toes to head and everywhere in between.

GEOFF MORRIS: Still trying not to be angry about the whole thing.

EMILY AMHERST: I'm fine, Geoff.

GEOFF MORRIS: You're not. Listen, I'm sorry. I'll settle down.

EMILY AMHERST: You're cute when you're angry.

GEOFF MORRIS: Yeah? Get used to it, Heart. I'm going to be cute for quite a while.

EMILY AMHERST: Thanks, Geoff. For everything. It was hard to sleep last night, but knowing I was safe helped me catch a few winks.

GEOFF MORRIS: I'm glad. I finally crashed around three. Up at five. At work around six.

EMILY AMHERST: Sounds like a long day.

GEOFF MORRIS: Thanks for giving me your number. Hearing you're okay will make the day easier. I'll try to get back to you in a bit, maybe carve out another ten minutes to get back to your message. I'll tell my boss it's work related or about the band. He's a fan, so that's cool.

EMILY AMHERST: Your boss is a fan of Sideshow? Must be nice.

GEOFF MORRIS: It's got its perks.

EMILY AMHERST: I like your letters. Let's keep writing them, okay? Even though we're only a few blocks away.

GEOFF MORRIS: I'll write every day if you want.

EMILY AMHERST: You're too good to me.

GEOFF MORRIS: About time someone was.

EMILY AMHERST: You better get back to work, Dimples. Don't want to get you in trouble with the boss. Don't want you to lose a fan.

GEOFF MORRIS: Take care of yourself, Heart.

EMILY AMHERST: I will. The time away is good. Helps me clear my head. Writing helps, too.

GEOFF MORRIS: Then get writing, baby.

G

To: Emily Amherst
Geoff Morris
Wednesday, January 4, 2012, 4:26 p.m.

Good to hear your voice at work today. Still here, but on my "lunch" break, ten and a half hours after clocking in. Didn't want to rush it, you know? Drove through a little Cuban place. Ever had fried plantains? If not, I'm bringing you some tonight. One of the nice things about LA: You never have to drive more than a few miles to sample the world's cuisines.

Glad to hear Yaz and Steph (Yaz's wife, if you haven't figured it out yet) are taking care of you. I knew they would. She was a nurse for a bit, back before Tripp came along. Besides, they've always taken care of me.

I didn't have the whole "family" thing going for me growing up. I could sit here and gripe about my drunk of a father and a mom who loved being miserable more than she loved me. Her goal was to make everyone in the house regret knowing her, hence, the drunk father. That's why I ran with Mark and Hailey. They had family—real family, and I was a part of it. Honestly, if not for them, I've no idea where I'd have ended up.

I tell you this because of Barry. Whatever it is between us, I gotta be up front. You need to know this now about me, and if you want to stop talking, I get it. But I'm hoping that innocence I see in you is equal parts mercy and hope. If it is, maybe you can forgive me.

So here it is. I used to drink pretty heavy. Came by it honest, from my pops. He drank to make life with Mom bearable. Eventually he figured it was a temporary solution to a permanent problem; he got wise and left me with her. I was eight. Had my first beer at nine. By high school, I'd drain tequila bottles after school.

Here's the good news: I haven't had a drop in years. Yaz got in my ear about it early on. The man speaks with the voice of my conscience. He sat me down with Mark, of all people, and had this intervention thing. Set me up with AA, all that. Glad he did, too. I'm a different person because of Mark, because of Yaz and Steph.

Steph, as you've discovered, is amazing. I get why Yaz is a rock and roll mercenary. I'd be too. His family is way better than any gig.

I like to roll over there on my days off and chill. We'll watch movies, play games, all that domestic crap. May not fit your idea of rock 'n' roll, but we've had some amazing writing sessions there late at night, Tripp all snuggled into bed, Yaz and I tearing it apart on our acoustics, Steph curled up at the foot of the couch, leaving the dishes for another day. Those nights, those are as close to Nirvana as I'll ever know (pun intended).

I could tell you Tripp stories to make you laugh and some to make you cry. Nothing as emotionally provocative as a two-year-old's mood swing, you know?

And if you dig my scent that much, flattering as it is, I've plenty of dirty laundry you're welcome to at any time.

I have to echo Yaz and Steph here about Seattle. I was hoping you weren't as bad off, maybe you exaggerated. Mom liked to make Everests out of ant hills. I've learned to underestimate. You got off the train, and I realized how wrong I was. I could've told you then you wouldn't be riding up with us. Probably a good thing. We're rolling through Ralley, and I don't want any chance of you mixing it up with Barry again.

I figured you'd be safe with me and Yaz. Gentle as he is, he's got a killer underneath the tats. Couple years back, he and Steph were having troubles. Had a mean drunk at a show try to mix it up with him. Yaz beats the guy within an inch of his life and makes him beg Yaz to finish it off, all in fifteen seconds. Most amazing thing I've seen. Full-on ninja. Spent a few weeks in jail for it, but I learned something that night: Don't mess with a black belt.

TBH, your kind words make me a little uneasy. I've got this thing about people complimenting me. Ask Yaz. He'll talk up my riff one night, and I'll act like he told me my cat died. Not sure why. Some crazy Freud stuff. Probably has to do with my mommy dearest. I crave recognition and praise, but when I get it, I get embarrassed and insecure, like people are taking shots, like they're being sarcastic. I'm a head case. No worries, though. I'll work on it.

As for the meeting re-do, it's a promise. Whenever you feel up to it. Wii bowling sounds great. Maybe even some "Call of Duty" on the Xbox?

Hailey's not returning my calls. Must be too busy or too worried about Mark. In my head, I see him laid up in bed, watching TV, counting his final hours in *Friends* reruns, Hailey by his side. Murderous images, depressing as all get out, but can't shake them.

"Time Passin' Man" was my first radio hit. Can't believe he remembers it. Must have written it when I was eighteen. Wrote it when I was heavy into Soul Asylum and Screaming Trees.

I doubt Hailey will let me take her out for dinner. Can't see her leaving Mark's side. But I'll try to talk her into it. She needs her mind on something other than Mark, needs a break.

See you soon.

Geoff

To: Geoff Morris
Emily Amherst
Thursday, January 5, 2012, 2:00 a.m.

Had a great time tonight. Can't believe I got to spend the whole evening with you. When you left, I immediately moved to the computer to write you. Wanted to call, but figured you'd crashed out already. You were falling asleep between frames and bad jokes. Already miss your warped sense of humor. You're all kinds of sick. I think Yaz and Steph are still hurting from the spanking we gave them bowling. Never bowled from a couch before. Should be an Olympic sport. I'm already feeling better, though you and Yaz made me laugh so hard I nearly split my sutures.

Steph got me a late appointment with her family doctor to get some antibiotics. She's not happy I'm running a slight fever. Doc asked me what happened, and I lied. Told him I was in a car accident. "Hate to see the car," he said. I couldn't go over the whole thing again. I hate lying, hate he made me do it. Hope God will forgive me.

The doctor gave me some hefty antibiotics, and I think they're helping already.

BTW, don't be smart. I was trying to be tender when I told you about the shirt. You blew it off and made some crack about dirty laundry, even after I told you Barry made me do his. I know you were joking, but it hurt a little. If it's all the same to you, I'll keep this one shirt and you can manage the rest.

I'm disappointed I can't go to Seattle. I wanted to see Hailey and Mark. Really, I wanted to spend time with you. Still, I was a bit surprised when you said you'd planned on taking Hailey out. I understand a nice dinner to take her mind off Mark, but how far do you plan on going to distract her? She's in a hard place now, but Hailey doesn't change. She's sweet, but she can be a hag. Maybe taking her out isn't a good idea. How about supper in the cafeteria? If you do take her out, may thoughts of me haunt your evening (hee hee).

Focus on Mark when you're there. Tell him I'm thinking of him and praying for him. Tell him I love him and I miss him.

I found a local classic rock station on the radio. Called the request line out of curiosity and asked for "Time Passin' Man." The guy said, "Sure, local favorite." Had no idea you were a "local favorite." The song was beautiful. Guess I'll be listening to the radio a bit more often.

And I'm a little concerned about this date your band is playing at Mitch's. I got the distinct impression you and Yaz have plans of visiting Barry. Between your email earlier and the testosterone-filled conversation tonight, it sounds like you guys have a plan. But I can fight my own battles. As much as I appreciate your intentions, I don't need you confronting Barry. I know Yaz has his black belt, but Barry's an ex-marine. He's been in war. He's a trained killer. You saw what he did to me. I don't want either of you hurt.

Even if you did handle him, you'll wind up in jail. I can't have you in jail. I need you here. I don't want you making a huge mistake on my part. Don't do anything that will jeopardize the band's chances of making it.

I'll confront Barry on my own terms. Found out earlier today he emptied my savings account. $40,000 gone. I'd been saving for years to buy a cabin up at Willow Creek. I knew I never should have given him access, but when he got back from the war, and he asked me to add him to my account, I couldn't say no. I felt so bad for him, and stupid me, thought it might mean he'd want to get married sooner rather than later.

I'm going to talk to him, going to demand my money back. Don't worry. I'll be smart. I'll do it at Mitch's so he won't try anything funny, not with so many witnesses and security around. You guys rock the stage and let me handle my affairs. I'm sure when he sees me, he'll sober up and come to his senses. He's not unreasonable.

I called a lawyer, though, in case he doesn't want to give the money back. My lawyer contacted the police. We'll all be there Friday. I'll let the long arm of the law punch Barry for me.

Steph's got a friend who needs help managing inventory for his business. It's a paperless company, and he said he'd be fine interviewing me on the phone. I can work from here for now. If things work well, it might turn into something a little more permanent. I haven't ruled out moving back to Ralley, but I want to keep my options open. Plus, it'll give me a bit of money to pay rent while I'm staying with Yaz and Steph.

Okay, sweet rocker, it's bedtime. Will I see you before you leave? Better yet, are you still speaking to me after my speech? I'll keep the shirt with you on it next to my pillow (don't burst my bubble). Cool thing is, your song is playing on the radio. Night, Dimples.

Love, Em

From the Journal of: Geoff Morris

Thursday, January 5, 2012, 6:51 a.m.

After taking a ration of grief from Steph, I push Em's door open. I'm gentle, a cat coming in unnoticed. Takes a certain amount of restraint on my part. Not used to sneaking around, tip-toeing, ninja walking. There's a charm to living alone, an unabashed selfishness that never requires apologizing. But I need to treat Em better.

I'm irritated with her letter. You think you get someone, you think they get you, and then you get the message. She's read my messages, but she hasn't heard my voice. Not her fault, I tell myself. Too much going on in her life. It's my fault. I wasn't clear enough. Story of my life. I've made a habit of sticking feet in my mouth. Looks like I'm still good at it.

But I have to see her before I leave, have to talk to her. It's not even seven. I left Yaz's just over five hours ago. Em's asleep in the guest room. Tripp's curled up at her feet like a cat. The room smells like some cross between hospital and hotel, freshness mingling with sterility. She's got a bottle of the antibiotics sitting on the table next to her. Pills look big enough for elephants.

Tripp stretches, rolls over, sticks a thumb in his mouth. Em's sleeping on her stomach. No wonder, with gouges like canyons on her back. I see those scratches, those bloody grooves, and I think about what I've heard of her Jesus, the whips on his back, the flesh all torn up. My uncle told me these stories, stories of Roman torture, a cat of nine tails. At least Em got bandages; she got medical care. She'll get better.

I kneel beside her, hope my presence here isn't too forward, doesn't embarrass her. Knowing her, it will, but she'd kill me if I left without saying good-bye.

The nascent sunlight spills in through the blinds, gets caught up in her hair like water on spider webs. I push it behind her ear and run my thumb over her cheek until her eyes open. She blinks a bit, moves to sit.

"Don't get up," I say.

She pulls the covers over her back, up to her neck. "Everything okay?"

I take my hand away. "We're leaving. I know you're tired. Steph wanted to let you sleep. Almost didn't let me in."

Em smiles. "How'd you get past the warden?"

"Called in a favor from Yaz. He looks at her and says, 'Girl, you want to be the one to tell her we're halfway to Ralley when she gets up?'"

Em giggles. "You guys are too much." She looks at me hard. "You're mad, aren't you?"

"I'm frustrated," I say.

"My letter?"

"Nothing to worry about," I say. She doesn't need me heaping grief on her before I roll out. "Didn't have time to write you back this morning, but I'll send you a message when we're on our way."

"Why don't you just call? Can I call once I'm up?"

I've worried her. I knew this was a bad idea. "Listen, Em. I suck at face-to-face. Not sure if you picked that up. My words come out better when I have a chance to think about them."

"Not always," she says.

I can't read her face. She's joking, has to be, but I can't see it in her eyes. "I want to read your letter again, make sure I get what you're saying. And I want to think about what I'm going to say. You can call after you have a chance to read the message."

"Why can't you just talk now?"

I've upset her. I want to kiss her, put her at ease, but the last thing she wants is someone forcing physical affection on her. We spent half last night sitting close, arms touching, fingers brushing tentatively, exploring, flirting with hand-holding, but neither of us acted on it. It's like we've died and woken up as high school freshmen. Instead, I brush my fingers on her cheek. That should be enough, should settle her nerves, but not threaten her. "No time. Tony's behind the wheel. Engine's running. Bus is packed. Band's drumming fingers waiting for me. Supposed to be driving right now."

"They can't wait five minutes?"

"What I have to say isn't a five-minute conversation."

"Well, now I'm worried, Dimples."

"Hakuna matata, Heart."

Her hand slithers out from beneath the covers. She takes my face in her hand. "Promise I didn't upset you."

"It's nothing. I wanted to say good-bye is all."

Her hand is warm, her thumb nearing my lips.

It's all I can do not to turn and kiss it.

"I don't want to say good bye," she says.

"Better than not saying it."

"Is it?"

I grin. "I'm coming back. It's just a week."

"I'm going to miss you."

"I already miss you," I say.

The bus honks, and I roll my eyes. Her hand's still on my face, and I don't want to move.

Tripp sits up, looks around, then collapses back on the bed.

I stand up, take her hand in mine, give it a gentle squeeze. "Sleep well, Heart. I'll be back soon. Rest up. Get better." I lean over, lips just over her cheek. Anyone else I'd kiss and take off, but Em needs something more, something less. "I love you," I say.

Before she can respond, I walk out the door. Guilt slaps me hard. I've been too rough on her. She'll worry all day. On my way out the front, I grab Steph. "I need to send her flowers, don't I?"

"She likes daisies," Steph says.

"I know. I'll order some on my way out."

"Same day delivery will be expensive," she sings.

I shake my head and sigh. "Should have ordered them last night."

G

To: Emily Amherst
Geoff Morris
Thursday, January 5, 2012, 11:11 a.m.

Four hours down, two to go before we hit Ralley. We stopped for lunch somewhere in Fresno. Little Café here off 99. Picked it because it's got a sign that advertises Wi-Fi.

I want to say this first: Tell me about this cabin in Willow Creek. Close your eyes; go there in your mind. Tell me everything. What's it look like? Smell like? How big is it? How is it furnished? Where in the mountains? What's the weather outside. Dream Emily, and tell me your dream. I want to know everything.

I want to be honest. Your letter has unintentionally embarrassed me in a number of ways. First of all, a classic rock station playing my music? I wrote it ten years ago, yeah, but, wow—classic?

I appreciate your candor and ferocity of spirit, but maybe you misunderstood. Yaz and I, we're not hunters. We're finishers. If Barry comes knocking, we'll knock back. But we're not going to hunt him down. We talk about it, sure, but we're not criminals. I'll admit, a part of me itches for him to do something, for him to push, just push, just a little. I never hit first. I won't start it, but I'll finish it until it's good and done. Sorry if that's TMI.

About the lying, here's how I see it. My uncle was a church kinda guy. We talked about stuff like this. If he were alive, he'd say Barry put you in a spot. It's his fault, not yours. If God's going to judge someone, it'll be him. At least, in a perfect world. Not even sure I believe in God. Don't want to if I'm going to feel guilty over doing something as simple as telling a white lie.

I'm a little disappointed you'd call Hailey a hag. Feels rude. I remember her as a sweet girl, gentle and caring, kinda like you.

Sure, she played a guy or two, but who didn't? It was high school. It was college. Why're you so vicious toward her all of a sudden? Her brother's dying, and you're calling her a hag. Not to be critical, but I expected more from you. Don't let your insecurity kill your innocence.

You got this purity, this sweetness, this "do what's best for everyone else" attitude, and TBH, it's sexy on you. That's what you should be wearing, that selfless concern. Wear it like it's a Grammy dress. But wearing this venomous name-calling? I'd rather see you naked (pun intended).

Good luck on the job. Sure you'll nail the interview. I'd write more but I'm frustrated still.

Not mad, frustrated.

All love,

Geoff

To: Geoff Morris
Emily Amherst
Thursday, January 5, 2012, 5:00 p.m.

Guess you told me what's what. But you don't have all the facts. I'll forgive you for slamming me unmercifully, but only because I haven't given you all the information. I'll do that soon, but first things first.

The huge box of flowers was the most wonderful gift I've ever gotten. How'd you know I love daisies? Did Steph let it slip? No one's given me flowers before. I was dumbfounded. When I saw the box, I nearly fell over. I'd say you're a romantic. You knocked my socks off.

About Hailey and name calling, I should have explained better. Hailey and I are friends, no matter what I call her. We slept over at each other's houses, sneaked out together in high school, roomed together in college. But she hurt me often. Never more than before she moved to Seattle. Our relationship is strained, to say the least. I don't want to get into all the details here because it'd feel like I was taking shots at her, and you're right. She doesn't deserve that now.

I don't like how she treats the men she dates. I don't like how selfish she is. She knows this. I call her a hag; she calls me a goody-two-shoes, a boring saint. It's in fun—most of the time. We love each other, but there are some wounds you can't see on the surface. I guess some of it is childish resentment. In high school, she was the pretty one, the skinny one, the popular one. I was "Hailey's friend," never more. I lived in her shadow. I know I sound jealous, but I'm not.

Hailey knew how I felt and took pleasure in rubbing it in. I'm not being overly sensitive. Even Mark and her parents saw it. Whenever

Hailey got a call from someone cooler than me, she'd leave me at her house. She'd find some cutting remark to make on her way out. And Mark would be there to pick up the pieces. He's the one who called her "Devil Hag." Not me.

He'd end up taking me down to The Factory, buy me a pizza, and insist I not let Hailey treat me like that. Can you imagine? A senior taking a dumpy sophomore out for pizza? Mark had the greatest heart. It kills me not to be able to see him now.

As we got older, I kinda felt sorry for her. She uses people until she gets what she wants, then dumps them. She's lonely and unhappy. I've seen her good and seen her bad, and I love her despite the flaws. Forgive me for calling her a hag. I shouldn't have.

I'm worried about you. I don't want you to fall for her and leave me, don't want you to get hurt by her. She'll play helpless, but she's not. If you want to take her out, I can't stop you. If you do, please be careful. Okay?

And I hope your "do what's best for everybody is sexy on me" wasn't a line. You made me blush and rebuked me in one graceful statement. I'm still blushing.

I apologize for assuming you and Yaz would intentionally pick a fight. As long as we're talking about what's sexy on us, your "finish it and finish it right," is smoking hot on you. But I can't bear to think that I'm causing you trouble. You've turned into something special (maybe it's what you said on your way out the door this morning), and I don't want to lose it. Barry doesn't know I'm here. Let's keep it that way. Let me handle him. I'll "finish him right." You worry about music, worry about making fans and getting signed. I'll handle the rest.

And what I thought was a classic rock station turned out to be "Yesterday's Favorites and Today's Top Hits." Nice to know where I can turn to hear your voice before I drift off to sleep at night.

You want to know about the cabin in Willow Creek? Mom and Dad bought a strip of land on Rickers Mountain just outside of Salyer, CA. It's in the middle of the Shasta National Forest, called Willow Creek. It's gorgeous. Sometimes I drive there to hide. Daddy always called me a tree hugger. His fault, though. He taught me outfitting skills for the mountain and the river.

I love Willow Creek because there's no place else to go but up. You can't climb any higher on the mountain once you crawl out on Moses Rock. I've been saving money to buy the cabin on the edge of the property. Nothing better than sitting on the side of a mountain peering into the sky. The clouds are at an arm's reach. It's the door to heaven. When I'm on Moses Rock, only clouds separate me and God. I can suck in the cool air and fill my lungs until they ache. A slow exhale raises chills on my arms. The redwoods are immeasurable, unimaginable. In the quiet, you can hear the animals breathing, almost feel their warm breath on your back. Light peeks through leaves and renews your spirit. Daisies grow wild in the fields and rocks. They've got their own story.

Nothing matters there. It's somewhere between fiction and reality. No one can touch me, can hurt me—not even Barry.

I don't understand why you don't believe in God. I know you didn't grow up in church learning about Jesus like I did, but maybe if you'd been to Willow Creek, you'd believe. Hard to see His creation, breathe in His air, and not believe. Someone had to make the trees and daisies, the rocks and river, the squirrels and bears. He birthed this planet, and even more amazingly, gave us forgiveness—which is why I don't hate Barry, why I still love Hailey.

Lean back and close your eyes. Imagine the cabin on a four-acre tract of land on the north side of Willow Creek. It climbs the side of Rickers Mountain. You can take a car up to Jerrod's Point, but from there you man your backpack and boots and hike. Forty minutes up, and you come to a clearing on the top of the mountain. Two bedrooms, one bath, small kitchenette. No power. Sale price, $250K, and worth every penny. I own an acre of it, but I want the other three.

The folks could only afford one tract twenty years ago. When Mom died a few years back, Daddy signed it over to me. He said, "Mom would want to be close, and there's no place closer to heaven than Willow Creek."

Call me selfish, but I've never told anyone about this land. It's always been my spot, my place, my piece of heaven. But now I want to share it with you. When you get back, we can drive up there. I guarantee you'll get a song or two out of it.

The cabin's pretty beat up now. The wraparound porch is weathered, and the handmade swing is rusted and warped. It hangs over the edge of the mountain, held up by equal parts rock and sky. When I buy it, I'm going to fix it up. Rebuild the porch and swing, plant a garden, sauté fresh zucchini in garlic and onion and chives I've grown out back. I'd eat outside in the crisp air—the sharp scents of pine and cut grass. I'd bring in cushy pillows to lie on beside the fire. I'd put a window by the bed, overlooking the mountain, and stare out until the sunset and the sky turned black and the stars popped on. You've never seen so many stars. I'd burn candles and oil lamps to keep the light tender. I'd have two dogs and a man who loved me. I'd can my vegetables and make jams and jellies and syrup from my fruit. Sounds silly, but you asked me to dream.

This is dumb. Why am I dreaming when Barry stole my money? I'll never get the cabin now.

When you think of me tonight, imagine me selfless and sexy, not selfish and petty. Tonight, instead of the cabin, I'll dream of a tender touch brushing the hair from my face, a gentle whisper waking me, and someone pressing their calloused finger against my lips and telling me they love me.

Tear it up tomorrow night, Dimples.

Miss you already.

Em

P.S. About the "I love you." Ditto.

PHONE TRANSCRIPT

Thursday, January 5, 6:19 p.m.

EMILY AMHERST: You got my message?

GEOFF MORRIS: All ten pages.

EMILY AMHERST: Stop it. It wasn't that long.

GEOFF MORRIS: Maybe double spaced.

EMILY AMHERST: Well?

GEOFF MORRIS: I wanted to hear your voice again. You've got that southern drawl of yours. Durned if it don't charm the spit right outta me.

EMILY AMHERST: Give it up, Dimples. You're a Left Coaster. You'll never get the accent or vocabulary right.

GEOFF MORRIS: Still, your voice.

EMILY AMHERST: Says the famous singer.

GEOFF MORRIS: Not famous yet, Heart. We've got a show tonight.

EMILY AMHERST: Another one? I didn't think you had one set up. Thought you were just going to get settled into the hotel.

GEOFF MORRIS: It's at the hotel. We're playing in the bar. Some unplugged stuff, background music really. Maybe a couple covers. Whatever strikes us—Nirvana, STP, Soundgarden, the classics. It's not paid. We're doing a favor for Riley Nelson.

EMILY AMHERST: From high school? Sweet kid with goofy hair?

GEOFF MORRIS: That's the one. We were in choir together. He's managing the Sunrise Express. Hooked Tony up with our rooms. Got us a good deal, so he called in a favor.

EMILY AMHERST: Look at you and Yaz. Chivalry is cute on you.

GEOFF MORRIS: I'm going to write you back.

EMILY AMHERST: Should I be worried?

GEOFF MORRIS: No.

EMILY AMHERST: I wish we could talk more. These five-minute phone calls and five-page messages are killing me.

GEOFF MORRIS: Me too. I miss you.

EMILY AMHERST: Ditto.

GEOFF MORRIS: I'd rather be Wii bowling with you.

EMILY AMHERST: You're a goofball.

GEOFF MORRIS: A goofball rock star with a gig lined up. Yaz is giving me the look.

EMILY AMHERST: Go rock the Sunrise Express, Dimples.

GEOFF MORRIS: Get better, okay?

EMILY AMHERST: I will.

G

To: Emily Amherst
Geoff Morris
Friday, January 6, 2012, 2:08 a.m.

I was going to call after our gig, but I got to talking with Riley. He had some drinks. I had a Coke Zero. Caught up on the last few years. He's married. Has two kids and one more on the way. Sunrise treats him well. Good for him.

As tired as I am, I'm getting the itch, getting antsy. Haven't been this excited since our first tour. We've got good fan support. Tony sold out most our shows, even a few after-parties. Looks like a fun, busy trip. We held a couple tickets for Hailey and Mark (terminal optimism, maybe, but a guy can hope).

You honestly think Steph had to tell me? Remember watching Tombstone over at Mark and Hailey's? Doc Holiday shoots Johnny Ringo in the head and says, "You're no daisy. You're not a daisy at all." You lean over, whisper in my ear, tell me daisies are your favorite flower. Here, a man's been shot in the head and you're telling me about your favorite flower. The whole thing sounded incongruous—it stuck in my head, a bullet in my brain. I've never forgotten.

I still say you're being harsh on Hailey. She was kind to me. Not sure what she did to make you bitter, but it must have been bad. Whatever it was, I'm sorry. Still, maybe it's time to move past it. We're adults now, yes? Let's let childish hurts go.

Imagine this. We've got one of the greatest drummers of this generation. Jason's so good, he doesn't pay for his kit. Tama gives him whatever he wants, and he talks them up whenever he can. Think anyone recognizes him on the street?

I get stopped sometimes. People want an autograph, want me to sing something or explain the lyrics, whatever. But without Jason, what am I? Without Jason, we're not playing a West Coast tour. It takes a lot of work to put something like this together. What do I do? I go along for the ride and let others do the work.

Think what you will about Hailey being out front, being the one who gets noticed, the one who's popular and sells out the people behind her. Here's what it boils down to: People in front—we're nothing without people backing us up. Where would Hailey be without you? Besides, you don't strike me as the spotlight type. I dig that. You can only run the Hollywood red carpet so long before you notice the dog hair and wine stains. You're better than that.

Something about your selflessness shames my selfishness into confession. I wanted you to share your dream because there's a part of me, a dark part, a buried part, that's a thief. I steal dreams, and I want to steal yours. I want to make it my own, want to fantasize about your fantasy, want to be with you in those mountains, want to smell the sun, want to look California and feel Minnesota.

I've been stealing Yaz's dream for years, while he lives it. Here's the tragedy: I can't dream anymore. I have no more dreams. Once, I dreamed of getting signed, making millions, cheap sex and booze, all that. What kind of dream is that? That's a borrowed dream, jacked from every wannabe rock star. Here we are on the cusp of something big, and all I can think about are the mountains because I can't dream for myself.

I'm tired and rambling. I'll see you tomorrow night. Take care of yourself. Be careful going home. Make sure someone is with you, like me or Yaz if possible.

All my love,
Geoff

To: Geoff Morris
Emily Amherst
Friday, January 6, 2012, 5:32 A.M.

Tripp had a bad night. Steph's exhausted, so I walked the floors with him. Took him a good hour to fall back asleep. He knows his daddy's gone, and he's very uneasy. He sat there, his head on my shoulder, his knuckle in his mouth, and whimpered. Yaz must be an incredible dad.

He finally went out, and I laid him back in bed but had to check the computer before I went back to sleep. I read your letter in the quiet pattering of rain. Is it raining in Ralley? How is the rain everywhere and nowhere?

I wish I could hear your voice, hear how you'd read the words you sent to me in your letter. Without inflection, I'm lost and a little disturbed.

I thought you wanted to know about me, not steal my dream. I trusted you with my intimate imaginings, and you say you want to steal it? Have I misunderstood what you meant? What are your intentions? I'm not angry. I'm sad.

And as far as Hailey is concerned, I think I'm a little better judge of her character than you. I've known her longer and better. Like you say, you always admired her from a distance. I think, once you get to know her better, you may not like what you find. When that happens, I'll be there to pick up your pieces.

Is this how you get in the mood to tour? Dr. Jekyll and Mr. Hyde? When you're home, you're sweet, tender, kind, and even romantic. And then tour time comes, and you shove everyone who cares about you into a box and stuff them on a shelf. Don't talk about being disappointed in me. Is this your way of telling me to shove off? If so, say it straight out. It'd hurt less.

I'm not Jennifer. Stop acting like I'm gonna yank your heart out and stomp it. I'm better than that.

I may be a lot of things, but I'm not dishonest or deceitful. When you talk to me, I am who I am. Call me naïve, call me ridiculous, call me blind, but I am who I am always. I don't use and abuse others. If that's what LA and the Hollywood red carpet is about, I want no part of it.

What you said in your message was mean-spirited. I'm hoping you'll say I misunderstood, hoping you'll better explain what you mean. There's another dream to steal.

I'm sorry. I'm out of line. Maybe I've misunderstood. I'm tired and hypersensitive right now. I'll hush now before I ruin any chance of seeing you again.

I'll see you tonight, if you're still talking to me. —Em

To: Geoff Morris
Emily Amherst
Friday, January 6, 2012, 6:07 a.m.

One more thing: I try never to lie. I'm no saint, but I am truthful. I'm also imperfect and sport a bit of a temper—I'm fallible and broken. I know I lied to the doctor, but I promise I'll never lie to you, even if you don't like what I have to say.

And I'm sorry about the Jennifer remark. It was uncalled for and mean-spirited. I was wrong and nasty. Please forgive me. I promise, when we don't get along, I'll make every effort to fight fair.

I shouldn't have sent that message. Mom always said regret is a nasty bedfellow, and she's right. Hope you can forgive me and still see me as likeable, loveable, sexy.

I'll let Steph wash my shirt today. Seems the scent went rank.

Later,

E

To: Geoff Morris
Emily Amherst
Friday, January 6, 2012, 7:31 a.m.

Look, Geoff, this is getting complicated. I'm falling head over heels for a strange and unique man, one who drives me insane with his ramblings about fame, money, and a woman a night. Someone a lot more stubborn than me, which is a remarkable talent.

We haven't had a quiet moment together. It's not fair, you know. Story of my life. I can't undo the hurt from Barry in one week, but this week with you has helped. You've rescued me, cared for me, provided for me, and I've been ungrateful.

I have to count my blessings. You cared enough to send for me. You made arrangements for me, bought me Ben & Jerry's ice cream, gave me daisies, teased with me, and caressed my face. What kind of rock star does that? We care for each other, but we're both scared.

But it doesn't excuse my behavior in my earlier message. I'm so guilty. I've written you three messages. I hope you don't use up all your data reading them.

I still don't get the part about stealing my dreams. I want to believe I misunderstood what you meant. If I did, I'll apologize. When I'm wrong, I admit it.

I can't take back what I wrote, but I can ask your forgiveness for my mean-spiritedness. Can you forgive me?

I've managed to put my foot in my mouth, swallow, and choke. I need your forgiveness to breathe.

I'm choking here.

Em

TEXT MESSAGE TRANSCRIPT
Friday, January 6, 2012, 3:19 p.m.

EMILY AMHERST: Did you get my messages?

GEOFF MORRIS: Yeah.

EMILY AMHERST: Forgive me?

GEOFF MORRIS: Can't talk now.

EMILY AMHERST: Please don't say that. Give me hope before you push me to the curb. Say something nice?

GEOFF MORRIS: We'll get through this.

EMILY AMHERST: I hurt so bad now.

GEOFF MORRIS: Wait till you read my letter. Pain always comes before healing.

EMILY AMHERST: I know I have it coming. Be easy on me, please?

GEOFF MORRIS: I'm always gentle. My words aren't.

EMILY AMHERST: I miss you.

GEOFF MORRIS: Yaz and I are talking with Riley now.

EMILY AMHERST: About?

GEOFF MORRIS: You. They're talking me down, so I don't say anything stupid.

EMILY AMHERST: Is it working?

GEOFF MORRIS: You'll know when I send my message.

EMILY AMHERST: This is torture.

GEOFF MORRIS: Sorry, Heart.

EMILY AMHERST: Tell Riley I said hey.

GEOFF MORRIS: Sure.

To: Emily Amherst
Geoff Morris
Friday, January 6, 2012, 3:53 p.m.

Foot in your mouth? Tell me how your toes taste. Maybe I could steal that dream too.

Let me apologize in advance for what follows.

Women complain men don't open up to them. They want to know what we're thinking and feeling and all that. I do that. I make myself vulnerable to you. I confide in you and tell you my darkest secret, my tragedy. I open my vein and bleed in front of you. You see the black in my blood, see how my heart pumps, how slow it is, how sick I am. And, like a woman, you twist it and throw it in my face, like I've done something wrong. I'd expect it from my mother, but hoped you'd be kinder.

I've never told anyone I can't dream anymore. I'm not an emotional rapist here. I'm sick and need help. I was hoping you might heal me. You might be the anti-Jennifer. You might understand and care. But that would require selflessness, wouldn't it? I'm wondering what happened to the sexy selflessness you wore so well.

I'm sorry. I can't blame you for being upset. I said it wrong. I don't want to steal your dream; I want to share it. I need you to dream for me because I can't imagine anything other than the life in front of me.

Here's the next chapter in my life: I go on tour. I play for suits. And because I've got no job (I quit Killer App) and no apartment (They wanted me to pay rent. I didn't.), I hope the suits dig us. Then, I get signed and leave Ralley and LA and live on a bus until I'm too old to rock.

Not a dream you want to steal, am I right?

Here's what I don't get about your Hailey thing: You keep saying it's a love/hate thing, but you've never said anything positive about her. Where's the love? Saying you love someone doesn't mean you do. Even Brutus loved Caesar, right?

Come tonight, put both feet on the ground, because you're forgiven. I can forgive you, but not myself. Expect a good show tonight. I'm always better when I'm angry.

—Dream Thief

TEXT MESSAGE TRANSCRIPT
Friday, January 6, 2012, 3:19 p.m.

EMILY AMHERST: Show time! Did I tell u, ur sexy when ur ticked? Look behind u.

From the Journal of: Geoff Morris

Friday, January 6, 2012, 3:19 p.m.

This is my church—Friday nights in a club heavy with smoke and booze, hot lights flashing, the band behind me. Tonight's special—first time Em gets to see me do my thing. I play it down, try not to get excited. She probably hates me after my last letter, but the glimpse I got of her before I took the stage—her hair all raptured in gold light, the swelling on her eye down, and her wicked southern grin—gets my blood going. I roll my anger and infatuation together and change up our set list a bit. "Let's open with 'Soul Eater,'" I say.

"Don't make me open with 'Eater,' man. That song kills me," Jason says. "It's double bass for eight minutes."

"Song's only six minutes, man. Don't exaggerate," I say.

"We're still polishing it," Yaz says. "Let's open with something cleaner."

"I like 'Eater,'" Nesmeth says, running his hands up and down the neck of his bass. By feel, he knows he's out of tune and gives the third machine-head a tight twist.

"Serious," I say. "First and last songs should be the strongest. 'Eater's' got fists. Shows what we can do."

Yaz says, "Whatever, man. Your town, your show."

"I hate you," Jason says. He spins a drum stick and lays down the four count. We all hit the low C# and let it ring for eight counts. Yaz crowds his stack, and the hum of feedback grabs the audience, pulls them to the stage. We don't announce our name before our set like most bands. Our music introduces us. The less I speak, the better. I'll sing all night, but filling the dead spots is where I'm weak. So, we don't leave dead spots. We go from song to song, and before I know it, we're about eight measures into "Asylum Antics." I find Em in the crowd again. She's not watching us. Barry's in her face, and she's holding her own.

Barry's a gorilla of a man and clearly the drunkest guy in Mitch's, which is saying something.

Back it up, I think. I'm about to drop the mic when I remind myself what she said—don't start anything. Let her fight her battle. Some suit's next to her. Probably her lawyer friend.

Yaz is beside me, shouting in my ear. "He the guy?"

I nod. We finish "Break Me," and Yaz moves directly into his fatty riff for "Hate Breed." I grab some water, and Yaz's guitar cuts out mid-riff. I turn back to see what's up, and Yaz is pointing to Em. Barry's got his fists up—he's dropped the lawyer and two security guards. A third tries to grab his arm, but Barry spins and crushes the guard in the face with an elbow. He pulls back, ready to swing at Em. Em covers her head. She dodges the first punch, and I'm grabbing Barry's arm as he pulls back again. I don't remember dropping the mic, leaping from the stage. I'm vaguely aware the music stops, and I hear people screaming.

Barry's left hand lands on my chest. I can't breathe, but I swing back. I've been in enough fights to know how to handle myself against a drunk. When he swings again, I step out of the way and counter. My fist connects with his chest and he takes a step back. I move with him, swinging again. He blocks, and when I look back to check Em, I feel his foot in my stomach.

This just got real.

Here's how you win a fight: you stop thinking about what you want to do to the other guy and worry about what he can do to you. Barry's an ex-marine, a trained killer. He's seen combat. He's killed men. But he's drunk, angry, and his swings are sloppy.

He moves to kick me again, and I grab his foot. I kick his other leg out and he falls, but gets himself up fast. I'm starting to wonder if I can win this fight. His movements are slow, exaggerated, but there's power behind them. I duck his next swing and come up with an uppercut. I graze his jaw; it's enough to stagger him a bit.

Now he's mad. He's not feeling pain. He's more than drunk; he's high. A hit like that would make anyone pause, but not Barry. He's got this look in his eyes, this animalistic stare, this murderous gaze.

But then Yaz shows up next to me, and I know this is a fight Barry can't win.

He swings wildly at Yaz.

Bad idea.

In one move, with one hand, Yaz deflects the punch and lands about thirteen of his own. Barry staggers back, and Yaz takes his knee out. Yaz pulls his foot up. This is the heel stomp—a very permanent end to a temporary problem. But before he lands it, Jason tackles him. Nesmeth helps me up. "He's done," Jason says.

Yaz paces over Barry's prone body. "Get up!" he spits at him. His adrenaline is pumping and he wants more. The fight was over too quickly to satisfy him.

Barry doesn't get up. Must have hit his head pretty hard on the way down, or the drugs are wearing off, or Yaz packs that much of a punch.

I turn to check Em—she's scared, but safe. She's shaking when I take her in my arms, crying, her arms swelling. The joy of a small town: Police are there minutes after the fights finish. They put their fat hands on my shoulders. "Let's go, Geoff," they say. Still know my name after all these years. It's a small victory for a night like this.

Rock that Packs a Punch

Ralley Times—John Acuff—Local bar owner Mitch Tompson briefly considered renaming his Friday night concerts to Friday Night Fights after yesterday's concert went sour.

Sideshow, a hard rock band from Los Angeles took the stage before a packed house and got the audience moving fast. It quickly became obvious front man Geoff Morris was distracted by an incident in the crowd. Morris tried to continue, but when an ex-marine drew his fist to hit a fan, Morris dove into the crowd. Lead guitarist Yaz made the leap as well as the crowd chanted "fight, fight, fight!"

Former Marine Lance Corporal Barry Waters attacked a young woman in the audience, and though authorities refused exact details, sources tell us the woman is linked to Morris. Attorney Wade Simpson was also attacked in the incident. The unnamed woman bore multiple injuries from an alleged dispute with Waters days before.

Bar owner Thompson would not comment on the details of the fight, only that "The guys saw a woman in trouble and stepped up. I got no plans to press charges on my end."

Though authorities arrested Morris and his band mate, charges were dropped when the details of the incident were brought before the court arraignment judge.

Thompson promises Sideshow will be back on his stage. "Where else do you get rock that packs a punch?" remarked Thompson.

G

To: Emily Amherst
Geoff Morris
Saturday, January 7, 2012, 11:32 a.m.

Hoping you'll still talk to me after last night. I ticked a lot of people off. Tony's hurt he had to bail me out. Five hundred bucks, and he gripes like it was five thousand. Had Yaz to keep me company. He used his one call to touch base with Steph, and she went off on him something fierce. Can't blame her. Said we had good motives, but were stupid. Should have thought with our heads and not our fists. Jason and Nesmeth are freaked out, thinking we'll have to cancel shows. Even if we don't, we'll have to reach deep into our pockets to help finance the rest of the trip. Whatever eating money we had went to bail for me and Yaz.

But it was like you said—Barry stepped up. I saw you from the stage; he was tearing into you, pointing his finger, and getting belligerent. I kept playing until he punched your lawyer and pulled back to hit you. I don't apologize for what I did. Don't think I should have to. Hope you can forgive me. Safe to say, Barry should think twice before he tries to lay a finger on you again.

You may get a kick out of this (pardon the pun). http://www.ralleytribune.com/article_id_8732446_rock_that_packs_a_punch.html

No such thing as bad press, right? Good news is you're not mentioned in the article.

Tony got a call this morning from Ninecore Records. They want to see us in Seattle. Say they'll take us to dinner before the show. Trying not to be excited about it. Don't want to get my hopes up. I'm tired of being the greatest band you've ever never heard of, you know?

It was good to see you. Appreciate your surprise before the show. Sorry I didn't get to kiss you good-bye.

Love,

Geoff

To: Geoff Morris
Emily Amherst
Saturday, January 7, 2012, 4:40 p.m.

Who was lucky enough to get your one phone call from jail? Tony? Jason? Curious. Maybe it's better I don't know.

I never finished my dream:

You wake up in the early morning, snuggled deep into a sleeping bag on the side of the mountain. Your toes tingle. Crickets chirp around you. Your eye opens, and as your vision adjusts, a single ray of light dodges the leaves of the trees over you and meets your stare.

You yawn, stretch just a bit, and roll to your stomach. The horizon takes your breath away. It's as though an artist has taken a full palette of color and brushed a stroke of each from the mountain to the dome of the sky—pink, lavender, gold, blue—streak after streak of rich, deep color; and you're so close, you can touch it with your fingers. You hold your hands up to the glow of the morning sun. Your skin changes from pink to sun-kissed orange.

There's a chill in the air, a whiff of a breeze. You breathe deep, and your head spins. It's a natural drug, engrossing, encompassing, encountering every cell in your body. Can you see it? Are you in my dream? I don't want you to walk away from it. Ever.

My dreams are yours, whenever and however you want them.

I thought I had things under control at Mitch's. I never dreamed Barry would consider hitting me or my attorney, especially in public. But he's toast now. No way he can worm out of the legal trouble he's in now.

What you and Yaz did tonight wasn't an attempt to cause trouble. It was an effort to save a life. I can be stubborn, though I've met my match in you. I thought I could approach Barry and lay the cards on the table—get my money back, my car, my respect. I had a lawyer and security. I believed he would listen. I had no idea he'd slipped to the point where he'd attack me in public.

I'm touched you and Yaz were watching me while you played. Impressive. Wish I looked better for you, gave you something better to stare at.

At least I got my car keys back from Barry. Grabbed them when the police dragged him off. But the money's long gone. Barry burned through most of it getting his "rocky mountain high." I pressed charges this time. I made sure to attend the arraignment this morning. The judge gave him eleven months in Rotherman Hospital for rehab and mental evaluation. Sad to see him fall so far, but hopefully he'll get the help he needs there.

He used to be gentle and quiet, like me. We spent our evenings at home mostly watching television. But when the doctor changed his meds, he changed. Wanted to go out more, do things, started drinking. Then, when he lost his job, he stopped eating, became obsessive, angry. I should have known better. I should have made him get help, should have told the doctor to switch him back to the old meds. Fear does a lot to you. I see that now.

Because of his history in the Marines and because of what he's done to me and how he attacked you and Yaz, Rotherman is going to put him under high security. I'm glad he's off the streets.

Tell Yaz I'll never forget how he broke the fist that fell. You say you two are Batman, but I think you're avenging guardian angels. What a team.

You should have seen Barry. He looked almost as bad as me. How are your knuckles, baby? Security pulled me out fast. I didn't have a chance to say goodbye, to see if you were hurt from the fight. I thought I'd die when they yanked me out of the club. I know they meant well, but the pain almost undid me. By the time I made it back into the club, they'd already pulled you and Yaz out and put you in the car. After all that, I wanted to hold you, wipe away the blood, hug you, maybe kiss you.

Good news is Mitch isn't pressing charges against you or Yaz. But I guess Barry got himself a lawyer and is planning on coming after you and Yaz. Said you went too far. Can you imagine? But my lawyer's grateful you two stepped in. He said he'd defend you both pro bono. Least he can do, he said. Should be an easy case. A no-brainer with Barry full of liquor and drugs. I doubt a judge will even hear it.

Frankie showed up at the arraignment. Small town news travels fast. He asked if I was coming back, and I told him no. I couldn't lie. He saw how beat up I was, and he understood. Said he didn't blame me for wanting to make a new start. But, bless his heart, he said I could still have the two weeks of pay. He kissed my forehead and asked if I'd seen Daddy lately. Said he wasn't doing well.

I ran over to Daddy's for lunch. He cried when he saw me. I'm not exactly the Emily he kissed good-bye two weeks ago. Even though the swelling is going down and the wounds are closing nicely, the scars are pretty horrifying. But, as bad as I am, Daddy may be worse. Not physically, but mentally. His mind's slipping; his memory's fading. He was confused and disoriented, even forgot he was in his house. I took him down to the doctor, and the nurse asked if I'd considered assisted living for him.

He was older when he had me. Most kids our age don't have to worry about these kinds of things. I wish I didn't have to.

How can I have let him get this bad? I was so focused on what was happening with me, so worried about Barry losing his mind, Mark being sick, falling for you, I forgot to check on Daddy. I think I'll stay here another day or two to tie up loose ends. Already, I find myself longing to get back to LA, anywhere other than Ralley.

Here's your song again on the radio. Makes me miss you more. Baby, I'm hooked on you. And, if you'll allow me to get to know you better, I'd love to share my dreams with you. I'm trying to keep a level head. I don't want what we have to be a rebound. I don't want you feeling sorry for the damsel in distress. That's not who I am.

One more dream. Close your eyes and imagine this:

I'm sitting next to you. You're tired from the show, from the fight. You lay down, put your head in my lap. I run my fingers through your hair, trace your eyebrows with my fingers, trail the tip of my finger over your ear, your cheek, your jaw, over your lips. You close your eyes. Rest up, hero. I'm here.

Yours always

—Em

PHONE TRANSCRIPT

Sunday, January 8, 2012, 5:00 p.m.

GEOFF MORRIS: Hey, Heart. Just pulled into Seattle. Tony's checking in at the Hard Rock now. Wanted to call you real quick before we go in and play.
EMILY AMHERST: I'm glad you did, Dimples. I miss you.
GEOFF MORRIS: Ditto. How's your dad?
EMILY AMHERST: I don't know. It's not looking good.
GEOFF MORRIS: Of all the things you need right now, this isn't one of them.
EMILY AMHERST: I know, right? When it rains, it pours.
GEOFF MORRIS: Should I tell the guys?
EMILY AMHERST: No. Don't bother them with it. I haven't told anyone but you.
GEOFF MORRIS: You're gonna tell Steph, right?
EMILY AMHERST: I should. She calls me every few hours to check on me. Love her heart. I told her I was helping Dad for a few days, but I didn't give her any details. It's killing her having Yaz gone. Tripp's a mess.
GEOFF MORRIS: I know. Yaz is a train wreck himself. He's quiet—not like him. I keep telling him only a few more days.
EMILY AMHERST: Only a few more days.
GEOFF MORRIS: Listen, I wanted to hear your voice again. Glad you're not mad about us stepping up.
EMILY AMHERST: You loved it.
GEOFF MORRIS: *Laughs* It felt good when I landed the uppercut.
EMILY AMHERST: Good luck tonight. Think of me.
GEOFF MORRIS: Always do, Heart. Night.

G

To: Emily Amherst
Geoff Morris
Monday, January 9, 2012, 1:10 a.m.

Posted some pics from our set tonight at the Hard Rock. I was hoping you'd be able to come up and see it, but I know you've got to get things straight.

Today's stories: We stopped at a KFC and as I'm ordering my chicken strips, the chick at the register looks at me and says, "Are you Morris? From Sideshow?" She's smiling when she asks, and I get embarrassed and nod. She tells me she's coming to the show, looking forward to it, and thought it was cool what I did for "that one girl," meaning you.

I'm thinking this chick must really follow us to read an article from a small newspaper a couple hundred miles away. I'm used to getting recognized in LA, but up here? It's a bit of a trip. Long story longer, she shows up at the show, and she's got friends out the door, and she wants to talk like we're close, like we're tight, like she grew up in Ralley. I'm thinking she's a case, but I don't say it. Not cool to insult fans. I nod all polite and talk with them, learn their names, make eye contact, all that, and then she asks the inevitable question. "You and that girl together or something?"

The question gave me pause.

Last night's a blur. I think back, and it's like seeing things through the haze of a hangover. I don't remember Yaz leaping off the stage. Of course, he left first. I was drinking water. You know what "Break Me" does to my voice. I remember seeing you, Barry's fist up, and I stop thinking. Next thing I know, I'm flying off the stage. I'm feeling the Dark Knight vibe. I black out for a bit. My senses get jumbled and confused—sounds and flashes, salty teeth cracking, brilliant pain in my chest, a choir of lights, octaves of knuckles, a yellow choking, satin screams, sandpaper shouts.

Then, all at once, I time jump. I'm ten minutes before the show. You're behind me. I turn around, and something happens, something unbelievable. I dream.

We're signed and millionaires, living it up and having the time of our lives.

I'm living quietly up in the mountains, and it's snowing. There's a tree in the front room all dressed up for Christmas, and I can taste the eggnog.

I'm in LA, Hollywood Hills, thirty-seven-room mansion with an underground recording studio.

I'm in my apartment in LA, broke as a joke, wishing I never quit Killer App and picking up applications at KFC.

These dreams, they're all similar, because in all of them, I'm happy, and in all of them, I'm with you. Simple. Your lips on mine, our fingers interlocked.

I need to get going. I'm amped from our show. Need to relax, unwind, sleep before visiting hours start. Want to be fresh when I see Mark, you know? Don't want to fall asleep halfway through our conversation.

Yaz is tucked in. He snaked my laptop an hour ago to put in a video call to Steph. Smoothed things over between them. She got Tripp up. They babbled for twenty minutes—the same thing over and again, but it made Tripp's night. They disconnected, and Yaz got all quiet again.

Anyway. I've got some voice mails here from Hailey. Probably directions to the hospital. I should check those before bed.

All love,

Geoff

To: Geoff Morris
Emily Amherst
Monday, January 9, 2012, 12:11 p.m.

Unbelievable photos. Hot and sweaty is sexy on you.

When I call you "dreamy," the description is accurate. You're not as crass as you imagined. Sometimes our dreams hide beneath the surface, waiting for the right moment to surface. Of all your dreams, I think I liked the snow in the mountains the best. I've been to Willow Creek in the snow. Tons of fun. Have you ever been sledding? Dad and I used to slide down the mountainside on our bellies when the snow was packed enough. He called it the "rip slide."

I fell boundless into your dreams, especially the part where my lips pressed yours. Delicious chills. Think it will ever happen? I've never kissed someone with lip studs, but I've thought about it a lot since I rediscovered you.

Super happy to hear you didn't wake up with KFC girl. Am I wrong to imagine some dedication for me in your heart? I don't want to push, but a girl can hope. And if you do have romantic feelings for me, I'll do what I can to water them and hope they grow. I'll dream you into my arms if I can. I feel like I'm sixteen again, giddy and goofy.

I've got a phone interview with Steph's friend on Monday. Guess he likes my degree and what I've done at Frankie's. If the interview goes well, he's talking $40K a year. Not much, but twice what Frankie's paid, and I can work from home, if I ever find one. For now, Steph says I'm welcome as long as I want, provided I help out with Tripp. It'll save her childcare; that can be my rent.

Doctor says he's testing Daddy for frontal lobe dementia. Not good. I thought heart issues were enough. I'd noticed his speech slurring the past couple of months, and he's been dragging his left foot for a couple weeks.

This type of dementia moves quick. He seems so tired these days, and I hate leaving him alone in Ralley. Steph said she'd look into some assisted living homes around LA. We both need a change. Besides, it's only two hours from Willow Creek. I can take him there to dream. The doctor didn't seem hopeful for a recovery. Told me to be ready for Daddy to lose sight of reality. Test results will be back on Wednesday. Until then, I have him at Miller Memorial Hospital. He won't wander or get hurt.

I get the sutures out of my back tomorrow. I'm scared there'll be a huge scar on my face. I can't believe we ever fought over whether or not you should have dinner with Hailey. Of course you should. She needs a familiar face, a good friend. You can be that for her. But promise me you won't let her suck you into her bed. I don't think I'd be able to recover from that. It'd hurt more than what Barry did to me.

One more dream to sweeten the deal: Imagine us walking along the beach, the tide rolling over our ankles, the sand sinking under our feet. We hold hands, press against each other. We get back to our towel and lie down. I put my head on your chest, feel it rising with your breath. You pull the hair out of my eyes and sing with the tide. It's a duet, you and the ocean, and you sing me to sleep.

Counting the days until I see you again.

Emily

G

To: Emily Amherst
Geoff Morris
Monday, January 9, 2012, 6:11 p.m.

Visiting hours are over now. I spent the whole day next to Mark. I hate to start off on a down note, but better bad news first for good news later, right?

Hailey's known for a while what was wrong with Mark, but didn't want to tell me. She knew I'd drop everything and race up here. I wish she had, but maybe she was looking out for my best interest. Still, what's in Mark's best interest?

Are you sitting down? The doctors gave a name for it, but I couldn't pronounce it or hope to spell it. It's a very rare, very aggressive form of MS. Drug resistant, messy, fast, ruthless. These are the doctor's words. I asked Hailey how long, and she started crying.

When I came in, he was watching TV. I said, "Hey," and he didn't even turn his head. He couldn't even if he wanted to. He rolled his eyes to me and said, "Hey, man." He said it all slow, like he was drunk or tired.

Hailey gave me a few minutes alone with him. He's frustrated, see? Can't even sit up on his own. I spent an hour helping him to sit up a bit, watching him struggle to drink some juice.

"Taking too long," he says, but he's not talking about getting better. He's done fighting—that's what I get. He's ready to move on. You know Mark—All-State half-back in high school. He's the only one of us who didn't pay for college, and now he can't put fork to mouth without help. He talks, and every slurred word is rimmed with resignation.

Today, I changed a bed pan and felt closer to a friend than I'd ever felt before. He gurgled a bit, and his head lolled over to the side. I wanted to say something but had no words. I'm the poet, the singer, the word artist, and I'm kneeling beside him without paint or canvas.

Why him? I pray to this God you say created the earth. At first, I'm angry. I'm mad God's doing this to Mark and not to me. I could handle it. I don't fear death. What do I have to lose? But Mark's got Hailey. He's got a real job, real friends, a life. Me? I'm crooked. I'm evil. I'm a waste of oxygen. I'm not fit to breathe the same air as this man. Why him? I ask God. Take me, take me instead.

The nurse came in and tells me hours are over. She hands me my coat. Subtle. I'm about to leave, and Mark says, "Don't worry. I'm ready."

"For what?" I ask.

"Won't be long now," he says.

How am I supposed to get ready for our show tonight? I want to cancel, but I've got nowhere to go. I tell myself I'll play for Mark tonight. It's all I can do.

Hailey and I had dinner together. Something the cafeteria called a hamburger. I had my doubts. Dinner was a quiet affair. Don't worry, Hailey spun no seductive webs.

Hard to focus on much, you know? Like when you first wake up, the sun's still sleeping, but you gotta roll out of bed and hope your legs are stable enough to hold you. I've got that sleep fog in my brain all day. I'm lucky to remember the songs we play. But we've played them so much, they're instinct now, like breathing.

And you, Em. If I could get this fog out of my head. Look, I love you. I know that. But I can't think about tonight, much less next week. Relationship, yeah, I'm interested, but we're so far away. I'll be back in a couple days, but I don't have a place to stay. I've got no idea what I'm going to do. I'm not in a place to take on a girlfriend, you know? If I were, it'd be you. I need you, and please don't think I'm using you, but I need your strength. If you can't do that without some sort of commitment, I understand.

I'm telling you, Em, I'm screwed up here. But I like the beach. The dream's sticking. Maybe the Pacific sunset can burn away the fog.

Love the job prospect. Should work out well for you. Tripp'll love seeing you. Yaz tells me how much Tripp's taken to you. It'll help Steph too. Poor girl's burning the candle at both ends. Yaz is too. He tells me he's worried they're not doing a good job with Tripp, like they're not there enough for him. Rips his heart out, you know? And I still have to wonder if he's going to end up quitting Sideshow sooner rather than later. Man, I'm getting an ulcer here.

And your dad—geez, Em. Sounds like you're dealing well with it. I hope he gets better soon. Having him nearby will be good for both of you.

Wish I could be with you when you get the sutures out. I'd love to be able to hold your hand, help ease the pain. Always nice to have a hand to hold. Hailey was telling me about Mark's spinal taps. Said they're the most painful thing anyone can endure. He's had about six of them over the last couple of weeks. Supposed to have another one tomorrow. I'll be there for it. Already told him. Doctor doesn't want me there? Too bad.

All love, Heart

—Geoff

TEXT MESSAGE TRANSCRIPT
Monday, January 9, 2012, 8:21 p.m.

GEOFF MORRIS: Mark's gone.

EMILY AMHERST: Gone?

EMILY AMHERST: Why won't you answer your phone? Talk to me.

EMILY AMHERST: Geoff, I'm sorry

EMILY AMHERST: Call me, Dimples. When you get a chance. I need to hear you.

GEOFF MORRIS: Can't talk now.

Book Two

She wants to dwell in everything
She's lost everything (she needs)
Everything he was going to be before he
Left her alone to swim with the woman in the
water.

—Sideshow, "Woman in the Water"

Emily Amherst's Journal

Monday, January 9, 2012, 8:30 p.m.

I get his text and my throat tightens. His words strangle me from two states away. Mark's death hits me hard, and I feel like I'm in the air again, seconds away from crashing through a glass coffee table. I'm terrified for Geoff, for Hailey, for me.

But this is no time for me to feel sorry for myself. I need to support Geoff. He needs me to be strong for him. But he won't let me. Not now. When he calls back, maybe.

The rain from LA has made its way up the state and drenches us. Any colder, and it'd be sleet. It's snowing on the mountains. The cloud stretches down and covers its peaks. Daddy would rather be there, instead of here. He'd rather be anywhere. The nurse left pamphlets for nursing homes across the state that could care for Daddy. I focus on two in LA. Both expensive. "What do you think of Glendale?" I ask him.

He stares at the wall, eyes glazed over, hand shaking.

"Glendale, Daddy. Think Mom would have liked it?"

A nurse walks in. She's young and beautiful. "You've got a sweet daughter, Mr. Amherst," she says.

Daddy doesn't blink.

"Have to take a bit of blood." She works a needle in his arm, and he hardly moves. Blood fills the tubes slowly. It's dark like wine.

I'd hoped to tell Daddy about Geoff, maybe introduce them when they come back down from Seattle, but I doubt Daddy will even remember me in a week.

What am I doing here? I should be in Seattle, should be with Geoff, should be holding his hand. But Daddy needs me too.

I listen to the patter of rain on glass, as if it has the answers, as if it can tell me what to do. I think again how nice it'd be to be the rain, to stretch over the state, move with the wind, to bring life.

The nurse shuffles out of the room with a smile. I hold my phone to my chest and sit next to Daddy.

To: Geoff Morris
Emily Amherst
Monday, January 9, 2012, 9:42 p.m.

I'm so sorry. I wish I could be there to help you stand. Death hurts. Cuts straight to the core. I remember the pain when Mom died, a panic building inside me, a scream that couldn't escape. My chest throbbed; my head hurt. Nothing seemed fair or right.

You said it best: fog, dense and deep. Nothing's recognizable. You can't cope, not for a while. You move out of habit. Your body lives out of habit. You never completely heal, but you learn to go on.

Crying helps. I know men think it's degrading, but tears can heal. Have a good cry. Let your tears pull out some of the pain.

I know you don't want to hear it, but God has a plan. I don't want to preach to you now. You don't want to hear it. But He is Almighty, and He knows more than us. He knows what's best for Mark. Mark's in a better place.

This is what Mark wanted, even though we didn't want it. Mom didn't fear death, and from what you say, neither did Mark. It kills me to have him gone. I'll miss him with all my heart. Already do.

I can't leave right now. If I could, I'd be on a plane tonight. But Daddy's sick. He's slipping, and I need to be here. I feel like I'm getting stabbed in two places. I need to be in Seattle for you and Hailey—for Mark—but I need to be here for Daddy too. I'll be up on Friday.

After Daddy goes, I won't have anyone left. All my aunts and uncles have passed. Never had a brother or sister. Haven't heard back from Steph's friend about the job. Barry took all my money. Even if I wanted to go to Seattle, there's no way I could get a ticket, and I doubt my car would make the trip.

Give Hailey a hug for me. Tell her I'm praying for her. For you too.

And I'm a little hurt you didn't tell me sooner about your financial troubles. Did you spend your rent money on my train ticket? I can't stand the thought of me putting you out of your apartment. I think you're right. Neither of us are really in a place to be able to start a relationship. But know this; I'll wait for you. As long as your heart is with me, that's enough for me.

Please let me know when you hear about the funeral. I'll do whatever I can to get up there. May take me a while to figure out how to do it, but I'll do what I can.

It's raining again. The steady hum of water against window puts me in a trance. Makes me want to be a drop, high in the sky, falling, freezing, then unfreezing. There's a cycle to it. Life and death, death and life.

Rain gets a bad rap, always means depression and gloom. But I see it as cleansing, refreshing, peaceful. I walked to my car from the hospital, took my jacket off, stared into the skies. I let the rain soak me, wash my depression away. I'm left, instead, with a hollow pang and emptiness, but a quiet contentedness.

We'll pull through, Geoff. We have to.

Is it raining there? It's Seattle, I'm sure it is. Walk out in the rain and imagine this short dream. If you close your eyes just right, squint into the gray haze, you'll see the vague shadow of a woman waving. That's me, moving toward you.

A heartbeat away,

—Em

G

To: Emily Amherst
Geoff Morris
Monday, January 9, 2012, 10:22 p.m.

I don't want to be pushy, but you need to come up for the funeral. You can fly up and back and only miss a couple of days. I'm sure Steph can look in on your dad for you. If money's an issue, we can help. Give the word, and we'll have a ticket in your mailbox by tomorrow afternoon. Hailey needs you up here. I need you too, because I'm not sure when I'll be able to see you again.

I'm staying with Hailey for the time being, sleeping on her couch, not in my car or her bed. Not exactly a romantic atmosphere up here. We're planning Marks' funeral for Tuesday. While we were working on the service, Tony called in. Ninecore Records liked our gig and wants us to join the West Coast Apocalypse Tour. It starts here in Seattle on Wednesday. I'll be gone for about a month, maybe more. If things go well, Ninecore will ink us. They're already marketing our self-produced album and, if we ink, will produce a new album when the tour stops in San Diego. Then, we'd be back on the road, to the East Coast for the better part of a year. This looks like the real deal, and I'm not excited about it, not in the least. I swear I'm getting an ulcer. Not sure I'm ready for this.

The sting of Mark's death is passing slowly. Helping with the funeral plans helps keep my mind, strangely enough, off him dying. Helps me remember him how he was. Here's something you'll find interesting: I found a ton of pictures of us in an old shoe box in the top of his closet. Not just you and me, but in the group. I'd forgotten we spent so much time together, or at least around each other. Can't believe we never talked like we are now.

There are a lot of pictures here without me, though. Stuff I missed after I bolted for LA. You guys stayed up here in Ralley for the summer, but, once I graduated, I got out of town. Remember? Didn't think there was anything up here for me. My mother made me miserable, and my dad was so drunk he didn't remember my name most days. I don't tell a lot of people that.

I also found a ton of pictures of you, and even more of you and Mark. Had a ring on your finger in a few of them. What's the story, Heart? What haven't you told me?

A few years back, we were playing the Whiskey. It was pouring that night. Record rain falls. Didn't expect much of a crowd, but we packed the place. Everyone's soaked to the bones. There was this connectedness unlike any other show. These were brave fans, true fans. Rock is more important than rain. We ended up chilling after the show for hours until they closed up, and then, we (me and the crowd) sat in the rain for another hour.

I took a walk like you suggested. It was after dinner. Hailey thought I was crazy, but I told her I needed to clear my head. It was raining. (When isn't it raining in Seattle?) I remembered the night at the Whiskey, and there it was again, that sense of connectedness that transcends space, like we were walking together, maybe on a rainy beach, my hands deep in my pockets, and, in my mind, I'm gently bumping your shoulder, and you mine.

Em. I miss you. I need you.

Come soon. Steph will watch your dad. Tell me when you can be packed and ready to fly to Seattle.

All my love,

Geoff

To: Geoff Morris
Emily Amherst
Tuesday, January 10, 2012, 11:00 a.m.

My heart breaks for you. It's ripped in half, part with you, part here with Daddy. But I guess you made my decision easy, didn't you? You've come to my rescue again. Steph showed up early this morning with a plane ticket. Guess you could only afford one-way, or you figure I'll drive back down with you. Must have cost a fortune on such short notice.

Someday, I won't need you to rescue me. I'll be strong and independent. For now, I'm grateful.

I need to tell you about Daddy, but I should do it in person. Right now, I need to pack for a flight.

Yours,

Em

TEXT MESSAGE TRANSCRIPT
Tuesday, January 10, 2012, 8:19 p.m.

EMILY AMHERST: You there? I'm at the airport.

EMILY AMHERST: Arriving 12:01 a.m. in Seattle. Delta Flight 3762

EMILY AMHERST: Pick me up?

EMILY AMHERST: Call me, I'm boarding the plane in an hour.

EMILY AMHERST: Where are you?

To: Geoff Morris
Emily Amherst
Tuesday, January 10, 2012, 10:21 p.m.

I'm on the plane. Never liked red-eyes, but I bet it was the best you could get for the time you had. I won't complain. And I will pay you back for them. I consider them a loan, not a gift. This is something I need to do. I got the onboard Wi-Fi, so I can see if you get back to me.

I spoke to Daddy's doctor before I left. Not good news. He doesn't expect Dad to get better. He's got a few heart problems to go with the dementia, but he should last a while. I'll be back before he gets worse. For now, he's stable.

Since Daddy can't make decisions, it's up to me. I've got power of attorney for him. Not something I wanted, but at least, with me, he's got a voice when his won't work.

You've mentioned an ulcer a few times. Geoff, are you sick? Or is this some figure of speech to describe your agony? It's hard to tell with you. If it's real, you should see a doctor. I can't have you getting sick too. Not after Mark, not with Daddy the way he is.

You probably don't remember me from the photos much because I was the quiet one. Plus, you were too hung up on Hailey to notice her friend. Besides, I wasn't exactly the cheerleader type that guys noticed. I was a little more athletic and didn't spend three hours on my make-up each morning.

As for me and Mark, we were close. I didn't want to tell you, but Mark and I were engaged for a while. Long story. No happy ending. You had so much on your mind, and I didn't want you worrying about me. For now, know I'm on my way to see you, to hold you, to comfort you.

I'm torn. I know I'm doing the right thing by coming to see you, but it hurts to leave Daddy when he needs me. If I were a better daughter, I'd have noticed the warning signs earlier. I'd have taken him in to the doctor months ago. But I was blinded by hope, distracted by Barry's slip into alcoholism and drug abuse. Even when I saw his house slipping, getting dirtier, him forgetting appointments and the like, I figured it was a sign of age, not of dementia. I'll have to have his home professionally cleaned when I get back. Eventually, I'll have to sell the house. But I don't want to think about that now.

I'll see you in a few hours. I can hardly sit still.

Soon in your arms,

Heart

From the Journal of: Geoff Morris

Wednesday, January 11, 2012, 12:19 a.m.

I told Hailey not to come. If she'd waited at home like I said, gone to bed to get some rest for the funeral this evening, I'd have been here on time. Instead, I wait for her to put make-up on, like she's picking up a man instead of Em. We scramble in to Seattle Tacoma International and check the flight board. Good news, bad news—her plane is late.

"Two hours?" Hailey says.

"It's raining," I say.

"It's always raining," she says. "I've seen more water in a shower."

I shrug. "Want me to take you back home?"

"I'm not waiting two hours."

I roll my eyes. "Let's go."

She grabs my hand as we walk to the car. I look at her; she looks at me. It's a short walk, and I open the door for her. She closes the umbrella, slides in, and when I crank the engine, she puts her hand on my knee. "Hailey," I say, pulling out of the airport and driving toward the freeway.

"Isn't this what you wanted?" she asks. "Haven't you always wanted me?"

I take her hand and put it on her knee instead. "You never wanted me."

"Things change," she says, putting her hand back and leaning toward me.

I contemplate pushing her away, telling her I have to drive. But her brother, my best friend, is dead. And we're here picking up an old friend who loves me and loved Mark. I love her, but right now, my heart's choked, any sort of feeling leaves me. Hailey needs a strong shoulder now. I need a strong shoulder now. "It's not right," I say.

We drive this way for miles, her eyes closed, her cheek on my shoulder. "Did you hear me?" I ask.

"Can't you shut up for a minute?"

"You never wanted me," I say again.

She sits up and folds her arms. She doesn't say anything the rest of the trip home. I let her out at her door and ask, "Is it cool if we stay here tonight?"

"You get the couch again," she says, as if I'd had a chance to sleep in her bed.

"I'm good with the couch."

"Em gets the floor," she says.

"Do you have any idea how beat up she is?"

"My brother's dead," she says softly, like it's a competition.

"He was my best friend," I say.

"Which is why you get the couch."

She slams the door. I shake my head and drive back to Seattle Tacoma.

Her plane is only delayed another hour before she finally lands at three. By now, my bones ache from sitting on the benches at the baggage claim. Emily comes down the steps really slowly, each step a challenge. She's wearing jeans, a loose shirt, and carrying a red backpack in her left hand. Her hair absolutely lights up the night. She doesn't smile when she sees me. She frowns.

I meet her halfway up, take her bag from her.

"How you feeling, Dimples?"

"Hurt a little less today. Too worried about details. Keeps my mind off the pain. You?"

"There are no words for how stiff I am."

She slips her arm around my waist, more for stability than

affection. I let her hold onto me, glad to be the strong one for a change. Tomorrow, I'll be leaning on her.

"About Hailey," I say.

"Hush. I don't want to hear it."

"You don't know what I was going to say."

"Whatever it is, it's not important. Let's get through tomorrow, you and me, and then we can talk about Hailey."

I hold the backpack over her head as we slosh through the parking lot to the car. We duck in, and I crank the heat. She's shivering.

"Car should warm in a bit," I say.

"This Hailey's car?"

"Yeah."

"Nice."

"Right? Guess the design work is doing okay for her up here. Wait till you see her apartment."

The rest of the drive is quiet, peppered with tired conversation about cramped airline seats and bad peanuts. I tell her our plans for tomorrow.

"You have songs picked out?" she asks.

I shrug. "Didn't think much about it."

"Can I suggest some?"

"Shoot," I say as we pull into Hailey's covered parking. We shuffle down the walkways to her place.

"Downstairs apartment? Nice," Em says. "I had two songs in mind. One's called 'I Can Only Imagine' by Mercy Me. It's Christian. Talks about Heaven. Beautiful song. Not exactly Sideshow rock, but you might like a soft song for the occasion."

"I'm open to it," I say. "The other song?"

"'Time Passin' Man.'"

I pause before turning the key to the apartment. We stand there, the rain falling around our feet. "I don't know," I say.

"We'll let Hailey decide."

I look at her, then, the rain behind her, her coat pulled around her shoulders, her warm smile, the light catching the drops of rain in her hair. They shine red. I think of Train's song, "Drops of Jupiter."

"Okay," I say.

When we go inside, Hailey's asleep on the couch, sprawled out in her pink flannel pajamas. She stirs as we shuffle in, stretches, and stands up. "Emily! Good to see you." She sounds real, but I wonder how fake the sentiment is. Less than three hours ago, she had her hand on my knee, made me think she wanted me in her bed. Now, she hugs Em so tight, Em grimaces.

Poor Em. Too kind to say how much it hurts. "Easy, Hailey. She's still pretty beat up."

Hailey releases her, and I see red spots forming on the back of her shirt.

I shake my head. "Em. Your back."

"Let me get cleaned up," she says. She takes her bag, and when she turns to the bathroom, Hailey's eyes widen.

"You're bleeding, Emily."

"I know."

"Let me help," Hailey says.

They disappear in the bathroom, talking softly. Can't make it out exactly, but I'm sure Emily's filling her in on the Barry incident. I pull the sleeper couch out, fluff up some pillows for Em.

When they get back out, Hailey says, "Goodnight, Geoff. We're going to bed now."

"We?" I say.

"Em's staying in my room."

I arch an eyebrow.

"What?" Hailey says.

"Goodnight," I say. "To you both. Sleep well."

I fall on the couch, flip on the television. Always easier to sleep with a little background noise.

Emily Amherst's Journal

Wednesday, January 11, 2012, 6:00 p.m.

The rain grows colder, never seems to stop. It mixes with sleet and makes slush on the sidewalk. I push open the door to the church and walk in. Beautiful sprays of light glisten off the stained-glass windows. And in the front of the church, Mark. I'm chilled, frozen. I want to walk closer, run my hand over the casket, see his face again, the face I caressed so many times.

It wouldn't be his face. It'd be some pale reflection of the face I loved, the lips I kissed, the man I almost married. It'd be his body, sure, but his soul, the desperately gentle, loving soul I fell for, is gone.

My throat tightens.

Geoff comes from the front of the sanctuary. Hailey clings to his arm. I can read the expression on his face when our eyes meet. I wasn't surprised. After all, this is how Hailey works. But now isn't the time.

Mark must have been well known in this church. A line forms from the back of the building up the center aisle to offer their condolences to Hailey, as members continue to pour through the door.

I sit on the third pew from the front and watch, but Geoff never looks at me. I'm feeling like I'm back in high school. Hailey in the front, me in the back, and this time, it's Geoff in the middle.

The minister steps to the pulpit. "Friends are the heartbeat of our souls." He motions at the filled sanctuary. "You are Mark's friends."

Geoff sits on the front row with Hailey. I didn't expect less; he's part of the ceremony. But it bothers me. He never looks around.

The minister describes the peace that passes understanding and the promise of eternal life. I watch Geoff from behind and wonder if he's getting this, taking in the message of peace and love, of God. Mark would have wanted him to hear.

The praise band played a beautiful rendition of "Amazing Grace."

I look around the sanctuary, take in a deep breath, and smell roses. Hailey sobs. Geoff puts his arm around her. It's awkward. Uncomfortable. There's no place for me here.

It's a beautiful service, a fitting tribute to Mark, an obvious proof of a life changed. Geoff stands and walks to the pulpit. His guitar strap drags the floor. He props his foot on the crossbar of a chair and rests the beat-up guitar on his knee. He's handsome. Nice shirt, dress slacks. I've never seen him in anything other than jeans and tee shirts. No facial adornments. Shaven. Breathtaking.

"When a man walks, he walks his own way. When he talks, he speaks his truth. But when he shares his heart, he gives it all. All to you." I'm not sure where the lyric comes from, but I'm thinking he made it up, maybe on the spot. He strums, then begins to pick the strings. A tender tune resonates through the church—tears cloud his eyes. He didn't sing one song he'd planned. Just like him, just like Mark, to change the program without warning. But it's beautiful. It's perfect. His voice is rough, but he sings with a strange, chilling passion. It's grittier, stirring. His voice summons my tears, and I break.

He finishes, presses his hand on the casket, his eyes red and swollen. I've never heard his voice this thick. He sits down again, and Hailey grabs him, grief-stricken. She tightens her grip on Geoff's arm. The funeral ends, and I stand close behind Geoff, try to offer him my hand as people pass by. He ignores me. Hailey steps between us, almost pushing me to the side. I can't fight a petty battle with these wounds.

I need air, so I wait on the front porch of the church. Geoff's inside, Hailey on his arm, talking to old friends I've never met. This is Mark's Seattle life. Other than me and Geoff, no one from Ralley showed.

I wait and wait, half expecting Mark to show up beside me like he always did in school. He'd put his arm around me and say, "Chin up, Em. God's got big plans for you." This is what he told me in school whenever Hailey abandoned me.

After college, he'd have taken me in his arms and kissed me so deeply, I'd forget whatever bothered me. I could have married him, could have been happy. Maybe that's why I'm bitter. I know I need to forgive her for what she did, but how can I when she took so much?

Oh Mark, I miss you.

The church door opens and a bear-sized hand reaches around me. It's Yaz, Jason beside him.

"Come on, babe. I'll get you out of here," Yaz says. He scoops up my backpack and pulls me toward a beat-up old car, a VW Beetle, opens the door and drops my bag in. "Go home, Em. Go back to Ralley and check on your dad." He kisses the top of my head.

"Whose car is this?"

"Mine," Jason says. He smiles sadly. "Family lives in Seattle. It's not much, but it got me through high school. Should get you home."

"But—"

"Go home, Em," Yaz says. "Trust me."

Trust is hard these days, with these wounds, with these old faces. I don't want to go. Geoff says he needs me, but it doesn't look like he needs much. Inside, Hailey hangs on him, and he laughs uneasily. No, he doesn't need me.

I start the car and head toward the interstate.

To: Geoff Morris
Emily Amherst
Wednesday, January 11, 2012, 10:24 p.m.

I'm not sure where to begin or what to say. Thanks for picking me up at the airport. I felt the tension, the awkwardness. There's no need for explanation. I can guess. I'm trying my best not to say anything brash, especially about Hailey. I stood on the porch after the service, waiting for you to come out, waiting for you to find me.

I knew before the service, before Yaz put me in Jason's Beetle and told me to drive. I knew before the apartment. I knew at the airport, when you looked at me. You were hiding something. When Hailey told me, it was the only confirmation I needed—she told me all about your dinner, how you kissed her, how you slept with her.

Some things never change.

It would have hurt less if I wasn't there for Mark's funeral. He was always there to pick up the pieces when Hailey shattered my life. Instead, I had to sit in the church, broken inside and out, and watch Hailey sink her nails into you. I should have known not to fall for you. I knew you were too good for me.

If you feel sorry for me, don't. I'm used to it. She's beautiful; I'm scarred. She's classy; I'm not. I get it. No worries. I'm good. I have too many things to worry about right now anyway.

I've driven until I can't hold my eyes open. The rain's turned to snow, and my phone's dying. Made it as far as the Hotel Arch in Dyersburg. Not the cheapest place, but I had enough from Daddy's account to pay for the room for the night. I'll pay him back. I'm getting close to Rickers Mountain. We used to stay here before and after Willow Creek trips. Anyway, the car's been sputtering. Figured it needed rest as much as me, so I stopped for the night.

I'll finish the trip tomorrow. Right now, I need sleep.

You did a great job today. Mark would be proud. You looked amazing and sounded better.

I guess you guys pull out tomorrow. Sorry I couldn't be there for you, like you said. I tried. I wanted to hold you, to comfort you, but it was obvious it wasn't the right time.

Yaz said Hailey would be traveling with you guys. She's good with promotion and advertising. She'll be a great addition for marketing. Plus, I'm sure she'll keep you happy.

I'm sorry if I pushed you too hard for a relationship. Whatever I did wrong, to push you to Hailey, I'm sorry. I thought we had something developing. I knew our timing was terrible, but hoped we could work something out after things settled down.

Thanks for all you've done for me. I'll be sure to pay you back for the train tickets and the plane ticket. If you need anything else, let me know. I don't want to be the reason you're broke.

Phone's almost dead.

One more dream before I go, for old times' sake. It's snowing. The path up the mountain is covered, but the sky's clear blue. The air's crisp, sharp. The smell of snow lingers in the atmosphere. The pine trees hang heavy with wet powder, and in the distance, you can hear the crack of branches. I'm sitting on a rock overhanging the bluff, wrapped in a blanket, sipping hot chocolate. I've dusted a spot next to me free of snow, if you still want to share my dream.

Be safe.

Em

G To: Emily Amherst
Geoff Morris
Wednesday, January 11, 2012, 11:19 p.m.

TBH, I'm more than a little upset right now. I come up here to see my friend and then to bury him. This whole trip was about Mark, and you and Hailey had to turn it into some sick battle over me? I'm sick, Em—that's how mad I am. You didn't even have the decency to tell me you were engaged to Mark? How do you not mention that?

And Yaz and Jason send you packing? And no one talks to me about it?

Look, I'm sorry you waited outside for me, but no one asked you to. Why didn't you stay inside where it was warm? I wanted you inside, needed you in there with me, needed you close enough to shame Hailey off my arm, because God knows I'm not strong enough to push her off, not at her brother's funeral.

We used to talk, Heart. Remember? Used to share our thoughts, our dreams, our fears, our hopes.

I buried my friend today, and I needed you, and you left. I can't blame you. Can't blame Yaz or Jason. They did what they thought was best, but why didn't anyone tell me? Why did everyone assume I'd fallen into Hailey's web?

Let me set the record straight: I'm not sure what she told you when we got back from the airport, but I can tell you what she said before.

She talked you up, Em. Told me what a great friend you were, how she was blessed to have you. Couldn't figure out why you hadn't stopped talking to her years ago. Talked about your faithfulness and forgiveness and love. I'm not making this up.

We talked about you at dinner, you and Mark. She always thought you two would end up married. When Mark died, she felt guilty. She'd been so mean to you, so loathsome, blamed herself for you not marrying him.

And at no point did we kiss. At no point did we hold hands or anything of the like. Not until the trip to the airport to get you. The first trip. She held my hand, tried to put her hand on my knee, to cuddle up.

I couldn't push her away. Mark's dead. I couldn't.

That's all that happened. I dropped her off at her apartment, picked you up, and you know what happened after that. The whole band stayed over at Hailey's tonight. She didn't want to be alone. That's why she's coming with us on tour. She's the one who called Ninecore and turned them on to us. If anything happens with them, we have her to thank for it.

Where are you, Em? Why aren't you answering my calls? I know you said your phone was dying, but you can charge it at the hotel, right? Call me. Text me. Message me. Whatever.

I'm not sure why Yaz and Jason sent you packing. Probably thought I'd hooked up with Hailey. They love you too, Em. They wanted to protect you. Still furious they didn't talk to me first. But I guess I put myself in this position, didn't I? A woman a night, right?

A woman a night and always alone.

Until I met you.

Don't give up on me, Em. Please. I get that you have to take care of your dad, and Steph needs you too. Save me a spot on the rock overhanging the bluff. Save me a spot in your heart.

Geoff

To: Geoff Morris
Emily Amherst
Thursday, January 12, 2012, 9:12 a.m.

FYI, I dropped my phone in a puddle in Seattle, and it hasn't been charging right since. If my angry rant cuts off half-way, you know why. But believe what you want. You seem to be good at jumping to conclusions.

I'm done with this whole Hailey thing. Got it? I don't care what crap she spit onto your dinner plate about me—you've got to trust me. I went to Seattle for Mark as much as I did for you. Last thing I wanted to do was cause a scene. So, I kept quiet, kept my distance. Hailey saw to that. I can't believe you think I'd take an opportunity like a funeral to throw a schoolgirl tantrum over a boyfriend or whatever you are.

What are we, anyway? You want me there, but when I show, there's no place for me. If I try to get close, you'll say I'm pushing Hailey away. How can I win with you? You can't handle a relationship now, but you want to lean on me for strength, want to steal my dreams? You want a level of intimacy without commitment. Tell me what you want, Geoff. Tell me how to win, how to give you what you need without scaring you off.

Since you "set the record straight," let me have the same chance. I waited inside the church. Stood right behind you, and even next to your side for a long time. You never glanced at me. If you needed me, all you had to do was look. Every time I tried to get closer, Hailey stepped between us.

I stepped out on the porch for a few minutes. It was killing me see you hurt and not being able to get close enough to help. I didn't abandon you. Yaz and Jason sent me away. I didn't want to hurt you.

I was hoping to avoid getting hurt.

Are we "you and me"? Or are we "you" and "me"?

Don't be mad at Yaz and Jason. They wouldn't send me away without cause. They did what they thought was best for me. They see Hailey for what she is, a lump of vanity. But at least she can make things happen for the band. That must be the price of love.

I'll call when I've had a chance to cool off.

Hope my phone lasts that long.

Em

PHONE TRANSCRIPT

Thursday, January 12, 2012, 9:23 a.m.

EMILY AMHERST: Hey. You answered.

GEOFF MORRIS: Why wouldn't I? At least I didn't leave.

EMILY AMHERST: You didn't talk to Yaz and Jason about why they made me go?

GEOFF MORRIS: I'd rather hear it from you, Em.

EMILY AMHERST: Do I have to explain it? Think about it.

GEOFF MORRIS: I didn't ask for her to hang all over me, Em. Her brother died. I didn't have the heart to push her away.

EMILY AMHERST: Neither did I, and that's why I left.

GEOFF MORRIS: Come on, Em. What do you want me to do?

EMILY AMHERST: Something. Anything. Tell her how you feel. Better yet, tell me how you feel.

GEOFF MORRIS: I don't know how I feel. I'm angry. I'm sad. I'm terrified. I'm confused. I've told you all that already. You're not listening.

EMILY AMHERST: I'm listening fine. I don't think you're saying what you think you are. Your words and actions don't match, and I don't know which I should believe.

GEOFF MORRIS: I could say the same thing.

EMILY AMHERST: Geoff.

GEOFF MORRIS: I'm sorry.

EMILY AMHERST: I have to go, Dimples. I got to get checked out and back down to Ralley to check on Dad.

GEOFF MORRIS: Don't hang up, Em. I'm not done talking.

GEOFF MORRIS: Em? You hung up?

> To: Emily Amherst
> Geoff Morris
> Thursday, January 12, 2012, 9:37 a.m.

I hope your phone died, because if you hung up on me, that'd be really low. I know you're mad. I don't blame you. Don't run away. Don't cut me out of your life. I'm sorry if I hurt you. I never meant to. I'm doing my best here, trying as hard as I can to make you happy, to please you. But this is new water for me. I haven't been this close to someone since Jennifer. And I'm worried this story will have the same ending.

I want us to be us, "you and me," but how can we when we're always apart? We've got this Apocalypse Tour lined up, and Hailey's riding with us. But I'd trade her for you in a heartbeat. Yeah, she's got connections with Ninecore, but the hard part is over. They like us. Now it's about selling merchandise. They see our disks move, see our downloads explode, and we're as good as inked, which means more travel.

You've got this life you're building in LA. That's great, but if we want to be us, we can't do this long-distance thing. You flew up to Seattle for me. You came to Mark's funeral for me. And what did I do? I let Hailey hang herself on my arm the whole time. I didn't have the guts to tell her to back off, didn't have the heart to reach out to you, my true heart. What kind of boyfriend would I be?

The fact that you're even interested in me still speaks to your selflessness. You've got an innocence of hope going for you. You look at me and see what I can be. No other reason you'd hang.

I'm worse than Barry. He had an excuse for the booze, the depression, the drugs. I'm no soldier. What have I ever done for anyone?

I'm sorry. You're right about everything. Forgive me. Tell me where you are. I'll come get you.

Answer your phone for once, okay? Send me a text or something. Let me know you're alive. We'll get past this, won't we?

Yaz is ticked at me. I came down on him hard for sending you off. Said some unpleasant things. He says things, you know, that cut through you. He looks at me and says, "Still thinking about yourself? I thought you were growing up."

Jason shakes his head. "Come on, Geoff," he says. "A girl a night, man. That's not what Em's about. She doesn't need to see it."

At first, I'm angry. How dare they, right?

"What were we supposed to think?" Nesmeth says. The rain's pouring down now. Hailey's in her car, waiting for me to drive her home. She's on her phone, pulling her hair back into a ponytail. She's got those dark glasses on even though it's late. I know she's been crying. Real tears, not fake. And here I am in the middle, breaking hearts on both sides.

"Let me stay with you," I say to Jason.

He nods. "I'll drive Hailey home."

Yaz socks my shoulder. Playful, but it stings. "Maybe you are growing up."

"Shut up," I say.

You see, Em. You talk about being stuck in the middle. So am I.

We leave for Vancouver tomorrow a.m. Work our way back to Seattle, Portland, Eugene, Boise, Sacramento, San Francisco, and on and on and on.

Hit me back, Heart. Miss you.

Geoff

TEXT MESSAGE TRANSCRIPT
Friday, January 13, 2012, 11:27 a.m.

GEOFF MORRIS: Made it to Vancouver. Steph overnighted our passports to us. You talking to me yet?

GEOFF MORRIS: Guess not.

To: Emily Amherst
Geoff Morris
Friday, January 13, 2012, 3:19 p.m.

You've made your point. I overstepped my bounds, and I'm sorry. What you want from me? An apology? More daisies? Because I'll do it. At some point, you have to talk to me again.

Apocalypse Tour is in full force. BC Place is all set up. We've already done our sound check. We'll be opening for Whisper. Gainsae will be there. Met up with the guys from Token. Good to see Jerry Erickson out of rehab. He's doing well. It's a who's who of rock up here, Heart. These are my idols, you know? Have all their albums. Been to their shows, and now I'll be sharing a stage with them. Something inside me stirs when I talk with these guys. It's like the dreaming part of me is healing—a process you started.

But there's still a part of me that's sick, a part that the lights of Vancouver spilling over False Creek can't fix. My stomach still roils. I can hardly eat.

Hailey's here. She's been snapping pictures nonstop. Can't get her camera out of her hand. Jason's stepped up. He's taken her under his wing. Maybe because she's single, and she's hot (his words, not mine). Whatever the case, they've been friendly this trip.

Spoke with Alison Blevins of Whisper. You've heard of her. She heard we were joining the tour and downloaded our album. Liked it and wants to sing a few songs with us. The plan is, she'll come out and sing a song or two with us since we're opening. Should help the crowd accept us a bit, rather than booing us off the stage to see the bigger name acts. Anyway, when Whisper headlines tonight, I'll come back out and do a couple songs with her. If it goes well, we might make it a regular thing.

I'm talking about singing with a dyed-in-the-wool rock goddess, the gasoline on every rocker's fiery fantasies, and what am I thinking? "Wait till I tell Em."

This is me telling you, Heart. Tonight's show should be good. But it's hard to be excited without you here to share the moment.

I'm sorry for what I said, for what I did. I got this Irish temper, but shouldn't have taken it out on you. Get back to me is what I'm saying. You don't forgive me? Fine. Just tell me, and I'll move on. I'll leave you alone, and you'll never hear from me again. Just give the word.

All my love,
Geoff

Emily Amherst's Journal

Friday, January 13, 2012, 4:19 p.m.

Jason's car chugs twice and cuts out. "Unbelievable," I whisper. I should have known better than to take the highway, but I wanted to go through the mountains, clear my head a bit, find some peace. The freeways are anything but peaceful.

I crank the engine again. Nothing. I'm not a gearhead, but I'm sure it's more than a dead battery. Something's very wrong with this car, and I've got no tools to fix it. I'm a good thirty miles from the nearest town, and angry clouds are gathering overhead. Whatever heat the car had built up vanishes in a breath. I've got my coat, but not much else, and I'm smart enough to know a gathering storm when I see one.

I've got no chance of making it to town, but maybe I'm close enough to the cabin. It'd be quite the hike, maybe six miles, but the turnout we take is close by. In another hour, the sun will set and the temperature will plummet. I can stay with the car and hope someone comes by, someone kind enough to give me a ride, but no one but locals would take this road, and they're smart enough not to stop before a storm. If I want a chance to survive, it will be at the cabin.

I step outside and the cold scratches my cheeks. My ears prickle. I find the sign marking the turn and hustle. If I want to have a chance of making it up the hill before I freeze, I'm going to need to move. My muscles ache in the cold, and I pull my jacket around me tighter. I flip up my hood, point my head down, and head into the wind. The wind hits my face, freezes my skin. I paw at it from time to time, only in spurts, then put my hands back in my pockets.

I've never felt cold like this before.

Where's Geoff when you need him? Where's Yaz? At this point, I'd be happy to see Hailey.

I find the stream that marks the hiking path. I keep the sound of running water to my right as I hike between ice-crusted trees.

The clouds break, and the snow comes down thick and heavy. It sticks immediately, sinking into the cracks of bark along the trees, melting only where it meets the running water of the stream. In minutes, there's a solid inch of snow. It seeps into my shoes, soaks my socks. At this point, I can't feel my feet. I'm walking on stumps, on prosthetic feet.

I move faster, fast as I can. The hustle keeps my torso warm, but my fingers tingle. My body convulses with cold and my back aches. The wounds on my back burn with ice. An hour into the walk, I hit the halfway mark—the knot of old pines beyond the stream. I'm making progress. It gives me the hope, the strength I need to keep moving.

The snow bunches together, makes walking difficult. If I'm not careful, I'll find a hole and break my ankle. I can't move fast anymore; I have to move cautiously.

I should have stayed with Geoff, should have pushed Hailey to the side.

The snow lets up a bit. Visibility gets better. I hear the voice of my father. He made sure to teach me whatever survival skills he thought I'd need. And since we were the only ones using the cabin in the winter, he figured he'd talk to me about snow safety. I take the opportunity of improved conditions to reevaluate my position, to get a bead on my location and my destination. In the distance, the cabin rises up like a gravestone in the snow.

Hunger sets in, distracts me from the numbing cold for a minute.

Foot after foot, mile after mile. My pants and jackets freeze. My body heat keeps them malleable enough for movement.

And then, it's there, just up the hill. I can hardly breathe for the thin, cold air. Each breath freezes my chest, chills my blood. My heart slows, beats sleepily.

Keep moving.

I press on toward the cabin, my vision darkening. I want to sleep. Gravity pulls at my heavy limbs. I don't want to die like this, not so close.

Push harder. Move faster. My legs resist; my shoulders pinch together.

When I make it to the cabin, I can hardly move, but I refuse to stop. The door's locked, and there's no way I'll find the spare key in this blizzard. Instead, as much as I don't want to, I break the window on the door. I reach in, my hand trembling with cold and fear, and unlock the doorknob. I push inside the squeaky door, slam it behind me.

The cabin doesn't have a heater, but at least I'm out of the cold, the snow and the wind. I move quickly, stacking some leftover kindling and firewood in the fireplace. There's enough for a night, but I'll have to find more in the morning.

I open the kitchen drawer and pull out a box of matches. I light the kindling with trembling fingers. The nascent flame warms my fingers, and I huddle as close as I can without burning myself. It takes far too long to get going, but when it does, the cabin starts to warm.

I strip off my wet clothes, put them by the fire to dry, and cover up with one of the blankets from the pine linen chest.

Now I can think about food. I check the small cabinets in the tiny kitchen. Not much. Just some cans of soup and vegetables. By the look of the storm, this will have to last me a few days. I'll have to wait until the snow starts to melt before I can make it into town.

I grab as many blankets as I can from the chest, spread them out near the fire. I take a pillow from the couch and make a tiny bed. Bundling up, I lay a few feet from the fire and allow it to warm me. Before I drift off to sleep, I try my phone one last time. No battery at all. No outlets here to charge it, either.

I close my eyes, feel a new wetness running down my cheeks.

When they don't hear from me, they'll look for me. They'll have to.

But they'd search the freeways, not the highway.

The fire flickers blue and orange. I add another log but don't want to put any more on. I'll need the other three logs to get me through the night.

My eyes get heavy; my stomach growls. I should have told Geoff how much I love him. We could've had something special, and I didn't play my cards right.

I close my eyes. If I never open them again, I pray Geoff will know I care.

PHONE TRANSCRIPT

Saturday, January 14, 2012, 1:19 a.m.

EMILY AMHERST: You've reached Emily Amherst. Leave me a message.

GEOFF MORRIS: Hey. About to turn in for the night. Show was amazing, Heart. Look, you're probably sleeping. You've got your phone off. It's busted like you say, maybe, and you can't get my calls. But you should be in Ralley by now. You could have made it to LA. I find it hard to believe you wouldn't stop somewhere and call. If you're mad at me, fine, but call Steph at least. Let her know you're okay. I'm worried, Heart. Yaz is worried, even Hailey. I just buried my best friend; don't make me bury this friendship. Em? Call, okay?

G

To: Emily Amherst
Geoff Morris
Saturday, January 14, 2012, 11:47 p.m.

Another day without email or a phone call. I'm past anger and into worry.

We're back in Seattle. Show at Key Arena. Sold out. Crowd loved us. Ninecore set some numbers for the tour. They're trying to minimize the "risk" they're taking on us, but they're kinda known for their risks. Remember Thirstmonger? What a colossal failure they turned out to be. They want to see us sell out our merch, and they've targeted 20,000 downloads of our songs. We hit that number, and they're thinking ink. We're already over four thousand on the first two nights.

Before the show, I was throwing up. People thought it was nerves, but I was thinking different. I swear, I've got an ulcer. Going to sleep, then getting it checked tomorrow.

Love,

Dimples

G

To: Emily Amherst
Geoff Morris
Sunday, January 15, 2012, 3:43 a.m.

Don't be angry. Hailey and I—we kissed tonight. Really kissed. She was a little drunk, and I was worried about you. Not sure that makes sense. Jason passed out, so Hailey sat on my lap. She gets pretty handsy when she's smashed.

Saw a doctor when we got into Portland this afternoon. Said I had an ulcer. He's got me drinking this silver sludge twice a day. Said if it gets irritated, the vomiting would continue and probably shred my vocal chords. Told me I should quit singing for a while. I told him he could quit dreaming.

Call me.

Geoff

To: Emily Amherst
Geoff Morris
Monday, January 16, 2012, 4:18 a.m.

I was joking about kissing Hailey. I wanted to get you ticked enough to call.

I wasn't joking about the ulcer.

We've called Olivia and Frankie. Neither has heard from you or can find you. Steph's out of her mind with worry. Heart, we've got cops searching all over for you. They're trying to find Jason's beat up car. We're thinking kidnapping at this point. I called Rotherman Hospital all freaked out. They still have Barry there, so at least I'm not worried about that. Seriously, Em. Did aliens abduct you?

You have to call or text someone, even if it's not me, okay?

If you're getting these messages, let me know.

Steph and Tripp are still in the hotel, still looking in on Dad. He asked about you yesterday. Steph cried.

I got to go, Heart. I'm breaking over here. We all are.

Geoff

From the Journal of: Geoff Morris

Tuesday, January 17, 2012, 11:41 a.m.

Yaz shakes his head when he sees the lump of white snow that used to be Jason's car. "You were right," he says, more sorrow than hope.

Hailey grabs my hand. "I'm sorry," she says. Her voice is fat with sadness.

They've given up. "She's not in there," I say.

"Geoff," Yaz says. "What else is around?"

"The cabin," I say. I get out of the rental car. We packed for heavy snow and moved on my hunch, on my hope. My boots crunch through icy snow. The sky's blue. The last remnants of the storm of the century have moved on. I knock the first fistful of snow off Jason's car when Yaz sticks his head out of the rental.

"Don't, Geoff. You won't want to see her like that. You can't unsee it, you know?" Hailey's beside him, nodding.

"I told you," I say, knocking another fistful of snow off the driver-side window. "She's not in here." I grin and point to the car. "Empty," I say.

Yaz's eyes get big. "I'll call search and rescue."

"You do that," I say, sliding back into the driver's seat. Yaz dials as I steer toward the sign I saw about a mile back—the turn out toward the mountain, toward the cabin. The chains on the tires bite into the ice as we move up the side of the mountain.

"Stop, Geoff," Hailey says. "If we find her body—"

"You stop," I say. "Give up all you want, but I won't."

"Search and Rescue will be here in twenty minutes," Yaz says. "A few more minutes won't make a difference. Let's wait for the experts."

I drive until the road ends and point to the stream. "She writes about this place all the time," I say. "We follow that stream uphill. There's a hiking trail along here. The path without trees. See it?"

"Geoff," Yaz says again.

I get out of the car and start walking. "Am I meeting you back here, or are you coming?"

They get out of the car, zip up their coats and pull up their hoods. I haven't felt cold like this since before I left Ralley. In minutes, my cheeks are numb. The snow's up to my shins. Trudging through it takes all the energy I have, and I wonder if we'll make it back to San Jose in time for tonight's show. If we don't make it, it'll cost us in merch and downloads, may even keep us from being signed.

Doesn't matter. Em does.

Yaz huffs behind me. "You grew up in this stuff?"

My breath billows out in bluish steam. "Didn't snow like this in Ralley."

"But it snowed." Hailey's teeth chatter. "That's why I left." She grabs Yaz's arm for support. She's shorter than us; the snow's up to her knees. "You're going to get us all killed," she says.

"The cabin will have food. It'll have blankets, wood for fire. I'm telling you, guys, she's up there and she's safe. Em's a survivor. Survived an attack by a very angry, very drunk, very high marine. You think a snow storm's going to stop her? She's resourceful."

Yaz's breaths come in puffs. "If Steph didn't make me come with you," he says.

"But she did."

We hike most the way in quiet. No words, just chattering teeth, shaking hands, glowing red cheeks, the stream bubbling and frothing with new water.

"I can't see anything," Hailey says. "It's all snow."

I point. "See that bump? Has to be the cabin." And there's smoke billowing up from it.

We pick up the pace. We've been out here an hour, easy, but the blip on the horizon has us hopeful. We pick up the pace, even Hailey, though the snow's nearly up to her hips now.

I point to the trees as we get closer to the cabin. "See that?" I say. "Lower branches have been snapped off. She's been here."

"What if it's not her?" Yaz asks.

Hailey snips, "Who else would it be?"

"Probably the dude that owns it," Yaz says.

"It's her," I say. The broken window pane on the door lends credibility to my argument. "Em?" I say, opening the door.

It squeals open, and there she is, bundled up in blankets, unmoving on the floor. I kneel beside her, check her pulse. It's faint, but it's there. Her skin is freezing. "Em," I say, louder this time.

Her eyes flutter.

Hailey cries.

"Geoff?" she says.

"You okay?"

She wraps her arms around me, kisses me on my lips.

To: Geoff Morris
Emily Amherst
Wednesday, January 18, 2012, 11:30 a.m.

Thank you doesn't seem enough for what you've done. You've saved me again. But I know I have other people I need to thank. Yaz and Hailey, of course. Steph for making Yaz go with you. Gainsae and Token for switching performance times so Sideshow could play later. You risked your life and the band's life for me.

Steph told me Yaz was horrified when you were digging the snow off the beetle. Said he didn't know what you'd do if you saw my body frozen behind the wheel. I'm glad Hailey came along, though I'm still not sure I trust her. Burned my hands on her stove too many times. But I'll give her the benefit of the doubt.

To think, you figured out where I went, and you came to find me. I'm humbled, honored, you paid such attention to me and my letters. It makes me think about this "you and me" thing.

When I kissed you, it wasn't simply because I was happy to see you. I kissed you because I'm falling in love with you.

In the cabin, I had a lot of time to stare death in the face. Daddy taught me survival skills, and his first lesson was this: The unprepared person stuck in nature loses every time. I was unprepared. I shouldn't have survived. I spent days in that cabin, waiting for the storm to break long enough to hunt up something to eat. It didn't break for days.

You make decisions when you think you're a stone's throw from death. Life is too short to live with regret.

Look, I'm far from perfect. I've lived with childhood fears all my life. Never stepped out of my comfort zone, never really lived. I've relied on others to tell me when to be happy, what to believe, when to weep.

You're not the kind of person others would want me to spend time with. You're an individual, and I'm a rubber stamp. You're piercings, chopped dark hair, tattoos. I'm ponytail and faded jeans. I'm a student; you're a rock star. You live life; I simply exist.

What I'm trying to say is this: I want to steal your dreams. I want to live. I want to do more than lock myself in a windowless office and bury my nose in inventory and spreadsheets.

You say I'm selfless and kind. But you're the one who put himself on the line for me. You're the one who risked your rent money, even your life, rescuing me. You've given me the benefit of the doubt. What have I done for you?

I won't let you walk away from me, Geoff. I don't know exactly what you want—any relationship between us would be tough, but I'm committed. I'm willing. We can make it work.

If I ever doubted the existence of God or His love for us, those doubts vanished when you came in the cabin. I'm done waiting, thinking, deliberating. I'd imagined it for days, my lips pressing yours, you gently brushing my hair from my face. In my mind, I could taste you, breathe in your warm breath, feel the chill of your emotion climb up my arms.

That's why I kissed you. I wanted to make it count.

If you're willing, I'll stand by your side. I love your quirks, your uniqueness, your joy, your view of life. I can't, at this point, imagine being without you.

Maybe you're not ready. But a man who digs a car out of the snow, then hikes an hour up a mountain in single digit weather on a hunch, is a man I think is willing to make an effort.

I'm placing an offer on the table. We start over. New. We blaze this trail of attraction, obsession, together. It won't be perfect. But isn't that half the fun?

I'm less as a person without you. I want to be more with you. Our whole relationship rolls like a bad movie. But I know what I feel now, and I know it's not just a fantasy for a rock star who came to my rescue. It's real.

I'm asking for your forgiveness for my assumptions, for the mean things I've said.

I want to share one more dream with you, and if it's the last one, I understand. Think of your show tonight. Look at the crowd from backstage and feel your heart pump in rhythm with the bass. Let the adrenaline boil. Do that little bounce where you bump up and down on your toes and crack your knuckles as you make a fist. Brush your hair back out of your face, and before you step out on that stage, close your eyes and remember our kiss. You drive me crazy. The thought of you makes my heart race and the heat inside my body rise. You make my palms sweat and words stumble. You make my knees weak and my body shake from excitement.

That's the dream I want you to take before you step on that stage tonight. Then sing. Blow the crowd away, but save the passion for me. I'm stepping out on faith here, but, sweetie, I love you.

Longing for you.

Your Heart

TEXT MESSAGE TRANSCRIPTS
Wednesday, January 18, 2012, 8:53 p.m.

EMILY AMHERST: Open with something pretty tonight, like "Surreal."

GEOFF MORRIS: Keep kissing like you do, and I'll open with any song you want.

EMILY AMHERST: Goof. Go get 'em, Dimples.

GEOFF MORRIS: Be safe. I'll message after our set. Gainsae's done. Gotta go.

G

To: Emily Amherst
Geoff Morris
Thursday, January 19, 2012, 1:19 a.m.

Tuesday was long. We left early to get down to the arena to sound check. We're driving down in the bus, and I'm glancing over the map, trying to get a feel for where in the world Salyer is when it hits me—that's not too far from Willow Creek. Sure enough, there it is on the map, looking like a smudge on my phone.

I tell them I'm making a stop. The band's ticked, but I tell Yaz I know where you are, and he and Hailey hop in the first rental car we find. We start driving, Hailey squinting at the map on her phone, Yaz mumbling about the snow. He's an LA kid—never seen real snow. Hailey stares at the map, then checks the road. "Doesn't look the same," she says.

"It's the snow," I tell her.

They were worried, Em. Terrified. Thought Hailey's tears would freeze to her face. That girl loves you, you know? I'm happy to hear you're willing to give her a second chance, a third chance, a fiftieth chance, whatever.

Anyway, we're shocked when we get inside the cabin. You'd torn the place apart. Smashed up all the furniture for firewood, made a nest of old wet bark stripped off tree branches. You really lived on soup and snow? That's full-on Man vs. Wild, and, if I can say it without sounding crass, also full-on sexy.

You'll want to know—I never doubted. I knew you were okay, but I also knew you needed help. Call it a hunch, a voice, an assurance. Whatever it was, it pointed me to you, and I'm smart enough to follow leads like that.

Putting you in the rental with Hailey and sending you back

down to Ralley was one of the toughest things I've done. If it were any other time, any other situation, I'd have driven you myself. But I couldn't let the band down, and I knew you were in good hands.

Rock stars dream of the tour, the music, the antics, the pulsing adrenaline. But the allure washes away fast. Never thought I'd be homesick for my old apartment, for the few days we had together before Mark died, before Ninecore took us to dinner.

We got back to the arena about three hours late. Security waves Yaz and me in. We head backstage, and Jason's twirling drumsticks. He's nervous, anxious. Nesmeth's pacing. We get in and they stare at us. "She okay?" Nesmeth asks.

"She's good," I say. "A little sick of soup."

Jason laughs. "Let's hit it," he says. And that's it. The roadies hand us our guitars, and we take the stage. I'm completely unprepared to sing. My mind's with you. My heart's with you. I know, by now, you're back in Ralley, eating the largest meal of your life. I look over the crowd anyway. Tony's at the sound booth, the guys from Gainsae are front and center. They like to be in the crowd for our sets. Alison's watching in the wings, waiting for our duet, a new number called "Underbelly," and I'm thinking, why can't Em be here? I almost expect to see your face in the crowd, and I search it all night, looking for you.

The crowd's come ready for us. They're wearing our shirts, singing our songs, throwing rock fists, pitting like gladiators. Fresno's a rocking place. The freaks come out at night. We've got no merch left. Sold out halfway through the tour. Tony's on the phone after the show putting in emergency orders. Ninecore tells us we're about a thousand downloads away from ink. I shake my head. It's happening too fast.

And then there's us. Heart, I don't know what to say. I'll lay it on the line, and ask you to listen gently, because it's late, I'm exhausted, and I'm still amped up on adrenaline from the show.

I put a lot on you the last few days. I demanded you come to the funeral, made you pick between me and your dad. You chose me, and we see how far that got you. But you come back from the cabin dripping with kindness, and my heart breaks that you could love a man like me. I want to tell you everything, Em, but I can't hurt you, and I wonder, if you knew me a little better, maybe you wouldn't love me. My heart hurts. I'm terrified, not to trust you, but for you to trust me.

You're the first woman I've fallen in love with before I've slept with her. Maybe that's not the romantic line you were hoping for, but it's true. I say it as a compliment. I want you to understand, to know me. I'm shallow, but I don't want to be. You make me want to be more, to be stronger. You're the first woman in my life that's normal, that's got a selfless heart. I can't ruin that for you.

Long story short, I love you. I want us to be us, but I'm afraid you don't really know what that means, not fully, not now. I don't want to lead you on, don't want you to think I'm someone I'm not.

Don't misunderstand. I've never lied to you (except the kissing Hailey thing), but I may not have been completely forthcoming with everything. If we're going to be "us," you need to know me better.

We're in Los Angeles Sunday. Hoping you can get things worked out with your dad before then. I'd love to see you again. I've saved you a backstage pass for Staples Center, if you're looking for a taste of the rock 'n' roll life.

I miss you; I love you; I'm terrified.

Counting days to LA.

—Geoff

TEXT MESSAGE TRANSCRIPT
Thursday, January 19, 2012, 1:30 a.m.

EMILY AMHERST: I love you too.

To: Geoff Morris
Emily Amherst
Thursday, January 19, 2012, 11:00 a.m.

Call me immature, but I love Winnie the Pooh. The book takes the heart of a child and translates it into the soul of an adult. Milne takes those simple, heartfelt, and innocent moments and makes them prodigious, awesome, wonderful. Like when Winnie the Pooh tells Christopher Robin, "If you live to be a hundred, I want to live to be a hundred minus one day, so I never have to live a day without you."

You don't have to be smart, or bold, or dumb to understand the depth of his love. Whatever you have to tell me about your past won't matter. The past is the past. We can figure out our future together as we go. I want you, and you want me. Let's start there and work forward. If we screw up along the way, we start over until we get it right. Love is do-overs, forgiveness.

When I was a kid, Mom used to take me to a church in Salyer. I had this Sunday school teacher who used to talk about forgiveness every week. "It's like tearing off all the messy pages in a notebook. You're left with new, clean paper." In the cabin, I got back in touch with God. When I closed my eyes, unsure if I'd ever open them again, I thought of all the paper I'd scribbled on that God ripped out. He's given me a clean sheet of paper. I need to do the same thing.

That's what Jesus did for all of us, and it's what he wants us to do too. I know you don't like hearing about him, but without Jesus, there is no forgiveness. I hope you understand that. Without Jesus, there is no Emily.

And then you walked in. I can't ignore the timing. We've got a new sheet of paper. I don't care about the Geoff of the past. I love the Geoff who trusted his gut enough to find me at the cabin, the man who cried over his best friend's death, the man who defended me from an angry ex-marine, the man who loves me and respects me and never pressures me to do things I'm not comfortable with.

I didn't forgive you when you took me in your arms in the cabin and carried me down that mountain, whispering, singing in my ear, or when you buried your face in my neck, or when you kissed me, or when you told me you loved me. I forgave you before all that, when you got on the bus. I knew you weren't leaving me. You were trying to make a better life for me.

You are a hero.

We'll both makes mistakes. Promise me we'll forgive each other and start again.

Hailey and I came to a few understandings when I was getting checked out at the ER. I told her I didn't appreciate the lie she told, and I didn't want her trying to take the one thing I love away from me again.

Here's the whole story on me and Mark. We got engaged a week before their parents died. Hailey took their deaths pretty hard and wanted Mark to move up to Seattle with her—to have family close by. But she knew he'd never leave me. We'd made plans to settle down in Ralley. She told Mark some pretty mean things about me. Said I'd been cheating on him for weeks, that I had a "secret boyfriend." He didn't believe her, so she paid a guy to hit on me and even kiss me in front of Mark. He never talked to me again. I didn't know it was her until a year later.

But I forgave her. She apologized, and I gave her a clean sheet of paper. It'll be tough, but I'm going to try to fix our relationship. But give us our space. Don't push me toward her. Let it happen naturally.

On that note, I need to tell you something else. Please don't be too mad. When Steph picked me up at the hospital, I told her I wanted to give Barry a new piece of paper too. I can't live my life afraid. On the way home, we stopped by Rotherman to see him. It wasn't easy. I nearly threw up on the stairs, I was so nervous. But I went in anyway. Steph came with me, and Barry's doctor and a security guard, too.

Honestly, Barry's pitiful. I knew the PTSD made things tough for him, but I had no idea how bad off he really was, how much of an escape and comfort he found in the haze of hangovers and highs. He cried and cried, took my hands and asked me to forgive him. He shook the whole time, either from withdrawal or grief. But he was gentle and tender. He looked more like the Barry I fell in love with two years ago than the one who attacked me a few weeks ago.

We only stayed ten minutes. I told him about the cabin and about the band. He told me about his rehab. When I left, he asked to hug me. My spine stiffened, but I had to beat my fears. I told him he could. Please don't be mad. The guards were right there. I was safe. And he was gentle. He saw the scarring on my neck and shoulders and face and shook his head. "I'm sorry, Em," he said. "I can't believe I did that." He must have apologized a hundred times.

I don't plan on going back, but I had to go this time, had to beat this demon. Maybe now I can put that part of my life behind me.

News on Daddy isn't good. Doctor thinks he'll make it another month, maybe. He's in a full-care facility now. Hospice. Good news is, we found a place called Ridgehaven Manor in Glendale, not too far from Yaz and Steph's. We're going to drive back to LA today and get everything set up for him. Wish he were coherent enough to know what was happening. All he can do is stare at me with wonder, as if he's seeing me for the first time.

I can't believe you have an ulcer. Please take care of yourself. I've had enough tragedy in my life lately. Last thing I need is for you to get sick. I did a little research on ulcers, and I'm going to send you a list of things you can eat. Diet is the first line of defense.

I've decided to do something with my hair. I need a change. What do you think? Short and sassy? Medium and professional? Stringy and messy? Red? Mahogany?

Good news is, I got a new phone today. Feel free to call anytime you want.

If you live to be a hundred, I want to live to be a hundred minus one day.

My love,

Emily

PHONE TRANSCRIPT

Thursday, January 19, 2012, 8:22 p.m.

EMILY AMHERST: Hey, Dimples!

GEOFF MORRIS: Hey, Heart. Wanted to call earlier, but Tony took me back to the doc. He wants me drinking more of the sludge. It's this experimental new thing they're doing.

EMILY AMHERST: You better do what he says.

GEOFF MORRIS: Yeah, I know.

EMILY AMHERST: What's wrong?

GEOFF MORRIS: I'm tired. This touring thing is brutal.

EMILY AMHERST: That's not it. What's wrong?

GEOFF MORRIS: Nothing. I'm just digesting.

EMILY AMHERST: It's Barry, isn't it?

GEOFF MORRIS: Yeah. And Hailey. And you and me and your dad and Ninecore and Tony.

EMILY AMHERST: And Mark too.

GEOFF MORRIS: Yes, Mark too.

EMILY AMHERST: You can't do anything about Hailey or my dad or Mark. All you can do is be the best Geoff you can be. Everything else will work itself out. I'm here for you.

GEOFF MORRIS: Bakersfield is three hours from LA. I could have driven down to see you before the show, but Tony doesn't want me leaving anymore. Freaked out after I grabbed you from the cabin.

EMILY AMHERST: Only a few more days until LA, baby.

GEOFF MORRIS: You can't come up to Vegas Saturday? Let Steph sit with your dad? We can get a room. It'd be nice not to have to sleep on the bus for once.

EMILY AMHERST: I can't, babe. My dad.

GEOFF MORRIS: I know. I shouldn't have asked. I'm sorry, Heart.

EMILY AMHERST: I wanted to talk to you before the show to get you going, get you excited. Now I'm depressing you.

GEOFF MORRIS: You're not.

EMILY AMHERST: You're not very convincing.

GEOFF MORRIS: I'm greedy is all. I want you and can't have you, so I'm throwing a tantrum. I'll grow up. I promise.

EMILY AMHERST: Not too fast, though, babe. I like you the way you are.

GEOFF MORRIS: Thanks, Heart. Gainsae's wrapping up. Tony's giving me the evil eye.

EMILY AMHERST: I love you, Geoff.

GEOFF MORRIS: Love you too, Heart.

G

To: Emily Amherst
Geoff Morris
Friday, January 20, 2012, 1:17 a.m.

Some good things happened tonight. Bakersfield's small, but we packed the arena out and sold the merch Tony ordered for us. We got the last thousand downloads we needed—plus. Ninecore's going to sign us. I've seen the contract, read the language, put my college learning to good use. Ninecore's not the biggest, but they're the real deal.

We've had other suits talk to us on this tour. Didn't tell you that, but want to tell you now. They all come with pens and contracts. I read through them, tell them we'd be happy to sign if they change the language in this clause, omit that clause—you get the idea. They all say the same thing, "You a musician or a lawyer?" That ends the talks.

Ninecore's different. They're cool. They watch the song and dance, and they know we're smart, and they know we're not going to sign a contract that asks us to make sacrifices we can't make. They set us up on this tour, took an incredible risk on us, and they know we're faithful to them.

But the tour is long, and it's taking its toll. Jason and Nesmeth are having the time of their lives. They're younger than me and Yaz, and they're enjoying their youth. Me and Yaz are different, though. We'll hang with the fans after the show, kick our feet up with the other bands, talk a little shop, but then we head back to the bus alone. We play video games while Jason and Hailey hang and Nesmeth drags in whoever else he can to engage in other activities. When they're done, Yaz calls Steph. They video chat for a bit. She brings the computer in Tripp's room, lets Yaz see his boy sleeping. He hangs up, then weeps.

Says he's a horrible father, and I've got to tell him five more days, four more days, three more days, and then you'll be home. Then, it's just San Diego. Steph'll pick him up after the gig and bring him home. If we lay down tracks in SD, he'll pack up the fam and bring them with him. I say, "What about the East Coast tour?" He says, "I'll lay down tracks. That's all I can promise."

See, without Yaz, I'm not sure this band works, so I'm freaking out.

He's a good father, I tell him, providing for his family, setting them up for a good life. I tell him one man in a million has a chance at the kind of life he's got at his fingertips. He can set his family up for a long time with the kind of money we can make playing our music.

This is the longest he's been away from his family. He's falling all to pieces. He holds together okay during the day, but I see it when we're gigging. Something's not there—the fire, the intensity. He goes through the motions, puts on an incredible show, absolutely shreds on the guitar, flawless solos and fatty riffs, but he doesn't enjoy it, not like he did when we gig in LA and he can sleep at home.

What's the story with paparazzi? Steph mentioned something about it to Yaz. We've had a few magazine interviews and cover spreads and the like, but nothing too big, we thought—not big enough for paparazzi. Crazy.

Alison and I sang "Underbelly" again tonight. Getting a lot of buzz from that tune, something she and I put together in about ten minutes about a week ago.

Listen, Heart, about your letter. I had no idea Hailey would do something so devious. I know you warned me, told me she wasn't a good person, but I thought it was a misunderstanding—high school drama stuff. I'll be more watchful of her. She's been cozying up to Jason of late. Maybe I should warn him.

I don't even know what to say about your dad. We started the week with a funeral, almost had to bury you, and now your dad? I'll be thinking of him, Em. I'll even pray for him, though I'm not sure what good it will do. Still trying to wrap my mind around this God of yours. Seems to me, if He were all powerful, He wouldn't let all this crap fall on you.

I like the idea of new paper. You describe the idea perfectly. But forgiveness isn't one of my strong suits. Let me apologize in advance for saying something I'll probably regret later, but this needs to be said.

People like you, Em, with a heart like yours, you need the chance for new paper. But some people are evil. They don't deserve new paper. Or, better yet, they've run out of paper. You can only pull out so many sheets before the notebook's empty, right?

What Barry did to you, what he did twice—he's used up his paper. I don't want you going back. He could have hurt you again, even with Steph and the doctor and the guard there. He's an ex-marine, a trained killer. He busted me up pretty good, and if Yaz hadn't stepped in, he probably could have ended me, you, and your lawyer. Don't go see him again, okay? Promise me. If you believe in God, you let God deal with him. I'm not trying to be bossy here, but I love you, and I can't stand to see you hurt again. PTSD isn't something you play around with, Heart. Read the news—you get the idea.

My mom's the same way. She's a head-case. She had this inferiority complex, so she had to find ways to put people down, to celebrate herself over everyone else. Constant criticism. And, on top of it all, she steals my college fund. There's no new paper for my mom or my dad. They were too busy arguing to raise me. I finished with them early. Ran away when I was sixteen. You didn't know that, did you? Ended up homeless for a couple of years. Finished high school living on the streets. Still got a scholarship to UCLA. I figure that wasn't too bad. Know who came to my graduation that year? Not my mom or my dad.

Every time I've given someone a new sheet, they scribble on it, ruin it again. I've learned—save your paper for those who will treat it well.

In context of your hair, I like the color already. That strawberry blond look is hot. I'd go short and sassy, something playful. Check Steph's front step tomorrow evening. Yaz and I may send an inking gift to you and her.

Until then, all my love, Heart.

Geoff

VIDEO CALL TRANSCRIPT
EAmherst connecting to Zombiecall.com
Friday, January 20, 2012, 3:18 p.m.

MorrisG: This is a surprise.
EAmherst: Bigger surprise you answered. I've tried video chat before, but you never answered. SURPRISE! Thanks for answering.
MorrisG: Installed this stupid program last year. Never used it. Didn't mean to ignore you on the video call, but it's been non-stop. Tours are brutal. Love the hair. Turn a bit, let me see the back. Nice, Heart.
EAmherst: You like? Wanted something playful. Kinda punk with the shave on this side, but I had to do something until it grows out.
MorrisG: Hot. You make a good punker.
EAmherst: Stop it. How you can say that with this staring you in the face?
MorrisG: What? The scar? Hardly notice. Besides, it'll heal. It can't touch your smile, your eyes, those perfect little ears of yours.
EAmherst: You resting?
MorrisG: Yeah. Schooling Yaz in Halo. Jason and Hailey are grabbing lunch. You should see her. She's all gothed out now. Little Ms. Pink herself.
EAmherst: Can we not talk about her right now?
MorrisG: Sure, Heart. I get it. What's up?
EAmherst: Great news about the contract.
MorrisG: Right? Still, dreading it a bit. Yaz isn't thrilled.
EAmherst: I know. Remember Steve Addison from college?
MorrisG: Preppy law kid?
EAmherst: Yeah. I gave him a call. We chatted a bit, and

I told him about you. His firm works with Ninecore. He gave me some sweet info. Contract language allows you to request tours in two week intervals. You know, two on, two off, that kind of thing. I guess Ratchet's on that schedule. Slows momentum, but their singer wants to spend what time she can with her new baby. Can't blame her for that. He said if you're having health issues, you should ask about it. I think it'd be a good thing to look into. You need it; I need it; Yaz needs it.

MorrisG: You serious right now?

EAmherst: Yeah, why? What's wrong? What'd I do now?

MorrisG: Heart, you can't go talking about my ulcer to people. That's gotta stay private. I don't need that in the news. I don't need Ninecore getting cold feet right now. We're a big enough risk as is. If they think I can't tour, they may not ink us. Tony and I have been very hush hush on the whole thing. Jason and Nesmeth don't even know. Just me and Tony and Yaz.

EAmherst: What about Hailey?

MorrisG: No clue, babe. I wouldn't tell her something like that.

EAmherst: I'm sorry.

MorrisG: Look, I'm sorry I snapped. I've been edgy lately. Shouldn't take it out on you.

EAmherst: I don't want to nag, Dimples, but do you think you can at least talk to Tony about the two-week thing?

MorrisG: We're newbs, babe. We don't get to make requests.

EAmherst: You said Ninecore was cool. You said they were legit. That's why you like them. They'll understand. You're an investment, and they'll want to make sure they get a good return.

MorrisG: But if I'm a risk, they won't invest in the first place.

EAmherst: Fine. Don't talk to them.

MorrisG: Don't be like that, Heart. I'm just trying to lay it on the line.
EAmherst: I know. Think about it, okay? It's built into the contract. You can make the request after you ink if you want.
MorrisG: I'll think about it. Listen, Em, about my email.
EAmherst: We'll talk about that later. How's your stomach?
MorrisG: Hurts. I got your list of foods. Doc agreed. I love you, Heart. You get that, right?
EAmherst: Yeah.
MorrisG: I'm not happy about the Barry thing.
EAmherst: Let it go. I thought you'd get why I went. I don't want to live in fear. Don't want to spend my life looking over my shoulder.
MorrisG: Don't go back. Please.
EAmherst: I told you I wouldn't. Sounds like you need to work on forgiveness.
MorrisG: There's a difference between forgiving and forgetting. He nearly beat you into a coma. Ripped your face and neck open. Shredded your back.
EAmherst: I remember every time I look in the mirror, every time I lie on my back, every time I shower.
MorrisG: We're not going to agree, are we?
EAmherst: Agree on what? I said I wasn't going back. I'm still pressing charges. What's not to agree on?
MorrisG: Truth?
EAmherst: Truth.
MorrisG: I hate him. I hate that he hurt you. I hate that he hurt me. I hate that you went back to see him. I hate that he touched you, and I hate that you let him. You let him touch you, Em. You should know better. I gotta go.
EAmherst: Geoff wait. Geoff.
MorrisG has disconnected from ZombieCall.com

To: Geoff Morris
Emily Amherst
Friday, January 20, 2012, 8:19 p.m.

You hung up on me? Seriously? Stop being a baby.

Let's start over. New paper.

I'm thrilled about the band being signed. Awesome about the downloads. Do Steph and I get t-shirts? Steph was all over the information Steve gave me. And she's passing it onto Yaz. Steve seemed to think you could negotiate the time of year too. All you can do is ask, right?

My point is, I'll do whatever I have to do to see you. If it means I drive to see you, take a train or fly, I'll make some of the shows. Stop worrying. Worry irritates the ulcer.

I think my sweet Geoff is a bit of a control freak. Relax. I'm the accountant. I should be the one sweating details, not you. If Ninecore's as good as you and Steve say, I bet you can negotiate.

About the paparazzi, Steph caught them in the elm tree in the back yard, shooting pictures of the baby. I'm a little under the radar. They haven't figured me out yet, but Steph says it won't be long. I'm with her, and when they see us together, they'll snoop.

We've thought about throwing a backyard BBQ and inviting them. :) Right now, they're all hung up on the fight with Barry. Your Batman leap and Yaz's Superman toss are all over the Entertainment News channel. Someone got it on video, put it on YouTube, and now it's viral. Might have something to do with the last thousand + downloads you got.

I heard the song with Alison on the radio today. Wow. They must have played it every twenty minutes. You're getting some good play.

As for Hailey, thanks for finally believing me. I didn't mention Mark because Mark never mentioned me. It was history. But I'd be less than honest if I said I never loved him. He's the one I made the mistake with. Shortly after we got close physically, Hailey pulled her stunt.

Don't say anything about her to Jason. She said some nice things about him, and she may be ready to settle down. That's the impression I got from her on our way back to Ralley. She seems pretty into him. No reason to ruin it. I don't want to do to her what she did to me.

Daddy gets weaker every day. Steph and I went to the funeral home yesterday. It was hard, picking out an urn, paying for a funeral, facing the future. I'm not going to put myself through that whole wake nonsense. Daddy hasn't been able to keep up with his friends. He'll go quietly—no need for much of a get-together.

Thank you for your prayers. That's a start. And if it makes you feel any better, I'm not sure anyone can wrap their head around God. But forgiveness is freeing.

I know you had a hard time as a kid, but you might feel a little better if you talked to your mom and dad. Make an effort to forgive. They may never change, but if you don't make the effort, you may end up regretting it later. My visit to Barry wasn't for him; it was for me. I feel better. Let it go. I can't change what he did to me, but I can change how I act. I choose to let go. I'm sure I'll get mad from time to time. I'll always have the reminders. But I don't have to keep being angry. Neither do you.

I understand why you're angry, but I'm safe. Forgiveness is a process. No one's too old to learn.

And as long as Barry is hospitalized, we have nothing to worry about. The paparazzi are a bigger threat than him.

I think forgiveness can help your ulcer, Dimples. Let your anger and resentment go. I know you don't like hearing about Jesus, but you could really use him now. We both do. I won't push. But think about it.

I'm waiting for the surprise. Can't wait to see it. Is it you? A girl can dream, can't she?

Put another pic up on Facebook for you. Short and sassy, like you wanted.

I'm sure the show will be awesome tonight. Get some sleep when you're done. Tomorrow, I'm going to see about trading in Daddy's truck. Time for a new start.

My love, babe.

Em

G

To: Emily Amherst
Geoff Morris
Saturday, January 21, 2012, 1:18 a.m.

You told Steph, and Steph told Yaz, and now Yaz is in Tony's ear, and Tony's sweating it because he doesn't want to bring it up to Ninecore yet, but Yaz is pushing like you've never seen him, like he's a boar in a corner.

I should have been clearer when we were chatting. It's too early to bring this stuff up. You say the viral video's good for us, but if Ninecore sees us as more of a risk, they pull the contract back. Get it? No ink. No dollars. No recouping the life savings I've dumped into this tour. Yaz has a back-up plan. He doesn't need the ink. Me and Jason and Nesmeth? Not so much.

This is our life, Heart—the diesel fumes, the practical jokes, a million miles of asphalt, hours of sound checks, running through songs backstage, making music with friends—with really talented people. The lights, the pyrotechnics, the crowd surfing, the dollar beers, the very rowdy, very drunk, very beautiful masses holding you up for no other reason than to say they touched you, they have connected with you, formed a bond in some way.

Maybe that sounds egotistical, but here's what I'm saying: It's beautiful to think my words, my voice, my strings have changed the course of strangers' lives. I'm doing something good on this tour. I don't do a lot of good things, but this, my music, my words, my voice—for whatever reason, they resonate in people. They need me, and if Ninecore pulls out, what do I have left?

No apartment. No car. I've sold everything I have. Am I supposed to call my mom? "Hey, haven't talked to you in the better part of a decade, but I was feeling pretty good about myself. Maybe you can bring me down a bit. Go ahead, wind up, and punch me with reality like a concrete brick. I need it. Also, remember all that money you stole from me? How about you give that back now?"

Should I call my dad? I don't even know where he's living right now. Might be dead. Could have died years ago, and I'd never know it.

I don't want to be homeless again, Heart. I did that for two years in high school—showering off in gym before everyone showed up, eating two meals a day in the cafeteria and scrounging for dinner, hanging in clubs until closing, then sneaking back on campus to curl up in the locker room before school. That's not a life for me anymore.

I get you want what's best for me, but why don't you listen when I tell you what's best? Why don't you believe me? If we're going to make this work, Heart, we gotta communicate.

I'm not good at communicating, am I? Can't believe I disconnected from the chat this afternoon. Classic jerk move. Man, I need a gallon of Pepto.

Why do I do this to myself? Every night's the same thing. Talk with Em, get pumped up for the show, rock a new city, hang with fans and bands, then check my messages. You have to know how exhausted I am at the end of a night. I don't think straight, and my emotions are frayed, and I think I can communicate coherently. But I can't, and I get angry and upset, and I say stupid things that probably hurt you, which is exactly what I'm trying to avoid.

I want you safe and happy is all. The paparazzi can undo that quick. Steph told Yaz, Yaz got on Tony. Tony put in a call to Ninecore, hence the very large men taking frequent walks down their street. Guess Steph's talking to your Steve friend about possible litigation against the tabloids sending the people onto her property. Dead end, he says. Public figures and all that. Shouldn't have "married famous" is the feeling Yaz gets, but she didn't, right? What was Sideshow when Yaz put a ring on Steph's finger? A garage band, a couple of friends hammering out some tunes because they were sick of their day jobs. They had big dreams, got caught up in it, and then found out the life wasn't exactly what they wanted. If you see the flashing cameras, babe, turn away. Find somewhere else to be, somewhere with a lot of people and cops.

You heard "Underbelly" finally? Alison's incredible. Sings like a harp. Voice like lightning. A real joy to harmonize with.

And your dad—man, Em. What's it like planning for death? With Mark, it all happened after, you know? We knew he wasn't going to make it, but you have to wait, wondering what day it will be. I'm not helping, am I? What I mean to say is, I'm sorry.

Praying feels weird, but I do it anyway. Yaz says I suck at it. What does he know, I say. I pray from my heart. Wrong or right, it's what I do, and I hope it helps. I know you'll get that. That's what you do to me, Em—you make me a praying man. You say Jesus is listening. I hope he is. Of course, I'm not sure why he'd listen to a guy like me. I'm far too screwed up.

Jason and Hailey are still friendly. She seems different. Sad, you know, like the whole Mark business is hitting her finally. She's tired, worn out. Quit her job. Full on freelance now. She's got about as much riding on this tour as we do. But Jason keeps her happy, and she keeps him from the line of women outside our bus. Now, Nesmeth is the only one making choices each night. You'll like this. Jason's cleaned up his mouth, too. Yaz and Nesmeth still curse like sailors, but you knew that.

New car, eh? What are you looking for exactly? I'll be in LA soon. Want to hang on a bit, and we'll look together?

I've been avoiding the Barry thing. You know why. I stand by what I said. Forgiveness is one thing, but I still hope a car hits him when he gets out. Maybe that's too much, too far, but it's truth, right? It's what he deserves. Not death, nothing quick. Something with a very long, very painful recovery process, say like getting thrown through a glass coffee table.

I'll forgive my mom when she forgives me for not being perfect, for always letting her down, for being too much like my old man. How's that sound?

Hate starting out and ending on a sour note. Know this: No matter how much I gripe, I still love you. For you, there's always new paper.

Love,

Geoff

To: Geoff Morris
Emily Amherst
Saturday, January 21, 2012, 8:04 a.m.

I went to college, and they taught me how to be an accountant. They showed me how to manage stacks of IRS forms and dishonest people who play the system. I graduated with honors.

There's no college for this lifestyle of yours. You're right. You don't communicate. You don't teach. You just fly off the handle and throw punches.

Dad taught me outfitting skills, how to survive in the mountains, how to hike, how to ride the rapids. No one taught me how to date a rock star.

I've never done anything exciting in my life. I've lived, taken steps, made choices, succeeded, and failed.

Forget I tried to help by talking to Steve. And the next time you feel like you need to fill me in, learn to freakin' communicate. I'm trying to help, and you make it out like I'm trying to ruin you.

I'm going to the nursing home. They called about Daddy. Guess I'll see if I can foul up what's left of his life too.

I hate fighting, but I still love you.

Later.

E

To: Emily Amherst
Geoff Morris
Saturday, January 21, 2012, 12:18 p.m.

I've hurt you.

I'm no better than Barry. This is what I was worried about—not you, not us, but about me screwing "us" up. If there's one thing I learned from my mom, it's how to screw up a relationship. It's ingrained in me; it's some sort of sick instinct. I finally get to the point where I'm ready to give up the promiscuity, the shallowness of simple physical touch, and really get to know someone, really fall in love. Then I'm lucky enough to talk with you, to rediscover you—a friend from the past I'd been stupid enough to overlook for years. Worse yet, you like me too, and what do I do?

I do what I'm good at—screwing up relationships. Trained by the best.

Last night, after we talked, Yaz got in Tony's ear. Tony bugged. Shut Yaz down, so Yaz pulled out the big guns. "Talk to Ninecore or I walk," he says. "You can play Vegas without me."

I get in Yaz's ear. He can't do this to us, to me, right? But he's set, he's not backing down. No way we can replace Yaz. Tony backs down and gets Ninecore on the horn. This is minutes after I blew up at you, so I'm listening in, and my ulcer's flaring, and I know this won't end well.

Tony's got Sterling Amundsten of Ninecore himself on the line. Woke him up at some ungodly hour to talk contract with him. Jason and Hailey are holding hands behind me. Nesmeth hands me a bottle of the silver sludge. We're all sweating, and Yaz is fuming. He's looking at Tony like he's Barry.

Long story short, this is what Amundsten tells Tony: "Make a list of what they need. We'll get it worked in the contract tomorrow before they sign."

Nesmeth pushes Yaz, calls him some names, but it's all in good fun now. The tension's broken. I go back to my bunk and sack out, hold my stomach, and pray to this God of yours for some relief—pray he doesn't let you run away from me—pray I haven't screwed everything up. I pray for your dad too. You should know that. They're awkward, my prayers, filled with thous and shalts and wilts. I've never talked to a deity. Don't know their language, so I borrow from what I gathered from my uncle, the only classy guy related to me by blood. I miss him like mad, you know?

***

We inked this morning, Heart. Just before we left for Vegas. Sideshow is Ninecore's newest act. So much stress off me now. I can finally think clear again.

Let me back up a step or two and try this again. I got irritated last night because I thought you'd gone behind my back. After our chat, I thought you understood I didn't want you talking to anyone about what you'd found. But that's not fair of me. I can't ask you not to share things with Steph. Come to think of it, I shouldn't hide things from Yaz either. Doesn't make me a very good friend if I do.

This is me apologizing. I'm not good at it, but I promise to get better. You've got too much on your mind right now to worry about a moody rock star. That's what Yaz told me last night. He read my message, and he got bent. "If this band doesn't work out for you, you know what you got? Em. Ink or no, platinum or no, you got Em, as long as you don't keep talking to her like that."

Yaz speaks with the voice of my conscience.

How's Dad? Almost don't want to ask.

We hit Vegas about four minutes ago. We're playing the Hard Rock Hotel. They're putting us up in rooms. I'll actually have a bed tonight, rather than my bunk.

Playing some tribute songs tonight. Stone Temple Pilots, Nirvana, classic Alice in Chains, a real 90s affair. We take their lesser known songs, try to breathe new life in them, let the fans get a sense of our musical DNA.

I don't want to fight, Heart. I'm sorry. Hope it helps.

For now, I won't talk about Barry or my mom or anything else.

While you're handing out new paper, you think you have any for me?

Miss you, Heart.

Geoff

TEXT MESSAGE TRANSCRIPT
Saturday, January 21, 2102 12:24 pm

EMILY AMHERST: Notice the white page.

Emily Amherst's Journal

Saturday, January 21, 21012 11:12 am

I need air. Space. I can't take another month like this. Barry. Mark. Hailey. Dad. I try to make Geoff happy, and all I do is make things worse. Every time I open my mouth, I find some new way to irritate him. But he drives me wild, and I can't stay away.

Daddy's so far gone, I can't even tell him I love him. I check Google Maps. Las Vegas isn't too bad of a drive. A little over four hours, but closer to six with traffic. Still plenty of time to make the show, and if we leave soon, maybe a little time before. I call Steph. "Up for a road trip?"

"Where?" she says.

"Vegas."

She screams. "Wondered how long it'd take you to wise up." We're packed in fifteen minutes, throw our bags in Steph's trunk, load Tripp up in his car seat with a baggie of Cheerios and a cup of apple juice. "Wanna see Daddy?" Steph asks.

Tripp squeals.

Steph drives fast. We hit the desert in a little over an hour. The city vanishes behind us; sage brush and Joshua trees dot the sides of the highway. We eat in the car and drive. We get past Baker and the flow of traffic and Steph bumps up to eighty.

Sitting in the car irritates my back. I twist and turn, lean the seat back, play peekaboo with Tripp to pass the time. Steph's playing Sideshow the whole way.

"Love this part," she says.

"Can't even tell what Geoff's saying here."

"Label me as a smear on the memory of a man."

"Well, isn't that pleasant? Why doesn't he post his lyrics like every other band?"

Steph shakes her head. "You talk to him about that. He's tightlipped about it. Won't even tell Yaz."

My neck throbs. I swallow a pain pill with the last of my Diet Coke. Maybe this will help the pulsing pain.

I try not to cry, but it's a losing battle. Steph puts her hand on my knee. "You cry. It's fine. Go on."

I do. I weep for Daddy, for myself, for Geoff, for Mark. I need this visit. I need something tangible, something real to hold on to, something more than words on a screen. I need Geoff's strength to get me through this, and he needs me to help him heal, help him navigate this new life.

I know they'll be in LA tomorrow, but they'll be busy, like always, getting ready for the show. And I've got this panic rising in me, this nauseating fear. I've lost so much, and I may lose more.

Steph veers into the inside lane and passes half a dozen cars. My eyes are swollen, and she pats my knee again. "It'll work out."

Tripp coos in the back.

"I'm all that's left, once Daddy's gone. No mom, no dad. No brothers or sisters."

"We're your family," Steph says. "Me and Yaz and Tripp and Geoff. We may not be much, but we're something."

"You're more than I deserve."

"Man, how hard did Barry hit you? You're more than we deserve."

Her kindness flattens me, and I dry my eyes as we exit the freeway onto the strip. The sun's setting, and the lights are already on. Purples and greens and yellows and blues.

Steph slips in her Bluetooth and calls Yaz. "Be there in five, honey. Meet us in the lobby? You didn't tell Geoff, right? Good."

We park at the Hard Rock Hotel and Yaz is outside, waiting to carry Tripp in. He grabs him, tosses him into the air, and catches him gently. "I've missed you, T," he says. Tripp's face almost splits with his smile. He wraps his arms around Yaz's neck and buries his face in his chest. He's chanting "Dada, Dada, Dada," and I try not to think of my dad, dying in LA while I'm in Sin City.

"You're here for Geoff," Steph says, her hand on my elbow. "Focus, babe." She kisses Yaz, and he takes her under one arm, me under the other, and Tripp firm on his back.

"Good to see you've pinked up, Em. Not so blue anymore," Yaz says.

"I'm warm now. Took a few days."

Yaz signs a few autographs on the way to the room. When we get there, Tony's waiting. Tripp immediately jumps on the bed while Tony shakes my hand. "Good to meet you finally, Emily."

"Em," I say.

"Glad you could make it up. Geoff's been pretty sour lately. Locked up in his room, writing lyrics."

I'm nervous. Maybe this was a bad idea. I upset Geoff pretty bad, and I'm not sure he's over it, especially if he's locked himself away. I should have stayed in LA. I could be with Dad, watching him die. But I can't do that, not without Geoff.

Yaz puts Tripp down long enough to really look at me. He runs his fingers over my scars, a surgeon inspecting an incision. "We'll get these fixed, you know." His voice is clear and calm when he speaks, but his words chill me. "Wish Jason and Nesmeth hadn't pulled me off him." His hands drop to his sides, make fists at his pockets.

"How's Geoff?" I ask Tony.

"Moody, but when isn't he? All the greats are."

"I mean the ulcer. How's that?"

I recognize his blank stare. Geoff hasn't told him. I look to Yaz. Yaz shrugs.

"Unbelievable," I whisper.

"He's been to the doctor," Tony says, as if it's worth anything. "He's a private guy. Doesn't like talking about his personal life. Took him a week to even mention you."

The room spins a bit, and I feel like my feet are pulled from beneath me. I'm in the air again, flying backward toward a glass coffee table.

Steph steadies me with a hand on my shoulder. "Look at me, girl. You let Geoff be Geoff. The fact he told you means he loves you. He hasn't lied to you, okay?"

"He told me Tony knew."

Tony speaks fast, exactly as a manager and agent would. "I knew he was sick, knew he was on some sort of medication. But he wasn't specific. Said it was nothing to worry about."

"Haven't you noticed how he looks?" I'm trying not to shout. "Check the pictures. He gets thinner and paler every day!"

"He hasn't been getting a lot of sleep," Yaz says.

I shake my head. "It's more than that. He should have told you."

Yaz sits me down. He speaks in his calm voice, his dad voice. "Listen. You're all worked up, and you've got a right. But you came up here to see Geoff. You can work out whatever drama you have later. Right now, be with him. Enjoy him. He needs you, and you need him. Have a night together before the show. Stay up after and watch the sunrise. Drive back to LA together. You can take our car. Steph and Tripp can come in the bus. Work it out then. Right now, have a good night. For you. For Geoff. Yeah?"

I sigh and wipe at my nose. I take my phone out and call Geoff. I'll play the game Steph and I thought of. Maybe it will cheer him up a bit. Maybe it will cheer me up.

PHONE TRANSCRIPT

Saturday, January 21, 2012, 5:37 p.m.

GEOFF MORRIS: Hey, Heart. Happy distraction to hear from you. Working on lyrics. Got your blank text. Nice touch.
EMILY AMHERST: Got your surprise.
GEOFF MORRIS: Too much?
EMILY AMHERST: About 1,000 daisies? It was half-romantic, half-funeral.
GEOFF MORRIS: You like them?
EMILY AMHERST: A bit much, but yes, I loved them.
GEOFF MORRIS: I have another surprise, but can't get it to you for a while.
EMILY AMHERST: I'm listening.
GEOFF MORRIS: It's a surprise. No hints.
EMILY AMHERST: I've got a surprise of my own.
GEOFF MORRIS: Do I get a hint?
EMILY AMHERST: No hints for me, no hints for you.
GEOFF MORRIS: Worth a shot at least. I miss you, Heart. One more day away and it feels like a century.
EMILY AMHERST: Yeah.
GEOFF MORRIS: You still mad? You're mad, aren't you?
EMILY AMHERST: No, not mad.
GEOFF MORRIS: You sound mad. Or sad. Oh no. Dad?
EMILY AMHERST: He's fine, for now.
GEOFF MORRIS: What is it, then?
EMILY AMHERST: It's been a long day.
GEOFF MORRIS: Sure it's not something I did?

EMILY AMHERST: I would very much like to spend one day without arguing over stupid things, without all the moodiness and walking on eggshells, without worrying about Dad or you or my maybe new job or the paparazzi.

GEOFF MORRIS: They find you, Heart?

EMILY AMHERST: Yeah, they found me. You called it. But that's the least of my worries. Geoff, I just need to hear your voice. Can we have one conversation where we're not interrupted or worried about misunderstanding each other? Can I just hear you sing?

GEOFF MORRIS: Sounds perfect. I'm in. What do you want me to sing?

EMILY AMHERST: I don't know. I haven't seen any of your lyrics.

GEOFF MORRIS: Yeah, that's a thing with me. How about "Surreal?" Nice little ballad with some kick in the chorus. You in? Oh, come on, really?

EMILY AMHERST: What? What's wrong?

GEOFF MORRIS: Someone's knocking. Go away! I'm busy!

EMILY AMHERST: Just answer it, Dimples. I get it.

GEOFF MORRIS: No, Heart. You said no interruptions, and I mean to keep that. Shut up! I don't need housekeeping! It's Nesmeth. This is something he'd do. He likes to play jokes, get under my skin, you know? I'm on the phone here!

EMILY AMHERST: Well, I'm deaf now.

GEOFF MORRIS: Sorry, Heart. Man, I'm calling the lobby.

EMILY AMHERST: Babe, get the door. Keep me on the line if you have to. Maybe they don't speak English.

GEOFF MORRIS: I've got a whole list of words for them in seven different languages if they don't stop knocking.

EMILY AMHERST: Mind your ulcer, Dimples. Get the door.

GEOFF MORRIS: Hang on. This will only take a minute. Em?

EMILY AMHERST: Now, what list of words do you have for me?

From the Journal of: Geoff Morris

Saturday, January 21, 2012, 5:44 p.m.

She's standing there, hair short and sassy, wry grin on her face. She's played a joke, surprised me in a way that makes my heart hurt. I grab her hard, remember her wounds, let up a bit, but I don't let go. I keep her pressed against me. She's holding me hard too. We could spend the whole night in this posture.

I pull back long enough to kiss her. Lip on lip, like I've never kissed anyone. There's a tenderness, an eagerness, a passion, a pain. Here is my kiss, my heart with lips. Everything I am, I pour into this kiss.

I swear the lights in Vegas flickered.

"Em," I say. "Heart."

"Surprised?"

I pick her up. "I'm an idiot. I'm a jerk. My message to you, when I blew up. Don't leave. Okay? I mean, wow, you drove here from LA?"

"I'm not leaving," she says, and I hear sadness in her voice.

"What is it? We should be happy now. Is it Dad?"

"I don't want to talk about it."

She sounds like me, but I won't do the pushy friend thing where I dig and dig until the person blows up. When someone doesn't want to talk, they don't want to talk. They want peace, they want a distraction. What Em needs is a night without worries.

"Hakuna matata," I say. I pull her inside, slip on my jacket, and call Tony. "I'm unreachable for a few hours. I'll make the gig on time. Sound check without me. You know how I like it."

"When were you going to tell me about the ulcer?" Tony asks.

Em told him. I swallow my anger. Not the time. I take a breath, think about the fun we're about to have. "It's under control," I say.

Worry haunts her eyes. Does she see Barry when she looks at me? I kiss her head and hang up. "Ever been to Italy?" I lead her by the hand to the lobby and grab a cab outside. The strip's all lit up. There's never night on the strip, only the second dawn. Dusk exists for minutes each day, when the sky gives up the blue, wallows in golds and pinks and oranges before true nightfall, when the world flips upside down, and Vegas sends its lights to the stars. Stay here long enough, you start to wonder what the casinos are like on the moon.

She rests her head on my shoulder. I feel some of her sadness melt away. I put my arm around her. Holding her calms me. I want to be angry with her, but I can't. "The Venetian," I say, and the cabbie pulls out. Before long, we walk into the lobby of the hotel. It's opulent, over the top, like everything else in Vegas. This city has never met subtlety. It's assertive, pushy in its demands for us to have a good time.

Em's under my arm, I've got a few hours before we gig, and I'm ready for a break. I take her to the gondolas, and we slip into the boat. The canal runs through the hotel, through the mall portion all built up to look like the streets of Italy. It's night, but inside the hotel, it's bright as day. She holds my hand.

The gondolier, or whatever you call him, starts to sing. It's Italian. I don't get much of it, but I pick up "beauty" and "love." Em's resting her head on my chest. "It's beautiful," she says. "Sounds sad."

The gondolier makes some comments about how beautiful Em is, and I agree. The whole ride is the span of ten minutes, but Em needs it. I need it. She's smiling when we get out, and I figure it's worth it just to see the sadness out of her eyes.

We walk hand-in-hand through the shops, and I want to buy

her everything—but, even with our new contract and the pocket money it comes with, I'm not used to dropping that kind of cash for a handbag. I'm thrifty, even though I wonder if I'll ever have to be again. And Em's not the big spender type. Nice to know we agree on something.

Instead, I take her into an art shop, and we explore the dogs playing poker, the winged women circling barber poles, the children playing in the river. We examine the impressionists, the abstract, the realists, and the surrealists. Those are my favorites.

"What's the deal with poker-playing dogs?" she says. She covers her mouth to control her laughter. And for some reason, she's giddy. Her snickers turn to outright laughter, and I wonder if she's tired or lost her mind.

"What?" I ask.

She laughs harder.

"What's so funny?"

She snorts, and I laugh. Not sure what got her started, but the laughter is amazing. Her giggle amuses me, but when she snorts, I lose it. Here's the joy I knew was in her, and I feed off it, let it heal my soul. Her laughter, I think, might save the world.

I think about taking her to the roller coaster, but that'd kill her back.

"My feet hurt," she says.

"Ever play roulette?" I say.

She shakes her head, so I walk her to the casino. We sit beside each other, hold hands, and I explain the game to her. "Don't spend too much," she says.

"A hundred dollars. That's all."

"You don't have that kind of money."

"I have money," I say. "Ninecore doesn't mess around. Cut me a check just after signing. Found a check cashing place off the strip.

When I get to LA, I'll open an account."

The numbers fall our way, and by the time we're ready to head back to Hard Rock, I've made a little. Not much, but enough to cover what Em lost.

My stomach burns, and I bump her toward an Italian Ice vendor. "Two please. Small," I tell the vendor. I flip him a ten and Em's eyes widen.

"That's a small?" She scoops a spoonful into her mouth.

I take her to the fountain in the gardens in the lobby. Water sprays from the center in tall columns. They move as if by wind, though we're inside. She kicks off her sandals and perches on the wall of the fountain, dangling her feet in.

"How much do you love me?" I ask.

"Enough," she says, poking another bite of Italian ice in her mouth.

"Enough to take your feet out of the fountain before security escorts us out?"

"Sounds like fun."

"You're in rare form tonight," I say.

"I'm not budging. If you want me to move, you'll have to move me yourself." She grins.

Something washes over me, the imp of the perverse, the wickedness, the playful romantic I try to keep buried. But the art gallery, the casino floor, the gondola—I'm in it deep now, and I give in. I grab gently under her arms, lift her, as if I'm taking her from the fountain, but then push her in. I'm gentle, but she stumbles and splashes. She gets up, her jeans soaked, the hem of her shirt heavy with water. I can't take my eyes off her, and if I thought she was beautiful before, she's drop-dead gorgeous now. Her shirt glued to her body, the cute bob of hair straightened from the water.

"And that's not going to get us kicked out?"

"You said it sounded like fun."

She grabs my shirt hard, pulls me to herself, presses her lips against mine. With a bit of a lift and a twist of her hip, she pulls me in. I trip over the wall of the fountain and fall butt-first in the water. "Oh, girl, you're going to get it now." I grab her wrists and she laughs, but there's still fear in those eyes. I turn her loose, pull her waist to me, nuzzle her neck.

Cameras flash behind us. The paparazzi's found us. I'm not surprised. I kiss her again, let the cameras get good and close. "This is Em," I say to them. "Em, meet the most obnoxious group of people you'll ever know."

They laugh, and she does too. That's all that matters.

"Sir, I need to ask you to get out of the fountain," a man says. He's dressed in a white shirt, black slacks. He's got a gun on his hip. I don't argue. I help Em step out. The cameras part in front of us.

"Thanks for making the moment special," I say to them. "I expect copies of the pictures. A little something for my desktop wallpaper."

They laugh again, and I hurry Em out to the front of the hotel. The Nevada night is cold, and the paparazzi press in on us. I let them stay, only because they block the wind.

The cab ride back is quiet, and I'm okay with that. We need some quiet, some time to be together, to appreciate being, a night without worry, without fear of Dad or ulcers or new jobs or contracts. Her hair's a bushel of peaches, and it makes me hungry for dessert.

"We're close," I say.

"To what? The hotel?"

"No."

"What are we close to?" she asks again.

"Life uninterrupted."

She smiles. "Sounds good, doesn't it?"

"Life without arguing, without worry or stress."

"Not sure we'll ever get there."

"We're already there. You here, under my arm, that's what I need. Life can throw what it wants at us. When we're together, Heart, there's nothing we can't overcome."

She kisses me, eyes closed, a deep kiss, a kiss to match the one I gave her when I first saw her tonight.

Emily Amherst's Journal

Saturday, January 21, 2012, 7:56 p.m.

Geoff swipes the lock with his keycard. He hands me his wallet, dripping wet. "Look what you did."

"You started it."

"You needed it." Geoff smiles, and those dimples deepen. He shoves the door open with his shoulder, pulls off his shirt as he enters the room. "Wanna trade shirts?"

I'm a little embarrassed, but I play his game. "Only if the one I get is dry." I slip into the bathroom and close the door. I hear him mumble something about being locked out again, and I lay my head against the door. This is real. I was right.

Geoff pops the door with his palm. "Open up, Heart."

"Why?" I tease.

"So, I can give you a dry shirt that smells like me."

"Does it smell good?" I ask.

He goes into a long explanation of how it depends on what cologne he wears. I crack the door and stick my hand through. He grabs my hand, and I feel him kissing my knuckles, my palm. Geoff wraps the shirt around my hand. "Steph left your bag in here. You want it?"

"Thank you."

He hangs the overnight bag on my fingers and calls me a tease. I hear him walk away.

I turn on the shower and strip off the wet clothes. It was fun. I see now his stress comes from the work. It's part of him. His shampoo sits on the edge of the tub, and I squeeze some into my palm then step into the shower. I grimace. It's been weeks, and the scars are still fresh and sore. The water, warm and comforting, stings. I lather my hair. Nice to know it will dry in minutes. An advantage to short.

Behind the shower curtain, I'm wondering why he's chosen me. I say a prayer. "Thank you, God. Thank you."

I hear the radio crank up and Geoff singing to the tunes. When I'm dried and dressed, I open the door, and there's Geoff. Black jeans, black tee, black leather jacket. A chain hangs from belt loop to belt loop. He's got his studs in, his hair ruffled. This is the showman I've not seen, the entertainer. He holds out his arms for me.

"Showtime," he says.

I grin. "Showtime."

From the Journal of: Geoff Morris

Saturday, January 21, 2012, 9:14 p.m.

Nerves tonight are worse. It's a big show, some familiar tunes, but ones we haven't played much. Wanted to run through them with Yaz, to brush up, but the night with Em was more meaningful. There'll be more people here than our other gigs combined, but I don't care. Em's here.

The lights dim as Gainsae comes off stage. My ulcer flares. Doing a cold open tonight, a few solo measures of "Soul Eater" stripped down so the crowd can sing. No sound check. Ninecore in the wings, Em watching from backstage. I leave her with Steph and Alison. They'll watch from the side.

The crowd dies down a bit. The crowd's boiling, ready to hear Sideshow. I walk on stage in the dark. Hum the first few bars. The mic's live.

The crowd energizes, a surge of anticipation.

I sing the first line, and the crowd takes over. They sing the next three. I join them in the chorus. Just us. No lights.

On the second verse, a light separates the dark. I'm lit up; a rapturous light pulls me straight into heaven. The crowd's too dark to see, but I know they're there. I kneel at the edge of the stage, hold my hand out, and a million hands reach back. There's a beauty in that, an awesome, electric connection words can't encompass. I stop after the second verse. We let the beat hang for a bit, before Jason gives us a down beat, and we hit the chorus hard and heavy.

The crowd erupts, and their wave of energy hits me.

I imagine Jennifer, think of how she ate my soul. Try not to remember how Em heals it. Whole rock stars can't vocalize desperation and pain and aggression. I let the wounds surface, let them fester, remind myself of the agony of the last few days.

The crowd feels it, they move, sway—they're a torrent, a flooded river carrying broken branches and limbs in the flotsam.

We don't stop between songs, but move directly into "Hate Breed." I think of Barry, his fist in my chest, his foot inside my knee. I think of his hands on Em's neck. My ulcer flares, and I swallow it down best I can, but it hits my voice. My pitch is off, not much, but Yaz notices. I clear my throat, get in the crowd's face. They're chanting the words with me. I hold the mic out to them. Their voices hit me with a chorus of my anger and aggression.

Em's eyeing me from the corner of backstage. She looks afraid. But "Hate Breed" is done, and I grab my Les Paul. She's black and beautiful and tuned perfectly. We've hit it hard for two songs, and while it's earlier than normal for us to mix it up and bring the pace down a bit, I know Em's chomping to hear "Surreal." We can move from that into "Purify."

So, on we play, the crowd vibing, moving, chanting, cheering. This show is good. Tony's worked magic with the digital screen behind us, flashing the images Yaz and I put together—fists and chains, caves and war paint. It's all very dramatic, very moving. This is my high, my addiction.

It goes fast. Two encores with Alison before we give up the stage to Whisper, and then I'm backstage with Em.

She's shaking. I grab her, pull her to me. "This is what I need," I say. "You here, instead of another message. I know what it cost you to be here, and I promise, I'll make it worth your while."

She says, "You already have."

Emily Amherst's Journal

Saturday January 21, 2012, 9:14 p.m.

Whatever restraint he's shown, whatever control or calm I've seen in him tonight vanishes when he steps on stage. Reason leaves him, and he becomes the embodiment of passion. I shiver, not from excitement, but from fear. I can't tell if this is a show for my benefit, or if he's like this every time he plays. I can tell he's angry. He's a pressure cooker, and instead of being the release valve, I've become more heat. He goes to his knees on stage, and the crowd sounds like a bomb. Sterling Amundsten from Ninecore nods, holds up his phone. My guess is he's letting the big dogs listen to the crowd.

Sweat drips from the strands of hair around Geoff's face. His voice cracks. My heart seizes. Tony tosses him a bottle of water, and he takes a swig, then pours it over his head. He shakes like a dog from a bath, and the girls in the crowd are pawing at the stage.

This is what Geoff is meant to do. I see it now. I see the animal in him, the passion fighting to get out. He takes another gulp of water, swishes his mouth and spits toward a box at side stage. I thought at first it was a reflection from a light. There's so much color, explosions.

He falls into my arms after the set, his grip so hard against the scar on my back that tears well. I can take it; Geoff can't. His legs are weak, but the muscles in his arms pulsate. I go to my knees with him hanging on to me. Slide my hand through his hair. And he cries in my ear. "This is what I need, you here, instead of another message. I know what it cost you to be here, and I promise, I'll make it worth your while."

"You already have," I say.

The band grabs his shoulders as they walk by, congratulating each other on a great show. They're excited, a dream realized. "Nailed it," Jason says.

Hailey grabs Jason's face and kisses him hard. Steph leaps in Yaz's arms, wraps her legs around his waist. Even Nesmeth finds a girl—someone I've never seen—and, taking her by the neck, leans her back and kisses her.

"Who's that?" I ask Geoff.

"Never met her," he says.

Alison kneels next to him. "You're killing yourself, you know that?"

He nods, then struggles to stand. I help him up, and we limp to the elevator.

Security opens Geoff's door, and I ask if they can send up a cot. The guy stares at me in surprise. Not sleeping with the rock star is perverse in this community. "I'm not leaving him," I say. He smiles and apologizes. Says he'll get a cot right away. And he does.

I rest Geoff against the bathroom vanity and turn on the shower. "Warm or cold?"

"What do you want?" he asks.

I grin and turn on the warm water. I've already been doused once in the fountain, but I kick off my shoes, untie Geoff's and pull his drenched shirt over his head. He can hardly stand, and it's killing me. The longer he stands, the harder it is to balance him. "Come on, Dimples. Step in."

"My jeans," he says.

"Jeans dry. We need to cool you off." I guide him into the shower. His head drops, and he presses both hands against the shower as the water drains over his face. My clothes get wet while I balance him, but it doesn't matter. He needs me.

"You okay?" I ask.

Geoff turns and pulls me under the water. He grabs a hand full of my hair. Not hard, but tender. I know he's not going to stand much longer.

I hit the water nozzle and shut down the shower, grab a man-sized towel and drape it over him. All the time he's saying, "Em, don't go. Please don't go."

"I won't go anywhere, baby."

He's sick, and that makes me sick. He heaves, and it's all I can do to get him to the toilet to vomit. More blood. I should call an ambulance, but he'd never forgive me. If he can get through tonight, I'll make sure he sees a doctor tomorrow. I'll go with him if I have to, make sure he's taking care of himself.

I manage to get him dressed and into the living area, and he pulls me onto the couch. His fingers intertwine with mine, and I realize just how big Geoff is. He's tall and thin, but massive. His hands swallow mine.

I lay my head on his chest, and he props his feet on the coffee table. It's glass, and for a moment, the hair on the back of my neck rises. Trickles of water drip off my nose, and he squeezes me in his arms. His heart slows to an even rhythm; his breaths get shallow. His muscles ease into rest.

I need to be on this tour, need to be on the bus every day. Away from him, I'm the source of strife. With him, I'm the release.

But with Dad the way he is, how can I leave him again?

Geoff's hand presses against my face, and he plays with a strand of hair. He needs quiet, needs to decompress. I don't speak. Before long, our breathing is synchronized. His head tips to the side in sleep.

The cot is up, but I can't move now, so I pull the navy throw from the back of the couch and cover us. He's completely relaxed.

I know what I need to do but can't until Daddy is at rest.

I close my eyes. When this nap ends, Geoff will make my few

hours left here amazing. He's good like that, always trying to please me. For now, I'm content to rest against his chest. I slip his phone out of his shirt pocket and press the off button. Maybe I can rest, too, in the arms of this demon angel, in the arms of the man I've grown to love.

The wake-up call comes at seven. Stiff from sitting all night, I roll my neck, and the bones crack. I make my way to the bathroom, brush my teeth, and try to straighten the mess of hair dried in true punk fashion. I grab a pillow, toss it on the couch, and ease Geoff's head toward it.

He rouses and pulls me down gently, kisses my lips. "Best dream ever."

"Feeling better?"

He stands and stumbles across the room, catching his toe on the cot. The language is colorful as he punches the bed. Instinct takes over, and I back across the room.

He notices my jumpiness. "Sorry, Heart," he says.

I smile, hope it puts him at ease.

He grins and vanishes into the bathroom. He leaves the door partly open, maybe habit, maybe an invitation. Either way, I ignore it, and as the shower begins to run, change my clothes and put on makeup. I switch on Entertainment Network, and replays of the show scream through the speakers. Geoff opens the door, rubbing a towel on his head. "We made EN?"

"You've been on EN, babe. Nothing new for Sideshow." I kiss his cheek. "I've never seen anyone put such fire into a performance."

"Too many fires."

"What's that mean?" I ask.

He shakes his head. "Jen. Barry. Dad. Me screwing things up with you. Channeled it all."

I speak gently. "You spit blood."

He smiles. "Yeah? Felt like it, you know. Great show. Spitting blood, spitting fire. Everything came out last night."

"No, Dimples, you spit blood."

He swallows a mouthful of antacid and winces. "It's fine, Heart. I got this."

Leave it to a man to shut down, to ignore it. He opens the curtains and shrinks away from the light. "So early," he moans. "Not used to getting up until noon."

"Where's the sludge?" I ask. "The stuff the doctor gave you. I haven't seen it around." I'm on shaky ground, but I have to ask. He needs to know what he's doing to himself.

"Finished if off last night."

A plausible excuse, but I can't read his face. He might be lying, and I'd never know. It kills me, not knowing his faces. I decide to trust him. Now's not the time to nag anyway. We're here to enjoy each other. "You should ride back with us. Skip the bus, come with Yaz and Steph and Tripp and me."

"Way too crowded. Can't fit my knees in that car of theirs."

My heart sinks.

He presses his finger against my nose and dials Yaz. "I know. Right? People get up at this hour? Ugly. Meet us in the lobby in five?"

"What are you up to, Dimples?" I ask when he hangs up.

"Breakfast. And a surprise."

"What kind of surprise?" I say, smiling and pressing my hand to his chest.

"You're adorable when you're clueless," he says, then leads me to the elevator.

"Seriously, what's up, and how much is it going to cost me?"

He grins. "No good, and nothing."

Yaz and Steph are already in the elevator. Yaz looks like he's been hit by a truck. "Next time you wake me up at this hour, remind me to kill you," he says to Geoff. Tripp sleeps comfortably in Steph's arms.

"I'll kill myself first," Geoff says.

"Stop it, you two," Steph says. She smacks Yaz's butt and hugs Geoff. "You look better. Had us worried last night, you and Em all slumped on the floor."

"Killer show," he says. He's good at evading, and that worries me. But I'll keep my mouth shut and take my cues from Steph and Yaz. They know him better. If they're worried, they'll say something.

"Where are we headed?" I ask.

"We need a car," Geoff says.

The elevator doors slide open to the lobby, and we pour out. "We?"

"You and me," Geoff says. His arm is around my shoulder, but he's stronger this morning. He's not using me as a crutch. It's a tender touch.

I lean my head on his shoulder. "Okay. Even though we're never together, we need a car?"

"More you than me, but when we get back to LA, I'll need a car to get around. You can drive it until then."

Yaz slides into the driver seat, and Steph and I climb in back. Geoff rides shotgun and continues his discourse. "We pick something you don't mind driving. Something sporty. Red. Hot. Like you."

I grin. "If I'm driving it, I'll need something that can handle the snow."

"Not funny," Yaz says. "You're never going to the snow again."

"I'm serious," I say. I rub Geoff's shoulders and he groans. "If I'm driving this while you're away, I may want to go up to the mountain. I need something that can handle the slope."

His jaw tightens. "Save the mountain for when we can go

together."

"Okay," I say, playing with Tripp's foot. He's awake now and babbling. "But if this is a car for us both, then we should think about it."

"We will," he says.

Yaz pulls into a café. We order breakfast, and I'm impressed with Geoff's order—scrambled egg, side of gravy, no greasy bacon or sausage. Still, as small as the meal is, he barely finishes. When he does, he drains his milk and swallows more antacid.

The dealership's on the same block. Yaz and Geoff must have had this planned for a while. It doesn't take us long to settle on a Yukon. I'm happy because it goes in the snow. Geoff's happy because it can run down the paparazzi. I check my watch and groan. "We better wrap this up fast if we're going to get you back to LA before sound check," I say.

Geoff nods. "Help Steph with Tripp. Yaz and I will deal with the paperwork."

"I'll have to sign papers, too, you know. They'll check our credit. It's an ordeal."

"This ain't my first rodeo," he says and kisses my cheek.

I roll my eyes, but help Steph change Tripp. "They're up to something."

"I know," she says.

By the time the diaper's done, Geoff's shaking hands with the suit. The greasy dealer hands Geoff the keys. "That was fast," I say.

He says, "Things go fast when you pay cash."

My eyes widen. "You didn't."

"Been saving a bit. Plus, Ninecore's signing bonus helped," he says and hands me the keys. "You drive. I'm too tired. Need a little sleep if I'm going to be coherent for my interview."

My breath catches in my throat. "Please tell me you didn't drop the last of your life savings into this car. I can't be the reason you're broke again."

"He's fine," Yaz says. "I wouldn't let him do something stupid."

I swallow and slide into the driver seat. I breathe deep, hold the new car smell in my lungs. "Interview?" I ask.

Geoff punches in Yaz's address on the onboard GPS, cranks the stereo, then leans back. "Stone Rock wants to ask me a few questions. Not thrilled about it, but it's publicity, right? Ninecore set it up." He sighs. "This will be a good car," he says.

I turn the key, then take his hand in mine.

Apocalypse Tour Shakes West Coast

Sunday, January 22, 2012, 12:00 p.m.

LOS ANGELES, AP—If you follow rock at all, you know the name Ninecore Records. Known for their high-risk, high-reward signing of talented but sometimes troubled bands (anyone remember the collapse of Thirstmonger three years ago?), Ninecore took another gamble with their Apocalypse tour. Combining the power of their platinum bands Whisper and Token, Ninecore added two lesser-known bands, Sideshow and Gainsae. While Gainsae has a ton of good reviews, it's Sideshow that's stolen the show.

Sterling Amundsten of Ninecore remarked, "It was a financial gamble, pulling in unknown bands with Whisper and Token, but both Gainsae and Sideshow have far surpassed our expectations."

The Apocalypse Tour began as a "West Coast only" tour, but when the bands hit Vegas, entertainment gurus immediately hit Ninecore with an offer for four-year runs in the major arenas. The agreement would see the four bands doing week-long stints in Vegas three times each year.

Amundsten said, "The Vegas deal attests to the power of our bands. It allows a semi-permanent home for some of our West Coast bands, and allows them a bit of a respite from the sometimes seven-month long national tour schedule."

When asked if the success of the tour surprised him, Amundsten said, "We knew the power of Whisper and Token. Even Gainsae had a devoted national following. But the overwhelming national reception of Sideshow has surprised us. They've already turned a million downloads, and about a tenth of it is worldwide. We've never seen anything like it."

The Apocalypse Tour continues in LA with two more stops, one in San Diego, and a recently added Phoenix date, before negotiations officially begin with Vegas Entertainment officials. "This would be the first of its kind," says Amundsten, "one we think will break the glass ceilings of band tours as we know them."

The Grammy nods their bands have gotten might be one reason why Amundsten is optimistic. The relatively new band Gainsae has earned two nominations, while rock veterans Whisper, with lead singer Alison Blevins, have scooped up three. Token continues their assault on the Grammys for the second year in a row, pulling in four nominations. But the upstarts Sideshow have outdone them all with five nominations. Will this be Ninecore's second straight year cleaning up at the Grammys? If the Apocalypse Tour is any indication, the answer is yes.

Tickets for the tour are available through www.ticketsnownotlater.com. Some venues still have open availability, but promoters expect sell-out crowds.

From the Journal of: Geoff Morris

Sunday, January 22, 2012, 3:13 p.m.

I wake up north of Barstow, some desert town off the 15 Freeway. Em's still holding my hand, and now that it's after three, I feel a little more normal. My stomach's knotted up and the pain moves into my esophagus. I swallow a bit, clear my throat, taste blood. "How long have I been asleep?" I ask.

"A few hours," she says. She's smiling at me. "We needed this, babe."

"The car?"

She smacks my shoulder. "The time together."

I sit up, clear my throat again, swallow down the nausea. "The car's nice too." Her hand's on my knee, and I hold it. "Didn't mean to sleep the whole way," I say.

"I've been enjoying listening to you snore."

I crack my knuckles, roll my neck. "I don't snore. I growl." The new car smell feels good in my nose. The leather seats have warmers. Even though it's cold outside, I don't notice. Em didn't want the warmers, said they were an unnecessary expense, but I have no intention of keeping this car for myself. It's hers. She just doesn't realize it, and I want what's best for her. "Want me to drive?"

"You want to, don't you?"

"It is my car," I say. "Besides, you're hungry."

"Point taken." She finds a small eatery, pulls over, and orders for me. A turkey sandwich on toasted sourdough, mayo and lettuce, no tomato or mustard. Not my ideal lunch, but I'll enjoy it for her.

Back on the road, we listen to the radio, talk about the show. It's good nothing talk. No drama to worry about. She never mentions

Barry or her dad. I don't mention Hailey or my ulcer or my mom. The conversation's pleasant enough, but tension lies under the surface. These are things we need to discuss, but things we won't—can't talk about now. Our time's limited and we're determined to enjoy it.

"Here's the thing about Vegas," I say.

"You always throw random facts into conversations?"

I turn the radio down a bit, though it's a Whisper tune I've come to love. The Yukon drives nice, and I have second thoughts about transferring the title into her name once we get to LA. "The whole city's intent on entertainment and enjoyment. You notice? It's almost threatening, 'Have a good time, or we'll call the mob.'"

She laughs, but I keep going. I've got a point to make.

"The whole place works hard to offer anything and everything you could ever want; it almost forgets those who don't really want anything. They want peace and quiet, they want the dark, they want the stars at night. No place for them, is there?"

"Is that what you want?"

The conversation's getting a little more real, and I can feel her tense up. She takes her hand away from mine, and I take it back. We're close to LA now, and I've got an interview to make before the show, but I still have a couple hours. "I want you," I say. "All of you."

"Is this about sex?"

I shake my head, "No, Heart. Don't get me wrong, I want that too, but it can wait. I respect your wishes."

"What then?"

"I want to know all of you. Even the messy stuff. That's how this whole thing started. I think of us, and I think of Union Station, you getting off the train. Then Mark, the tour, the ulcer. One mess after another. We had a great time in Vegas not talking about the mess, but we shouldn't force ourselves not to. It should be natural.

We should work through the messes, so we can get to the good times lying out of reach, you know? Otherwise, we're trying to enjoy niceties with all these heavy messes hanging over our heads."

I've ruined the mood. She's upset now. "You're not happy?"

"Of course I am. This has been an awesome day. But imagine how many more nice days we have ahead of us." I take the 5 North toward Glendale.

She sighs. "First of all, you need to work on your communication skills. Second, you took the wrong exit. We're on the wrong freeway."

I shrug. "You're not getting what I'm saying."

"Where are we going?" she says, pulling her jacket tighter around her.

"We shouldn't be afraid of our messes anymore. I can't be as defensive. I want to work on me. I want to be a better me."

"I love the you you are," she says, and to her credit, I believe it.

I kiss her hand, exit Hyperion and steer toward Ridgehaven. She gets wise, figures out where we're going. "Why are you taking me here?"

"Who says I'm taking you?" I ask.

"You're starting to scare me," she says.

"Relax, Heart." I clear my throat, swallow down the bile. "I need to talk with someone."

I escort her into the hospital, and she signs us in. I'm a little surprised at the condition her father's in, how old he is. But she's told me this. He married late in life. He's got to be as old as my grandfather. If the doctors hadn't told us he was alive, I'd have assumed he'd already passed. But the heart monitor beeps at odd intervals, slow and lethargic, a lazy heartbeat. His eyes are closed, and he's got a week's worth of white stubble covering his face. The nurses open the curtains to let in what's left of the sunlight. Before long, the sun will set, and we'll be in the dark again.

Em sits down beside him, takes his hand, presses his fingers to her forehead. “Daddy,” she says. “I want you to meet Geoff.”

No response from her father. Hadn’t expected one, but I’d hoped. The monitor beeps again, and his IV drips. “Pleased to meet you,” I say. He’s not going to talk back, but Em needs this, needs me to see him. I need to step in her mess to help pull her out of it, to help her through the grieving process. I can’t do it and stay clean.

I sit next to him on the other side and take his hand. It’s something I’d never imagined doing. For a second, my father’s face interposes itself over Em’s dad, and I’m left with this surreal relief. Something in the moment makes humanity swell in me. It won’t be put down. I start to think about calling my dad—something I haven’t done since he left me when I was eight.

I clear my throat again, something I’ve been doing a lot. I push down the emotion, the fear and self-loathing, the blood and bile, and hope something new and beautiful will grow in me. “Em,” I say, not knowing exactly what I want to tell her. “Let me have a minute?”

“With me?” she says.

“With him.”

She furrows her brow, her pixie hair slumping forward. “Okay,” she says, a little distrustful. She leaves the room slow, looks back over her shoulder half a dozen times before she makes it out the door.

And then I’m alone with him, this man who fathered the woman I love, the man she loves with all her heart. Here is what a father should be, and I’m a little resentful she had something I couldn’t. But I turn away the selfishness and open my mouth, praying the words will come out the right way. “Good job,” I say, feeling stupid. “Em’s quite the girl.”

I pause, give the man a chance to respond, but he doesn’t so much as flutter his eyelids.

“What you’ve done with Em is incredible. She loves you, you

know. Whole heart. That's what I call her—Heart. I like it. Fits her, you know, because she's full of love and trust and innocence and patience. God knows how she puts up with me. But listen, I want you to hear this. This is important. I love her. Whole heart devoted to her. I know what kind of man you are because she tells me. She tells me how you took her camping, how your love of the mountain turned to hers, and the skills you taught her ended up saving her life. Did she tell you that? Even now, even like this, you saved her life."

I take a breath, wonder if Em's listening at the door, but I can't stop talking. How long before she bursts in? "Here it is, man. I want to date your daughter, want your blessing on what we have, what we're working toward. I know you can't really give it now, but I want to ask for it anyway. I want us to know you'll be happy with us being together."

I twist in my chair. "I can't really ask my father. No idea where he is, or if he's even alive. He was a drinker. Haven't talked to my mom in a decade. You're the family I've got now. You ..." I pause here, try to collect my thoughts, will my stomach to stop trying to push out of my gut. "You're the man I want to become."

His eyelids flutter, and I swear I see his eyes move under his lids, as if he's watching me, eyes wide shut. The monitor beeps twice, quick, rapid. His finger twitches, brushes mine. "Em!" I say. "Get in here!"

The door flies open. "What's wrong? Daddy?"

I stand up, point to his hand. "His finger," I say.

She grabs his hand. "Daddy?" she says, and her eyes fill with tears. I kneel beside her, put my arm around her, my hand on the old man's chest. Here, knees bent, Em under my arm, my heart filled to bursting, I understand what it is to pray, what it is to seek God, to petition the Almighty with a request that transcends words.

Welcome to the Sideshow

Melody Rolfs, *Stone Rock* staff writer
Sunday, January 22, 2012, 8:02 p.m.

When Sterling Amundsten, Ninecore's public relations director, contacted me with free tickets to their latest showing, I wanted to maintain a professional demeanor. I didn't know I'd be front and center at the Apocalypse Tour, awestruck by the mix of perfectly orchestrated bands: Ninecore's big three, Whisper, Token, the relatively new Gainsae, and a band that, less than a month ago, practiced in their guitarist's garage.

Unsurprisingly, Whisper, Gainsae, and Token delivered killer shows, but I had no idea what to expect from Sideshow. I downloaded their album and listened to it a half-dozen times before the show. I loved the tracks, but doubted any band could live up to the hype I'd heard from those who'd seen Sideshow play live.

I sat down with front man Geoff Morris in LA to find out exactly who Sideshow is and what kick-started this phenomenon—one that scored a nobody band from Los Angeles, California, five Grammy nominations.

SR: Where do we begin? You're an overnight sensation. What happened?

GM: It's not fair to classify us as an overnight success. Even before the Apocalypse Tour, we've had a devoted following. We've been playing LA and the southland for years, waiting for our moment. Same story you've heard a million times, but this one has a happy ending.

SR: Is there some significance to the name Sideshow?

GM: We never really felt like we fit in growing up, you know? We had friends, sure, but we were the ones who weren't in the spotlight. We weren't the main attraction. We've always just been the sideshow.

(Morris is a giant. He sits slouched in a chair and his legs stretch across the room.)

SR: I've been there. I always seem to be the butt of someone's joke.

GM: We all are at some point. I took my share of ridicule in high school, junior high. You get the idea.

SR: I find that hard to believe. What did they tease you about?

GM: (Laughs) Truth? I was a smart kid. Guess I intimidated the bullies.

SR: I can imagine. You've got a college degree, right? Computer science, isn't it?

GM: From UCLA, but I spent more time writing music than code.

SR: Which has paid off for you.

GM: So far. We'll see how long it lasts.

SR: You don't sound very confident.

GM: It's all happened so fast. One month, we're playing LA, hoping someone inks us. The next, we're in Seattle, inking with Ninecore and talking national tour.

SR: Seems the logical choice. You've already turned over a million downloads in the span of two weeks. You've racked up five Grammy nominations a month before final selections are made. I'd say your future's solid.

GM: But that's not me; that's Sideshow.

SR: You don't think it has something to do with you?

GM: Maybe, but not nearly as much as it has to do with Yaz (lead guitar) and Jason (drums) and Nesmeth (bass). Those guys could have solo careers as long as they don't have to sing (laughs).

SR: Humility's nice to see in a rock star. Don't see much of it in my line of work.

GM: (grins) Thanks.

SR: How long had you been playing before Ninecore

picked you up?
GM: We've been playing for about five years, pretty solid. Tony, our manager, decided to help us out about three years ago. He's been good for us, lining up some pretty nice gigs. Even before Ninecore got wind of us, we had a good following in LA among the celebrities and the like. You'd be surprised what a few tweets from a tier-one actress can do for a band's career.
SR: Sounds like you're about to name drop.
GM: (Shakes his head) The only names I drop are Yaz, Jason, Nesmeth, and Tony. They're the ones putting in the work. I guess I can drop Ninecore too.
SR: You won't spill the names of the celebrities that tweeted you to stardom?
GM: They'll claim it if they want, but I'm not about to pin it on them. Not my place.
SR: Humble and loyal? Haven't been in the rock scene long, have you?
GM: (Laughs) Here's the thing with Ninecore: They're meticulous with the bands they sign. They learned from the Thirstmonger ordeal. Everyone on Ninecore is talented and good. Look them up, you don't see their bands in the news, you don't see them making scenes, you don't get the prima donna attitude you see from other labels. We're level-headed; we work together. Ninecore's a team, not a competition.
SR: Are you sure you're not running for office?
GM: (Laughs) Slim chance getting me into politics.
SR: How does it feel to stare at five Grammy nominations?
GM: Tony told me yesterday. It's hard to wrap my brain around. Still living in the fog of touring. I'm pretty near-sighted when I'm on the bus. For me, it's hanging with the guys, sure, but it's more about making music, perfecting our show, writing new riffs, new lyrics. The Grammys

don't even feel real right now. Maybe you should ask me in February.

SR: Can you tell us what it's like to play with three of the biggest rock acts on any label.

GM: It's a bit of a trip, honestly. These bands are my heroes. I'd have been happy to open for any one of these bands, but now we're sharing a label, sharing billing with them. There's a part of me that thinks we're not on their level, even now, even though they've been totally welcoming and encouraging. And then to sing with Alison Blevins—man. What budding rock star hasn't fantasized about that? We've got chemistry, not just me and Alison, but Sideshow and Whisper and Token and Gainsae. We feed off each other. Nobody says, "It's our tour." We want to make amazing music. We're all different, and we end up sorta marrying influences. Each of us is stronger together than we are alone, you know?

SR: Have these influences affected your lyrics at all? Because, in the digital age, we're all prone to overshare. But you're quiet. This is your first interview, and unlike all the other bands on the planet, you can't find the lyrics to your songs, other than fan translations. You have plans to put up what you write?

GM: None. It's a neurosis. I write for me. It's the only way my words can mean anything to anyone. If they're not personal, they're not universal.

SR: (I lean forward) Let's talk dirty.

GM: (Winking) Now you're talking my language.

SR: (I blush) The video of you and Yaz busting up the marine during one of your shows. Seems a little harsh, doesn't it? This guy served his country.

GM: (He's silent, and then leans in to me) I've got all respect for those who serve our country. It wasn't a political statement; it wasn't some rock anthem about the man keeping us down. We get that reputation about being above the law, but me and Yaz went to jail for it. We paid our bail, and no charges were pressed. Fact? He's not a marine anymore. Discharged. And he wasn't a good guy.

SR: So, the rumor he attacked a woman, and you know the girl?

GM: I thought this interview was about music.

SR: It is. I'm sorry. I wanted you to have a chance to clear the air.

GM: (Grins again) That's what Tony's for. (He hands me Tony's card). Fair warning, he loves to talk dirty.

SR: (I blush again, but take the card. Gainsae plays their last few notes and Geoff stands up, rolls his neck from side to side, fists his hands, knuckles and neck cracking.) Looks like you've got to go.

GM: I appreciate the interview.

If Sideshow is half what this guy is, they're in for a long and prosperous run.

Sideshow and the Apocalypse Tour play the Rotherwood Arena tomorrow night.

Download "Underbelly," Morris' duet with Alison Blevins of Whisper, and other songs from the Apocalypse Tour from iTunes.com/NinecoreRecords

TEXT MESSAGE TRANSCRIPT
Sunday, January 22, 2012, 8:58 p.m.

EMILY AMHERST: SHOWTIME! Sing your heart out, not your guts.

EMILY AMHERST: Front row, middle, hands in the air.

EMILY AMHERST: You're mine, Dimples. Every piece of you. Now sing.

Emily Amherst's Journal

Sunday, January 22, 2012, 9:10 p.m.

Nesmeth walks out first, lays down the bass line for "Hate Breed."

My pocket vibrates. I check my phone. It's a heart.

Geoff walks out, brushes his hair from his eyes, squints over the crowd. He spots me, grins, points me out. He strides across the stage. The crowd cheers him, a wild chant of "Morris, Morris!" But he's got no mic, no guitar, and the crowd gets suspicious.

Nesmeth and Jason keep the beat steady, recycling the intro riff to the song that's helped launch them to fame. Yaz plays over the top, something melodic and sorrowful, something dark and menacing. They're not surprised. By now, they're used to his showmanship. He likes to change it up, so they're always ready.

He comes to the edge of the stage, curls his finger at me, and calls me toward him. I move with a mass of women, but it's me he reaches for at the edge of the stage. Security lifts me over the barrier. Geoff wraps his hands around my wrists and lifts me onto the stage. Hard not to feel like a crazed fan living their dream, but my dream is bigger. I'm not a random woman from the crowd. I get to keep him.

Maybe this is show. Maybe he wants to work the crowd up. He bends down, mouth to ear, clears his throat, and says, "You're mine, Heart. Every inch." He kisses me, a passionate rock kiss. This, I know, is half-show, half-love. He walks me backstage where Alison stands in the wings. So cute. Hair pulled up in a ponytail on top of her head, black daisy dukes, and spiked heels. She slides a stool for me to sit on and gives me a hug. Geoff shouts. "You ready, Em?"

I nod.

He slaps his hand on his leg to the beat. His head bobs in time.

He picks up his Gibson SG, which he's explained to me, is the perfect rock guitar. Before he plays, he steps to his mic and grins. "Hard to get up for a song like this after a moment like that, but I think I can manage." The crowd cheers, sending up an offering of cat calls and whistles. He hits the first note—a long strum echoes through the building, and the crowd starts to chant. Geoff shakes his head from side to side, moves in front of Yaz, and they sway.

"One-two-three, two-two-three."

The band hits that low chord, and I feel it, like knuckles in my chest. The crowd takes a step back, then up. The pit circles, and Geoff blasts his lyrics.

There's no controlling the crowd. They sing with a voice as loud as Geoff's. "Blister and bleed, a leech on a freak."

Tony brings me a set of earplugs. "You want to hear anything tomorrow, you use these." I slip them in, and for the next hour, I see Geoff transform into a musical maniac. I can't wipe the smile off my face. It thrills me to see him so happy.

It hits me: He could have pulled any woman from the crowd. And what could I do but watch and weep? But he picked me, pulled me onstage, kissed me in front of a sold-out crowd.

What's he see in me? Why would he latch onto a girl he'd not seen in years? Why would he send a stranger a train ticket? Did he think he could save me? Am I that needy? Maybe it's fate, the answer I'd prayed for, the escape I couldn't make alone?

The music quiets for a minute, and the stage goes dark. I think they're done, but Alison moves onstage. She makes her way to her mark perfectly. She's done this before. Already, the crowd chants her name. They know what's waiting for them, and the anticipation in silence drives them into a frenzy.

She starts the song, her voice a melody of jazz and blues, of rock and folk. It's a sharp contrast to the raspy, angry, passionate voice

Geoff uses. But they work together, the beauty and the beast, and play a rendition of "Underbelly" that'd make angels weep.

Geoff sits on a wooden stool, trades his SG for his Les Paul. His face is split with worry and hope, the face he wore at the hospital. Whatever he told Dad got him moving again. I hadn't seen Dad move in a week, but I got to talk to him today, got to tell him I loved him, got to tell him I loved Geoff.

The reality haunts me, and the fear and hope he wore creeps into me. In my darkest imaginings, I pray for it to be over, for Daddy to move on. Not to get rid of him, but for him to escape his body. Heaven awaits, a place without pain, without worry or fear or glass coffee tables.

I've been greedy. I've hoarded my messes. Worse, I've tried to stay out of Geoff's. He's reached out to me, told me about his mom, confided in me his deepest insecurities, and I was too mired in my mess to see how much drowned him. I've let him rescue me twice. Maybe it's time for me to get messy, time for me to rescue him.

When he comes off stage, I have his dose of the sludge measured out. No matter how much he says he's taking it, I have to wonder if he's telling me everything.

He sees me, the sludge, and shakes his head. He throws it back, drains the cup fast, takes me under his arm, and kisses my head. "So?"

I hand him some water. "You're everything they say you are."

"I haven't heard," he says, a wry grin. "What do they say?"

I smile back, hold him close. "Amazing. Astonishing. Alluring. Irresistible."

He laughs. "What do the men say?"

I smile and smack his chest.

He coughs, opens the water bottle, and drains half in one pull.

"Come sit down," I say.

"Can't," he says. "Hear them?"

The chant from the crowd is unmistakable. "Sideshow. Sideshow. Sideshow. Sideshow."

"Another song?" I ask. "Can you handle it?"

"Handles it every night," Alison says with a wink. "We all do. Part of the job."

"But your voice."

Yaz slips his guitar over his neck and starts to play. It's still live. The crowd cheers and then quiets. Yaz walks to center stage, stands, legs apart, playing a beautiful, almost classical movement. The distortion adds crunch and chaos to an otherwise clean riff.

Geoff kisses my forehead again and hands me the bottle. He walks on with Nesmeth and Jason, and they pick up halfway through the solo, until everyone cuts out but Geoff and Jason. He sings over a simple four-four, but Jason adds spice, and I think for a minute the two of them alone could make it on a label.

Geoff's lyrics are tender, gentle, but the backbeat's angry, aggressive. They finish out the song like this, let the silence hang for a moment, allow the crowd to catch their breath before Jason counts out the next song and knocks the wind from the crowd again.

This is why Ninecore signed them. They'd be stupid not to.

When Geoff comes off the stage this time, he's in a hurry. He grabs me, moves to a quiet room. He's pale, and his hand is clammy. He slams the door behind us, drops to his knees, and wretches.

I grab a trashcan and hold his forehead as he spits yellow foam tinged with red. He convulses as he heaves. I pull his hair back. "I got you, Dimples," I say. He lurches again, and I shake my head. "I'm calling the paramedics."

"Don't," he says between coughs and gags. "Tomorrow, okay? I'll go to the doctor tomorrow."

I stroke his pallid cheek. "I'm going with you."

Once he's settled down enough, I drive him home to Yaz's and wish we had someplace else to go. Steph doesn't need us here, taking up space and eating her food. I'll look for a house tomorrow, but for now, I need to get Geoff cleaned up. I put him in the shower, help him get into bed in the guest room. I'll take the couch tonight.

"Em?" he whispers.

"Right here." I wonder if this is a side effect of the show or the ulcer. I grab the trashcan and drag it to the bed. I slip him some ice from the freezer. "Take a bite of ice." He opens his mouth, and I see sores on his tongue. This is worse than I thought. "Open up. One more bite." I slip the ice in and he rolls to his side. Exhausted.

He pulls his knees toward his chest in pain. I get his meds. He's had the sludge, but he gets a pill for the acid and one to relax the muscles in his stomach to stop the vomiting.

He's cold. I stuff pillows around him and shove the bedspread tight between the mattress and box springs. He quiets as the meds take hold.

Someone knocks on the front door, and I check the peephole expecting to see Jason or Nesmeth, maybe even Alison or Hailey. Instead, it's Tony. "Hey," I say as I pull open the door.

"He okay?"

"No. But I got him his meds and tucked him in. He's sleeping."

"He talks to you, Em. I need you to talk to me. I'm a little stressed out. He's like this at the end of every show, and then he knocks the crowd out the next night. I go to bed every night wondering if he'll wake up. But he doesn't talk. I send him to doctors, and he goes, but I'm not sure he follows what they tell him. You send him a list of foods, and he changes his diet. If anyone can save him, Em, it's you."

I shake my head. "I don't know if I can."

"Let me help," he says.

I chew on my knuckle a minute, thinking of how to handle

Geoff properly without irritating him. Ultimately, his health is most important. Even if it gets him angry, he needs to see a doctor. "Get him into an internist tomorrow. Use whatever pull you have and get him a morning appointment."

"This your idea or mine?"

I grin. He gets Geoff. "Ours. But mostly mine."

He gives me a hug and heads out the door. "This guy feeds off you. I've never seen anything like it."

I smile and shut the door. I pull the door latch closed and turn the lock. The room's muggy, and I hit the dimmer switch on the lights. The blinds are open, and I see the lower half of a full moon. Stars hang low enough to touch.

I grab my blanket and pillow and curl up on the lounger. My fingers touch his. I close my eyes, and he says, "Em?" His voice is weak. He hums, then whispers, "The night sky glows with the eyes of angels. I'm pulled under her wings. Heart, oh Heart, cover me."

For an instant, I understand romance. It's not physical, not movies or cheap novels. It's give and take, thoughtless efforts to express the depth of emotion. This is romance, and Geoff owns it.

From the Journal of: Geoff Morris

Monday, January 23, 2012, 8:14 a.m.

I'm holding Em's hand when I say it. I hope she doesn't take it wrong. I want her to know it's a joke, so I put on my best grin, though what I feel like doing is throwing up. "This is the second straight morning you've gotten me up early."

"I didn't get you up yesterday," she says, face straight. "It was your alarm clock. Your car shopping scheme. Blame your brofriend, not your girlfriend."

I laugh, and it hurts and heals. "Brofriend?"

"You and Yaz," she says, her straight face cracking.

"I figured." I stretch out my legs, fold my arms over my stomach, and lean forward. "I hate hospitals."

"This isn't a hospital. It's a doctor's office."

"Same thing." I groan. "You didn't have to come."

"Would you be here if I didn't?"

"Fair point." I check the magazine she's reading. "*Cosmo*? Really?"

"It was this or *Car and Driver*."

"Easy choice." By now, the other people in the room are eyeing me. Maybe it's the tattoos or the long hair, or because I look like I may slump over dead at any moment. But hey, they're here too, right? Maybe they're a stone's throw from death's door too.

When they call my name, Em takes me back, leads me by the hand. I clear my throat, swallow down the blood. I'm not happy she's making me come here, but I let it go. She's trying to help. She's stepping into my mess. She could be with her father now, talking with him, encouraging him. Instead, she's leading me by the hand to the back office to talk with an internist. I don't even know what kind of doctor that is, but Em says he's the best at what he does, whatever that is.

"What'd you say to my dad?" she asks as we wait in the room for the doctor to appear. We hear him next door, consulting with someone about constipation issues, and I wish the thin walls of this joint understood what patient-doctor confidentiality meant.

"That's between me and him," I say.

"You're not going to tell me?"

"Can we do this later?" I ask. "Not exactly looking forward to being poked and prodded. Is he going to do the rubber glove test?"

"Stop it." Em's laugh is punch-drunk, an overtired child trying not to giggle. She's out of control, and she snorts again.

I'm laughing too, now, despite the knotting in my stomach, despite my esophagus tightening like a fist.

We recover from our laughing fit moments before the doctor walks in. He checks my chart, arches an eyebrow. "How long have you had symptoms?" he asks.

"Few weeks. Maybe a couple of months."

"Which is it?" he says.

I shrug. "Don't know. Didn't really keep track of when it started."

He looks at Em. "When did he start complaining about it?"

Nice how he assumes we're married or whatever. She could be my sister for all he knows. But still, she answers like a good wife. "A couple weeks ago."

"Think he had symptoms before he complained?"

"Probably. He doesn't talk much about stuff like this. For him to mention it, it must have been bad."

She's figured me out. I'm trying to decide if I should be angry or flattered, but the doctor interrupts. "Open up," he says.

I yawn wide and let him examine my mouth with his little camp flashlight. "You have sores," he says. "Have you been taking your medication?"

"The sludge?" I say. "Sometimes."

"Not enough," the doctor says. "Cheeks, tongue, gums. They painful?"

I nod.

"Hard to eat," he says.

"You're on a roll," I say.

"How long have you been bleeding?" he asks.

I shrug.

"I noticed it last night, but I'm wondering if it's been longer."

"Well?" he says.

"Longer," Em says.

"This blood isn't from the gums and mouth, I assume." He sits down on a chair and marks in my chart, a look of concern on his face. "Vomiting blood?"

"Yes," Em says.

He shakes his head. "Lie down on the table for me."

I do, and he slides on latex gloves. I clench up for a minute before he starts pressing on my abdomen. It hurts, like getting punched, but he's not pressing hard.

"Any pain?"

"Keep pushing. You'll find out."

"That's a yes," Em says. She takes my hand, kisses my forehead. "Why didn't you tell us you were this bad?"

"These things go away," I say.

The doctor shakes his head. "Not if you don't take care of them." He stops pressing and sits back down. "I'm going to need a better look. I want you to get an ultrasound and come back and see me when it's done. There's a place up the street that does them." He scrawls an address on a paper along with an order for the imaging he needs.

"I'll get this done next week," I say.

"Today," he says. "Now."

"Excuse me?" I ask.

"Should we be worried?" Em asks.

"Not now, no. Precautionary," he says.

We go right away. Em holds my hand and doesn't talk. Doctor's put a rush order on it, and we get right in. The process is faster than any medical procedure should be. No one talks directly to me. They look at Em like she should know more than she does. This, more than anything else, worries me.

When we get back to the internist, he sits us down. He pushes his lips together. He's a fish in the mood for a kiss, but his eyes are serious. He stares at the ultrasound. "Ulcer's usually aren't a big deal, but with one like yours, they can get pretty nasty."

"Okay," Em says. "What's that mean? More medication? Surgery?"

The doctor points to a small white blip near what looks like my stomach. "These are lesions," he says. "You can see—you've got a ton of them. They're all over the stomach, a couple going down toward the intestines, some up near the esophagus. Most aren't bad, but there are so many, they start to add up. Did you have an ultrasound when your last doctor diagnosed you?"

I shake my head. What he's saying is heavy, hurts my shoulders, and my ulcer flares like fireworks.

"I've been a doctor for a number of years now, Geoff, and it's never easy to give bad news."

"I'm a big boy," I say, nervous. "Lay it out, man."

"This," he points to another white blob, "is cancer."

I blink.

Em says, "What?"

"I can't tell for sure just from the ultrasound, but I'm ninety percent. We need to deal with this immediately."

"No," I say. "Dude, I'm 26."

Em covers her mouth with her hand, and I wish she hadn't come, wish she hadn't heard, not so I could hide it from her, but so I could protect her from what she's feeling now.

But there's no protection for me.

Book Three

Lies are the language of love
And promises are precursors to pain
I was born to breathe on borrowed time
Born to live, was that my crime?
—Sideshow, "Soul Eater"

Emily Amherst's Journal

Monday January 23, 2012, 10:11 a.m.

Saying I'm furious when we leave the room is an understatement. "You said you loved me. How can you do this to yourself?"

"I didn't give myself cancer," he says.

I pull my arm away and walk ahead.

"Em, wait."

"For what? To plan your funeral too? You want a black casket with chains? How about a simple cremation? Open casket so we can see what the cancer has done to you?"

"Heart," he says, his voice irritatingly in control. He coughs and spits. "No one hears about this."

I'm beyond angry; my eyes fill with tears. "You're a pompous jerk."

He grabs my arm.

"Let go!" Instinct kicks in. I wheel around and point my finger at him. "Never grab me again." I start to shake. My voice quivers, and my hands come up in defense. I'm no longer in control. It's fear, hurt, anger all balled into one explosive moment.

He stares at me. The nurses watch, shocked. The doctor comes out of his office. "Is everything okay?"

I can't stop. Geoff's staring at me, eyes rimmed red. "You going to ignore this too? You ignored your ulcer and look where it got you. You told me you had it under control. Liar! Daddy's hours from death, and now I'm going to lose you too." People in the office are staring, but I don't care.

"I'm not dead," he says. "Don't kill me yet."

The doctor chimes in. "We have a good shot of fixing it … if he takes care of it."

"But he won't!" I wonder when I lost all control. "His stupid band is more important than his life."

"Enough, Heart." Geoff comes close, towers over me, but he leans down, to eye level. "Let's talk this out."

"You're a stubborn jerk."

He holds his hands up like I've asked him to put down a weapon. He moves slowly, methodically.

My gut says run. My heart says stay. My anger screams.

Geoff inches his hand toward my cheek, and I slap it away and walk out of the building.

He follows me, tries to take my shoulders, but I spin around and swipe at him again. He grabs my wrist and pulls me to him, strong and gentle.

"Let go!" I slap his chest, but he holds on. I twist and scream, try to pull away. Barry's face flashes in my mind. I have to get out, have to get away.

The wounds on my back burn. I'm tearing myself apart fighting against him. He finally turns me loose, puts his hands up again, and hums.

"Shut up!" People in the parking lot look at me, but I can't stop.

Neither does he. He hums again, whispering between my screams. "The night sky glows with the eyes of angels. I'm pulled under her wings. Heart, oh heart, cover me."

"Don't you 'Heart' me!"

"I'm not Barry," he says.

"No. You're Jennifer."

He stops for a minute. I see anger sway in his eyes, but his cool calm washes it out. I want him angry, want him to hit me, so I can leave and be done with him and not have to worry about what the next months will look like.

"I'm not Barry," he says again.

"You're selfish, too in love with yourself to get help!"

"People depend on me, Em. I can't let them down. Two shows, and then I get whatever surgery, whatever treatment the doctor orders. I promise."

"Skip the shows. Get the treatment now."

He grins, and I wonder how he can smile right now. "He's a doctor. Immediately for him means sometime in the next five years."

"Don't joke about this," I say.

He opens the door for me, and I slide into the Yukon. "It's an early catch. Treatable, he says. We're not at the panic stage yet." He starts the car and drives back toward Yaz and Steph's. He's trying to be gentle, but I'm pushing.

"Let me tell the band."

"No one hears about this," he says again.

"Isn't that what Jennifer said?"

"Stop!" he snaps. I've not seen him lose his cool like this, not even on stage in his manic performances. "I'm not Barry. I'm not Jennifer. Don't turn me into them."

I try to lower my voice, try to get some element of control. "She wouldn't get help, and that drove you crazy."

"This is different."

"How?"

"Jen was killing herself."

"You're not?"

"Jen was selfish. I'm thinking of the band."

"What will they do when you die?" For an instant, he's quiet. He knows I'm right, but he won't relent.

He looks at me, passionate anger flickering in his eyes. He flips on the radio, and I turn it off. "I'm not done."

Instead of turning onto Yaz's road, he keeps driving up Maple.

"Fine." He spits again and clenches the wheel. "Listen, I don't want to die. I'll do whatever the doctor asks, after the shows. We have to do this on my terms, Em. The band doesn't hear about this until after Phoenix."

"How can you manage treatments if you don't tell Tony? You can't do them while you're on tour running full speed."

"Ninecore will get a doctor to come with us."

"Do you realize how dumb you sound? You won't tell anyone, but Ninecore can get a doctor?"

"Don't call me stupid." His anger flashes again. "You sound like my mother," he says, his voice thin.

I'm on shaky ground, but I can't stop. He's hurt me, and I want him to hurt.

"You going to run away from me too?"

He hits the brakes hard and screams like I've never heard anyone scream. My heart clenches. Blood runs down his lips. He's breathing hard, like he just finished a set. He pulls the Yukon over and gets out. He paces around the car, hands fisted, shoulders tensed.

I'm in real danger here, but I'm done running. I want to make this work. "We've done everything on your terms. Let's try my terms for once. Show me you love me more than the band."

"Don't make me choose," he says.

"I'm not," I say, because if I do, he'll choose them. "Compromise?"

He sits on the curb, face in hands. "Make me an offer."

"We tell the band. If they think you can make it through San Diego and Phoenix, fine. If they want you to start treatments immediately, you respect our wishes."

He wipes his eyes. "Do you have any idea how terrified I am?"

I slide out of the car, walk beside him slowly, my heart in my throat. He's so tense, so volatile. I push the image of Barry out of my mind, stretch out to him with quaking hands. "I know exactly."

From the Journal of: Geoff Morris

Monday, January 23, 2012, 12:42 p.m.

Funny how things work. Before we get back to Yaz's, Tony calls. He wants to meet us on the bus fifteen minutes early to give us some news. Not sure what news can't wait fifteen minutes when we leave LA for SD, but he's talking at half the speed of light when he leaves me a message. I tell Em, and she decides to come with me. We've had a chance to settle down, to cry on the curb, to hash out a bit of the trouble between us. If I didn't love her like I do, I'd have walked, sent her on her way, and turned my attention to the next girl. But I'm in this for the long haul, so I stick around and work at it.

I'm still angry with her, still mad about her calling me dumb, insulting me the way my mom used to. I wanted to bring it up to her. She wanted to talk about Barry. We compromised and talked about Vegas, the gondolas, the art gallery, roulette, the cab.

When we get to the bus, Tony has us sit down. "I've got news," he says.

"So does Geoff," Em says.

Tony looks at me. "Yeah?"

"You first," I say.

Yaz shakes his head. "Let's hear your news, Geoff."

I sit down, hang my head. This isn't how I wanted to do it, but I'm not surprised Em's forcing the issue. Probably figures I won't want to tell them if I hear whatever news Tony has. "It's nothing, really."

"It is something," Em says. She takes my hand in hers as she sits next to me. "Are you going to tell them, or do I have to do it?"

I think about it a minute, weigh the options. Better for the band to hear from her or from me? Better for Em if she says it, or if I do? I know what she wants, but I'm still a little sore, a little bitter. She talks like I'm killing her instead of myself. I figure there's no way to win, so I step up. "Doctor had some bad news."

Jason folds his arms. "How bad?"

Hailey holds onto his arms. "Is it the ulcer?"

Nesmeth puts his phone away and listens intently for once.

I stare at the floor. It's easier if I'm not looking at them, but I feel their eyes pressing. "I don't want you guys to freak out about this. Nothing's for sure right now. He wants to run a couple tests. No big deal. I'll get it done when we get back from Phoenix."

"Hold up," Tony says. "What kind of tests?"

"Nothing big. A scope is all."

"And a biopsy," Em says.

I swallow iron, clear my throat.

"A biopsy?" Hailey asks. She sits on Jason's bunk, sits cross-legged. "Like for cancer?"

"He's twenty-six," Nesmeth says. "It's not cancer."

"Exactly," I say.

Em says, "The doctor thinks it is."

Tony folds his hands behind his neck. "Cancer? You for real right now?"

"He thinks," I say. "Nothing's for sure. We'll know more after the tests."

"There's more," Em says.

I shake my head, but she keeps on talking.

"He thinks Geoff should have the scope and biopsy right away."

I stand up. "He doesn't want to get sued. That's what it boils down to. It's not cancer."

"You're bleeding," Hailey says.

"It's the ulcer," I say, wiping my mouth.

Em's quiet, and I wonder where the verbal MMA fighter is I saw an hour ago.

"Dude," Nesmeth says, "what if it's not?"

"Then I get some treatments, and we move on with our life."

Tony arches an eyebrow. "Cancer's not a cold, man. You don't take care of it with Nyquil."

"I'm not saying that."

"Geoff," Jason says, "this needs to get fixed."

"It will. Why's everyone talking like I'm going to let it slide."

"Because you're talking about it like it's no big deal," Hailey says. "It's a big deal."

"It's not. It's tiny. It's the size of a cockroach."

"Cancer kills," Tony says. His voice is low, a whisper, a threat.

"Not me, it doesn't."

Em stands up, "Tell him he has to get checked now. Today. Tomorrow. Tell him to rest and not play San Diego and Phoenix. He needs rest."

"I'm fine," I say. "I want to play."

"I don't know," Jason says.

"You can't be serious. I need to play. Non-negotiable."

"There's something else we need to consider," Tony says. He's cautious, exploring the ice sheet over a frozen lake with a gentle step.

"Your news," I say. "What is it?"

He scratches his eyebrow and rubs the bridge of his nose. "Doesn't seem as important anymore."

"We need good news," I say.

He sighs. "Two things: Ninecore's hired me on full time. They want me to set up a national tour."

Nesmeth runs his hands through his hair. "National? For real? When do we leave?"

He says, "There's more. They pulled some strings. They want us to play 'Hate Breed' at the Grammys."

My stomach lurches, crawls up my throat. "The Grammys are next week," I say.

Em says, "No way. He's not well enough."

I kneel in front of her, my eyes wide. I'm moving on adrenaline, the high of good news strengthening me. "Heart, you don't turn down the Grammys."

"You do when you're bleeding to death," she says, her voice heavy.

"I finish San Diego and Phoenix. I do nothing but rest and play. You have my word. I'll get the scope done before the Grammys. If I need treatment, I start after next week. It's perfect."

"It's not perfect," she says.

Hailey's voice is quiet, as if she's not sure she should even be in the bus, if she should speak up. "Em's right, Geoff."

I turn around, look at Yaz. "Tell her I can do this, man."

He shakes his head. "It's a bad idea," he says. "You're more important than a couple shows."

"The Grammys, Yaz."

He says nothing.

"Jason? Nesmeth?"

They shrug, one after the other. "You think you can do it?" Jason asks, and Hailey slaps him.

"I've been doing it every night for the last week. What's two more nights?"

"If you die," Nesmeth says, "I'll kill you."

"I won't," I say.

"Then I'm in."

Tony pales a bit and sits down. "Cancer?" he says again.

"Maybe," I say. "I think he's wrong."

"Please don't be stupid," Em whispers. She stares at Jason, at

Nesmeth. "Don't do this. Don't be selfish. Think of Geoff. Where's Sideshow without him? You need him healthy. Don't let him push himself to death."

"They voted, Heart. Jason and Nesmeth are with me."

"Hailey and Yaz and I aren't," she says.

"But only Yaz is in the band." I know it's a mistake when it comes out of my mouth, and I want to take it back, want to grab the words in mid-air and swallow them down like bile, like blood, like pride.

She stands up slow. Brushes her fingers across my cheek. "I love you."

She walks out of the bus.

To: Geoff Morris
Emily Amherst
Monday, January 23, 2012, 5:00 p.m.

I lost my head this morning. Can't remember the last time I lost control like that. I wanted my words to hurt you as much as you hurt me. I should have handled things better. I apologize.

I'm not sure where to begin. No word is right, no emotion on target—the only thing I know for sure is I love you, and I'm fighting for you.

When I lost it this morning, I was worried about me. What would I do without you? How could I breathe without you? Now it's about you, about us, about the band. It's about priorities.

This month has been heaven and hell. Steph was right: separation kills. I understand why Yaz fears touring. I understand his tears when he hangs up.

I owe you my life. You gave me a safe place to stay. You found me on the mountain. There aren't enough thank yous in the world to show my gratitude. You risked your life, the band's chance at getting signed, to save my life. But now you won't risk the same things to save yourself.

I guess we see love differently. To me, it's sacrifice, joy, give and take. You've lived your life with a chip on your shoulder, determined to prove you will not be taken down. You've lived through so much already and pulled yourself up. You've made something of yourself, turned yourself into a good man. You raised yourself, learned how to survive, but not to love.

Love is learned, and you haven't had anyone teach you. I'm sorry your father was a drunk, sorry your mother was jaded and manipulative. I'm sorrier I messed up. I wanted to show you what love was, but I've been a pretty bad example myself.

You are the most amazing man I've met, one worthy of something more than me, a woman as fearless as you, who can walk through flames and not care if she gets burned.

I'm sick. I'm spent, broken. Outside, my scars are healing. Inside, they're raw and bleeding.

I was wrong to push. Maybe I was being selfish. You're right; it's only two more shows. But after Phoenix and San Diego, it'll be Baltimore and St. Louis, then Philly and New York, and then they'll call me and say, "Em, Geoff's gone."

I don't say this out of anger or frustration, or because I lost the battle—I say this because I lost the war. Call me naïve, foolish, dumb, but I believed you when you said you loved me.

If you did, you would have chosen your life over two more shows. You would have followed me off the bus. But you didn't.

I still love every part of you, from the freaky tats to your face piercings to your dry humor. I love how you spit a little when you laugh, how you flex your muscles in your sleep. I love your ocean-green eyes. I love how your lips tip up when you sing, love your little bounce before you play, love how you slap your leg to the beat. I love how your laugh digs deep into my being. I love how you hold me and how you say you're sorry. I love your tenderness and, more than anything, I love when you call me Heart.

I didn't walk away because I don't love you. I walked because I do—because with me, you're nailed to the floor. Without me, you can soar.

As much as it will hurt, I'll watch every second of your flight.

Please take your meds. You won't sleep if you don't. I can't take care of you because you won't let me.

I'll be out of Yaz and Steph's in a couple days. I need to make a fresh start. You do, too. The keys to your car are on the nightstand in the guest room.

With all my love forever,

Emily

To: Emily Amherst
Geoff Morris
Monday, January 23, 2012, 6:08 p.m.

Am I supposed to feel sorry for you? Who walked out on whom, Em?

Last I checked, I was still on the bus. You were here too. Remember when I asked you to be with me? When I called you up on stage, kissed you in front of thousands of screaming fans? I could have pulled anyone up on stage with me. I pulled you.

Don't put this on me. I'm not the one pushing you away. I'm putting myself on the line for my friends, and I needed you with me.

Are we doing the pity party thing now? Are we doing truth?

Here's truth: My uncle, the good one, the one who loved God. He died my sophomore year in high school. My mother's brother. He leaves me a boatload of money for college. "For UCLA," he says in his letter to me, because he knows how much I wanted to go there. But I'm not eighteen, so the money goes into a trust, and my mom's the executor of the trust. This is when she leaves my dad, drags me by the ear to live with her. So, I refuse, and how does she manage to get herself an apartment? A new car? A new life? My UCLA money.

Hold on, it gets better. She goes to court, wins full custody of me because my dad was drunk in the courtroom. At least he showed. This is why I left, why I finished high school on my own, working odd jobs at clubs to buy whatever food I needed to get by. I earned my way to UCLA with grades. I slept two or three hours a night, showered in the gym, and made straight As. I made who I am by leaving.

A woman a night, remember? Why? Because I knew they wouldn't stick around. I got rid of them before they could get rid of me, before they could steal from me, break my heart, whatever.

And then you came along.

You called me stupid and dumb. Maybe you were right, because I trusted you to stay. And I stayed with you. I believed in you, Em, right up until the moment you walked out on me.

Don't talk to me about being broken when you've got half my heart in each of your hands. —Geoff

TEXT MESSAGE TRANSCRIPT
Monday, January 23, 2012,—7:00 p.m.

EMILY AMHERST: You're right.

G

To: Emily Amherst
Geoff Morris
Tuesday, January 24, 2012, 1:22 a.m.

Good show tonight, Heart. Missed you, though. Took my meds because I know you want me to.

I was out of line in my last message. I'm sorry. You won't take my calls, so this is what I have to offer: my words, my stories, my soul. None as beautiful as you deserve.

Here's what happened tonight. Nesmeth shows up to the bus, a woman under each arm. "Something to forget Em by," he says. "Your pick."

Maybe I was in the half-dazed dream of the post-show flare up, but I swear to you, the girl under his left arm has tattoos of flames running up her arms. They're moving, crackling, licking her skin. She's getting burned, but she doesn't care. She's got platinum blond hair, perfect teeth, the skin of a bronze idol. She's wearing a bikini top and a skirt shorter than my fingers. She's San Diego in a body. "What's her name?" I ask Nesmeth.

No lie, she leans toward me and whispers, "Fearless."

I'm hurting, in heart and stomach. I think a woman would be nice. But this girl isn't you. "Thanks," I say to Nesmeth. "But I'm tired. I need to sleep."

He nods, and takes Fearless and the other girl to his bunk.

I pull out my computer and write you to apologize for my earlier message, which I can't take back, which you can't unread. I've asked you for new paper too many times, maybe. Maybe now you get why I say there's not enough paper for some people. Maybe I'm one.

Forgive me, Heart?

How's your dad? I want to know.

You want to talk about Barry, and I never let you.
Talk, Heart.
I'm listening.
Geoff

To: Geoff Morris
Emily Amherst
Tuesday, January 24, 2012, 9:32 a.m.

Thanks for the story about Fearless, for slinging mud at me, for tacking my face on her "flame."

If this is your way of apologizing, try again.

You want me to pat you on the back for refusing her? News flash: People rarely say, "Good choice, not hopping into the sack with the first floozy the guys pass your way."

I tried to give you freedom. I tried to give you the option to live without worrying about me hounding you over obviously bad choices.

You want me to talk? I'll talk.

I was wrong to walk away. It was selfish. Let's forget your bad decision. (Notice I didn't say stupid or dumb?)

Whatever I fought for, whatever "us" I'd hoped for, was a lost war. You justify every action. It's your way or no way. You've got no give, no flexibility.

I shouldn't have walked. No matter how angry I am, my love for you stomps out the fire.

As for Fearless Flames, how dare you? If you were here, I'd punch you square in the nose, you and Nesmeth both. How dare he tempt you, and how dare you flaunt her in my face. You can have any woman you want, and I'll never find another man, I get it. Point taken. Now shut up.

Ready for round two?

I'm tired of you sidestepping what happened to me. I don't want a Poor Emily moment—this isn't a pity party. I appreciate what you did for me, getting me away, and defending me at Mitch's.

You say you don't see the scars, but you do. You wince every time you brush my hair from my face. You stutter when you search for a compliment. You put yourself between me and every mirror we pass. You're casual, like I don't notice, but I do.

I live with them, with relentless pain. I wonder if I'll ever have smooth skin again. Can I ever walk down the beach without people staring at the scarring on my back? Every time I pull my arm over my head, I feel the agony of pulling skin. I'm furious, but you ignore it. You never discuss it or Barry. This isn't something you can blow off.

For all the kind things you've done to try and make me feel better, the cruelest thing you've done is ignore this.

I've tried to be brave. I went to the hospital to visit Barry, to offer him a clean sheet. But the fact is, when I close my door at night, I lock it—move the nightstand against the door. I sleep as far as I can from windows. I keep my shades drawn, even during the day. As hard as I've tried, I still jump when anyone touches me.

I'm broke mentally, physically, and financially. My lawyer said he can't get back the money Barry stole. The job Steph set me up with never panned out. Daddy needs full-time care, which his insurance doesn't cover.

I thought I'd be fine. God provides. But then I fell for you. I've kept this to myself because I didn't want to dump on your dream. But your dream always needs more—one more show, one more session, one more interview. Does it matter that I need you, Geoff?

You love me, you say, but only on your terms, on your tour.

You mad? Probably. That's what you do when things get tough. You throw a tantrum until you get your way, twist what I say to make me look selfish and ugly, when the truth is, I love you.

No matter how much you insist you're being selfless by playing the shows "for the band," it's a selfish choice. You're putting yourself, the band, Ninecore, me, us, at risk. If you die, what do any of us have?

A novella of anger and hurt, but you said you'd listen. You wanted me to talk.

I guess I need some clean paper too.

If you took me back, Geoff, I'd never walk out on you again. If you die, I die.

But if you ever bring up anything about Ms. Short Skirt Bikini Top, I will become fearless.

Give me space. Let me digest the "mess" you've thrown me into.

I hope you believe me when I say, "I love you."

Emily

G

To: Emily Amherst
Geoff Morris
Tuesday, January 24, 2012, 6:19 p.m.

You've got every right to be angry. Your Irish temper's sexy on you.

My story about Fearless wasn't meant to make you feel inferior, to threaten you. In fact, I meant it as a compliment. Moral of the story: I love you, Heart. No other woman compares.

But you want space. You'll notice I haven't called or texted. I'm honoring your request. I'd been thinking the same thing for a while now. As much as I love being with you, being near you, smelling your cucumber melon perfume, holding your hand, kissing you hard on the lips, I think we need a break. Our relationship started through the space and time of the Internet. Maybe we need to explore that again. It might give us the distance we need to speak to each other without taking verbal swings.

Yaz and Tony sat me down shortly after you walked. They had what you might call a heart-to-heart. I called it an intervention. They're worried, they say. Tony made a phone call and set me up with a doctor in Phoenix. Not an ulcer doctor, a head shrink. Yaz says it's counseling or he walks. You must have got under their skin. They'd never have pulled anything like this pre-Em.

So, I agree. No matter how much my mother disagrees, I'm not dumb. I sit down in his plush office expecting him to ask me about my mother. I've lined up an earful for him, but he doesn't. He says, "Why are you here?"

"To save my friend," I say.

He smirks. "That's what your friend told me about you."

I figure, if I've got to do this, I might as well make the most of it. I got an hour with this guy, and he's got more degrees on his wall than I have songs. "Can't figure out what's wrong with me." I have him read through our messages. He gives me the normal lines—I'm stressed out, got a lot on my plate, it'd be weird if I didn't blow up occasionally. I say, "Not good enough. Tony's paying you well enough to tell me something I can't get from some six-dollar-an-hour roadie. You've been to school for this. Tell me why I'm so hard on her?"

He gets into this bit about love and hate not being opposites. They're neighbors, two houses sharing a fence and a gate with well-oiled hinges, swinging both ways. It's easy to go from one to the other, natural.

"The opposite of love?" I ask.

"Apathy," he says.

It makes sense. Love and hate are passion pointed in opposite directions.

Long story short, I say, "How do I fix it?"

He says, "Talk about nothing. Especially don't talk about you and her, your relationship, or whatever it is."

"I gotta," I say. "She's mad because I don't talk about us, about her, about what happened."

He says, "What do I know? These degrees came with the office." Sarcasm is seldom pretty, but it's downright ugly on a psychologist.

Anyway, I say, "I have to fix us."

He says I'm too busy fixing what isn't broke, and I wonder if this guy can be any more cliché. So, I decide something. I'm going to take his advice and ignore it at the same time. I'm going to write you a couple messages. One is about "us," and the other will have nothing to do with "us." I figure this way, it can take our minds off all the drama sitting like elephants on our chests. Don't know about you, but I could use a chance to take a breath.

My "nothing" message will come later, after my show. For now, let's talk "us," because you deserve it, and I owe it to you.

You were right. I never talked about your scars. Never wanted to. When I was with you, those few days in Vegas and LA, I wasn't about to ruin it by bringing up the past. And I didn't want you to be self-conscious about your injuries.

I do notice them. I wince, sure. What else can I do? They're a reminder of what he did to you, what I couldn't stop. I see them, and I fester with anger, my ulcer flares, and I'm nearly overcome with a get-in-my-car-and-hunt-him-down urge.

I screwed up with my ulcer. It's my body, but I never considered it affecting other people. Last thing I want is people looking at me. I don't need pitying looks, the "are you taking your meds?" nagging. I'm nothing, Em. The band's everything. I may get out on stage, put on a good show, but when they cut the lights and my mic, I'm finished. I want to crawl into a hole and hibernate for a year or two. Each show's a week's worth of energy, and it takes its toll.

But you're right. I have to take care of it. I called the doctor, set up a scope Thursday afternoon. Ninecore wants us recording on Tuesday. Should have time to do both. I'll balance my medical responsibilities with my band responsibilities.

Don't worry about me. You've got enough to worry about with your dad. I'm still praying for him. Don't know if I'm doing it right, but I'm trying.

Here's a new page.

If it's not too much, I'd like another sheet for myself.

Always,

Geoff

G

To: Emily Amherst
Geoff Morris
Wednesday, January 25, 2012, 12:22 a.m.

"Not Us"

Phoenix is beautiful. You'd like it. Sunset, purple clouds feathered over an orange horizon. The buildings silhouette, drop to deep black and windows glint with moonlight. It's hot and dry, not muggy like LA. The whole city's flat, spread out, mountains rippling up in the distance like worms crawling across cardboard.

Sent you something. Should be arriving tomorrow morning.

What's going on with this job? You said it never came through? If you need a job, and you're not too proud to take one from me, I can get you set up with Ninecore. They're based in Seattle, but they're opening an LA office. When he's not on tour, Tony will work from there. He likes you, wants to see you in a good job.

Grammys coming up in less than a week. Hoping to be well enough to play. Yaz and I are putting together some tricks to play while we're on stage. Make the show unforgettable, you know? Leave a mark.

Got a few full weeks post Grammys. Tony's lined up interviews, articles, PR stuff, photo shoots, launching a new website, creating content for social media. Get this—he wants me to make a Sideshow app. I told him I quit the business. Anyway, the big project is cutting the final tracks for the full-length album, the first of three we'll do with Ninecore. Things go well, we'll stick with them for three more. Should take us a week or so. After tracks are put down, Tony wants us back on the road.

Alison says "hey." She misses you. So does Hailey. They look at me sideways sometimes, like "How'd you screw it up with her?"

I'm not too good at this "nothing" message. I miss you. Give your dad my best. Hope to see him soon.

Always,

Geoff

To: Geoff Morris
Emily Amherst
Wednesday, January 25, 2012, 5:00 a.m.

Not us.

If you were trying to impress me, good job.

A nothing email? Back to the basics? I think your psychologist gave you a lesson in defusement (if that's a word). We both need to take it down a notch.

I'll play along, as long as "not us" emails don't mean "not us." I asked for space to calm down, not to walk away. We said horrible things in our fear and anger, and I'm sorry.

Here's the "not us." I'll write the "us" in a few. Hard to put distance between the two.

I stayed at the hospital until 11:00 last night. Dad's not doing well. Still don't know what you said to him that jolted him back to reality, but he's still in and out of consciousness. One minute he's lucid; the next, a zombie. He's not eating. Doctor says that's the ugly part of this disease. The body forgets to do its job.

The hospital chaplain has been visiting. Dad seems to respond to him. I told the chaplain how Daddy worked at the food pantry in Ralley. Told him how he seemed to connect with the folks who were nameless to the rest of the world.

He was a marine too. Did I tell you that? Career guy. Maybe that's why I was attracted to Barry in the first place—the man in the uniform. When he retired from the military, he took a factory job in California. Said he was tired of "shouting." Funny thing is, he still gets letters from the men in his platoons. They never mention him shouting, only his willingness to help them along, lead them, encourage them.

The doctor says I should be prepared. Enjoy the coherent moments, because when he goes, it'll be fast. It's just a matter of time when his heart forgets to take the next beat.

I remembered you talking once about the shoreline in LA. Before I went to the hospital, I stopped by the beach. It's so different than the East Coast. We were in Beaufort, SC, while Dad was stationed at Paris Island. Whole different look, this Pacific. I saw a whale in the distance. In SC, the best I could hope for was a great white. The ocean here is rough. On the East Coast, it's rolling, gentle. No smashing itself into sharp rocks, like suicide waves.

I worked my way through the skaters, cyclists, and weirdos, took my shoes off, and stepped into the sand. It was colder than I'd imagined. I stood at the edge of the tide and let the water wash over my ankles. I thought of the rain, spreading itself across the sky, being everywhere and nowhere, the drops always falling, freezing and unfreezing, an unending cycle. The ocean is the same, a giant upside-down storm, everywhere and nowhere. I want to be the rain; I want to be the ocean.

The ocean moves, swells, unceasingly. It's a give and take, a push and a shove. It's love.

The sunset caught my breath in my throat. Golden streaks intertwined with lavender and pink. It reached into forever, something I've been imagining a lot since Daddy's so close to eternity, and you're within arm's reach of it yourself. I sat in the waning sunlight, dreaming until the tide came in.

Sweet of you to offer a job. Normally I'd say no, but if they have some accounting or off-site work at Ninecore, I'd be willing to swallow my pride. Beats going hungry. I'd need to be available for Daddy, but I could work on contract. I'm great at managing schedules and spreadsheets, budgets, inventory, all that. Might help me avoid homelessness. Had a friend who lived out of his high school at night. He says it sucks. :)

I've been thinking about what your mom did. She must have had a reason. I'm not justifying what she did; I'm playing devil's advocate. You were young, and kids don't always see the whole picture. It's hard to be in a relationship with a drunk. Maybe she was trying to protect you? Either way, she should have talked to you about it.

My mom was good. She used to say regret was a nasty bedfellow. Imagine if your mom passed. If she did, you'd never have a chance to set things right. If the doctors can't work this cancer thing out, she may not have a chance to fix things with you. Either way, someone's left with regret.

I've got plenty of regret these days. I should never have walked off the bus. I thought I was lonely in Ralley, but it doesn't compare to now. I'll do whatever I can, explore every path of hope, until I know none are left. I hope you do the same.

I'm taking Tripp to the park this morning. Maybe he and I can get in a few twirls on the merry-go-round before the paparazzi wake up. Last time I took Tripp on some errands, the evening StarShot posted an article titled "Morris' Girl Sports Yaz's Baby." Really? How do you sport a baby? I'm not a journalist, but I could come up with something catchier.

I miss you and love you more than I could have ever imagined.

Emily

To: Geoff Morris
Emily Amherst
Wednesday, January 25, 2012, 11:50 a.m.

US

This won't shock you, but I'm a bit obsessive and little prideful. I can't sleep. You consume me. I want you, but I'm too proud to let you be who you are. When I lay down at night, my eyes widen, and I can't get you out of my head. I worry. I wonder. I get up and pace.

I bought some melatonin, switched to decaf tea, and tried a new radio station, but they play "Underbelly" every ten minutes. Hard to sleep with your voice so close and you so far. Plus, I'm a little jealous. Wherever you are, there's Alison, there's Hailey, but there's not Em.

I find myself in a vicious cycle of sleep deprivation and depression. All I want is to snuggle up with you.

I asked you to give me space; I didn't think it would be this deafening. We needed air. I've never heard you scream like you did in the Yukon. Your eyes lit up with an intimidating violence, but a strange self-control. You didn't look at me when you screamed. The yell tore your throat, and blood spattered the steering wheel. I was terrified. I'd do anything to get that image out of my head, but it's not your fault. It's mine. I promise, I'll never force that animal out of you again. I'm sorry. I'm ashamed, and I need your forgiveness.

I want to forget your scream and remember your crazy, impulsive moments—your happy, carefree spirit.

We're carved out of the same mold. We're two sad misfits, who, when brought together, make one incredible person. You're the vision, I'm the practical. We have to marry those qualities, imagine us as one instead of two. I'm not pushing marriage. I'm realizing the reason you fall into my arms after a show, why your passion burns on stage when I'm watching, why my hand fits in yours perfectly, your lips on mine. If we want this to work, we gotta give up ourselves and think of us as one.

When the doctor said cancer, I lost all control. I forgot you had to absorb the information too. We digest things differently. This isn't happening to me; it's happening to you. As much as I'd like to say I understand, I don't. I know you're scared. Me too, baby. Can we start over? New sheet of paper?

I want to be with you when you get treatment. I can be a second set of ears in case fear blurs whatever news the doctor has for you. But if you don't want me there, I understand. I didn't do a very good job of keeping my cool last time, did I?

Thank you for respecting my request for space, but I think I've had enough of it now. I want you back, if you'll have me.

I need you.

Emily

P.S. Your box arrived today. The dress is amazing.

To: Emily Amherst
Geoff Morris
Thursday, January 26, 2012, 4:19 p.m.

US

I'll admit—I've been stalking your Facebook. Steph tagged your photo of you in Lish Park near all those roses. The sun caught in your hair like water through a net. You're a little silhouetted and look pensive. And the tilt of your head, the line of your jaw soft and clear, I'm not sure what's up and to the left, but I want to know. I want to look with you. Beauty, when she looks at this photo, is shamed and a little jealous.

Here's a dream: We're at the cabin, early spring. We take a dip in the stream. The water's near ice. We goof around a bit, relaxing, enjoying the chilling bite on our skin. We get out, shivering like eight-year-olds after a warm shower on a cold winter's morning. I pull you in my arms, hold you tight, let our bodies warm each other. My chin rests on your head, and you press your ear to my chest. Then, you tilt your head back, and the sun catches your hair the way it did in the photo. You close your eyes, gently part your lips as I lower my head closer to yours.

I went to the doctor today. Had my scope somewhere around the time I should've been eating lunch. It would have been nice to have you there, but I'm glad you weren't. No matter how much I want you with me, I've got to do this on my own. I'm terrified, and when I'm scared, I tend to snap. You've seen that—the scream in the Yukon. Better for me to be alone. I'm good at it. At least I was, until I met you.

That said, I don't think it's a good idea for us to get back together right now, no matter how much we want to. We need to figure out who we are on our own before we can make "us" work. I've got a lot of things to think about. I'm taking this time to do some searching—something I should've done a while back. Call it a rite of passage, call it growing up, call it what you want. I'm not leaving. I'm not breaking up with you. Space and time is all. It's what the snide doctor said, and I want to do it right, for "us."

If you're tight on funds, let me help. Put your pride aside for a bit and let a friend help. Inking the deal with Ninecore left me with some spending money. Not a ton, but enough to recoup what I'd dropped into this band over the years. We've already earned out our advance on downloads, somewhere around two million now. Tony says we've passed the threshold and the growth now will be viral. Point is, money's coming to me, and I've got nothing to buy but things for you and some gear for the band. I'm putting some away for medical insurance, BTW. Your responsibility is rubbing off on me.

Here's the story with the dress. The white and yellow reminded me of a daisy, and they should complement your hair and eyes. It's got a full back, so you won't have to worry about your scars. There'll be a lot of photographers around when you wear it to the Grammys. I'm targeting that as our big night. I should have everything sorted out by then. My soul should be searched. I'll know about the possible cancer by then. We should be able to be "us" then, if that's okay with you. Can you wait another five days?

The pink slip is something I worked out with the dealer in Vegas. The Yukon is yours. You need it more than I do anyway.

I have another email to write to an awfully beautiful woman.

All love,

Geoff

G

To: Emily Amherst
Geoff Morris
Thursday, January 26, 2012, 4:31 p.m.

NOTHING

Here's a few notes from my journal, something Snide Doctor suggested:

GOOD MEMORY OF DAD: He's a crazy functional drunk, the guy who goes through life sloshed because a sober world is too scary. But today, he's less sloshed than normal and wants to teach me to throw a baseball. He throws the dumb thing twelve feet over my head. I chase it down and throw it back and, I swear, it catches him right in the nose. I'm eight, but I've got a good arm. He drops to his knees, bleeding in the grass and laughing. I'm apologizing as much as I can, and he's laughing. Finally, he gets up, rubs my head with a bloody hand, and says, "Killer arm, kid."

GOOD MEMORY OF MOM: I'm young. Don't remember exactly how old. I haven't started school, and things at home don't suck yet. My mom does motherly things because she's expected to, but I don't know that at the time. Right then, I'm thinking she loves me. This was before I knew better. Anyway, I'm on the couch, and she's cutting my nails. Don't know what it was about the moment, the television on in the background, the light of the dirty old lamp with the dusty shade, or her hands. Must've been her hands, the way she held mine in hers, gently but firmly, enough to keep me still, but not enough to hurt. She clips them all without drawing blood. This didn't happen often, but I think I remember it best because it was a time I trusted her.

This won't shock you, but I'm not good with trust. It's the elephant that sits on our chest. If we can't figure it out, it'll separate us and make us miserable. I'm stepping out here, extending a hand for you to hold gently and firmly, and I'm hoping you won't draw blood.

I'm putting together some lyrics. This line came to me in San Diego:

In her cloudy eyes
burn all the world's beauty;
her passion, like a knife,
is hard to ignore,
harder still to feel.

You already know my thing with lyrics. I better not find these online. Here's the elephant named Trust. Here's words for a tune I call Purify:

A rouge tide washes over her peach cheeks
Here passion is never more
Than a passing whisper
Slowly evaporating
Into a chlorine gas
She is a black rose
Hung on a red stem
She is a red raven
Feasting on the dead
She is the leech that cures my disease
She is the saran that I breathe
She wanted, needed me
I held her, helped her
To move, to stand again
Satin sheets went sliding by the bedside
Where she waits for me
Rain purifies
Lust lets love die

Snide Doctor prescribed fish. Not to eat, but to watch. So, I got a goldfish. Named him Cobain. I have to feed him once a day and keep him away from shotguns and women named Courtney. Fish are soothing. They mellow me out. I've decided home is where the fish are. For now, my home's in Ninecore Studios for another five days. After the Grammys, we're back on the road, and home will be the bus.

My other doctor—the ulcer one—said he'd have the results of the scope back in a couple days. He put a rush on it. I promise you'll be the first to hear.

Always,

Geoff

To: Geoff Morris
Emily Amherst
Friday, January 27, 2012, 12:00 a.m.

US

I wish I understood you. I try, but whenever I think I've got you figured out, you do what you do best: fix things.

The Yukon? I don't deserve such kindness. It's too much. I want to thank you, tell you I can't accept it, but Steph said if I told you no, she'd kick me out. She said, "Let Geoff be Geoff." This is me, letting you be you.

I'm trying to learn to accept gifts as an act of love, not pity. Can we meet in the middle? Call it our car?

Thank you is not good enough. I'm not the word weaver. I can't find something profound and beautiful to say. I'm so in love with you, I can't stand it.

I'm trying to understand why you didn't want me at the doctor, why you need to do this alone. Why do you need to do anything alone? I promised I'd respect your wishes, but this is killing me. I'm scared to death.

I'm learning to trust too. I trust you'll tell me everything. No secrets.

I gotta admit, I got giddy when you said you'd been stalking my Facebook page. I try to be careful what I post since the paparazzi peruse it too. But yes, that picture was for you. I'm glad it gives you sweet thoughts.

I'm having a hard time forgiving myself, waiting for your forgiveness. Being away from you is like having glass shards in my heart. I have to remind myself I asked for the space. But I never thought you'd agree. Now I feel like I've driven you away.

But I get the rite of passage, the growing up. Something I need to do too. If we don't, we'll never survive this business. I want you to be the king, so I can be your queen. Your greatest success is not the band, but your selfless heart. I love the musician, but worship the man.

I'm thrilled you've gotten your money back. At least one of us has. I admire your financial responsibility. It's sexy. :) I know lots of places you can invest your money. The taxes will still be horrendous, but fairly assessed. Let me know if you want help saving right.

I was dumbfounded when the dress arrived. I found myself speechless again, trying to find an appropriate thank you. It's beautiful, a poem. Chiffon. Flows like an angel's robe.

We were out shopping for dresses when it came in. Yaz picked out a dress and necklace for Steph. Hers is a long, deep purple, off the shoulder, and what a beautiful necklace he sent. He went with us to look for me. Insisted they help me find something right for me. I guess you never told him your plan. Anyway, I wasn't comfortable with them spending money on me, so I found a respectable, bargain-priced, black tea-length dress. It had a scoop back, which was nice, but wouldn't look good on me. We searched for a coverlet, but couldn't find one, so we gave up and went home.

And there was the box with my name on it. Steph couldn't stop smiling when I tried it on. It fits perfectly, and it's so soft. I must have stared at myself in the mirror for thirty minutes, trying out the perfect pose for when you see me for the first time again. Grammy night will be our "do over," and we can finally put Union Station behind us.

So, here's your dream: It's evening. A soft breeze, candlelight, and strawberries. You hear a voice. It's quiet, timid, shy. "Hey, baby." I walk across the room, the train of the dress you gave me fluttering in the breeze. No scar, nothing to mess up the moment. I come to you, take your hand, and you pull me close. We gently sway to the music.

I can't keep this up much longer. It's only four more days, but it feels like an eternity. I can't breathe.

Every day, I say a prayer. "God, grant him peace. Grant us love." And when I send it sailing into the sky, I trust.

You are the air that fills my lungs, the blood that warms my soul, and the hope that keeps me going.

My heart aches for you.

Em

To: Geoff Morris
Emily Amherst
Friday, January 27, 2012, 2:25 p.m.

NOTHING

My phone rings today, and it's Sterling Amundsten. "Ms. Amherst, Geoff Morris recommended you for a position with Ninecore." I'm wondering what position you recommended me for when he said, "Morris says you're fully apt in online merchandising and retail."

I had to laugh. Looks like seven years of running Frankie's Market paid off.

We talked for forty minutes. He blistered me with questions. I fired back. Told him how he could improve their online store sales, inventory, and increase their intake by forty-eight percent. He was impressed and offered me a starting position working for the online sales team. They'll start me at $45K. Not much for an accounting degree, but way better than what Frankie paid me. Plus, I can work from home, help Steph with Tripp, be available to Daddy, and travel with you, if you'll let me. The job comes with full benefits, insurance, 401K, new computer.

Before he hangs up, I ask, "Are you doing this because Geoff asked you to?"

"We had an open position. He overheard me interviewing a candidate between tracks and gave me your number."

Feels good knowing I landed the job on my own.

Steph was chatting with the lady who owns the house behind them today. I guess she's moving to New York and wants to rent her house out. Of course, my ears perked up. She's leaving in a few days and agreed to let me move in now and pay her the first month's rent after my first check comes in. She said it's better than renting to a stranger.

She's converted the garage to an apartment. If you ever get tired of the bus or the studio, you have a place to rest your head. It's got plenty of room for your guitars and mics. Visit anytime you want. I'm looking forward to being on my own again. I've enjoyed the time with Yaz and Steph, but they need their house back.

Daddy was awake today. Yesterday he couldn't speak, couldn't keep his eyes open, but this morning, the nurse called and said to come down while he was alert. I took him out on the patio for a bit, and he asked about you. Remembered your name and everything. Asked if you were feeling better. He said, "The boy'd be a good Marine." I didn't tell him you were better at beating up Marines. For a minute, it was like having Daddy back.

The doctor reminded me we'd have days like this, but the prognosis hasn't changed. Who knows how he'll be tomorrow. For now, I'll take what I can get.

Rock&Roll Magazine featured Sideshow in this month's issue. The cover is monumental. You on stage, legs apart, no shirt, dragon tats winding around your abs and up your arm, fists clinched, begging for a fight, hair stringy and long, clinging to your neck and back. Got me a little weak in the knees. My heart raced, and I broke out in a sweat. To think you love me—that you call me Heart—that you called me up onstage. Sexy, baby.

Fun memory about your dad. "Killer arm!" He knew what you were made of.

You never said anything about playing sports. I was never much at sports, but Daddy trained a pretty awesome outfitter. I can run the river better than most men. When you get better, I'm taking you to Willow Creek, and we're going to raft. You can swim, right?

I'm glad you found a good memory of your mom. Hold on to it;

cherish it. More may come. Think about what I said. Maybe you'll be able to find a clean sheet of paper for her.

Amazing lyrics. I slipped them in my pillowcase. They make it tough to sleep.

I spent many a morning watching fish cut through rivers and streams. Nothing's more relaxing. I'm sure Cobain will help settle you down. Great name, btw.

I miss you, Dimples; miss hearing you sing. I can't stand not texting after shows or seeing you point at me and pat your heart. Hurry up. Find what you need because I'm dying here.

Counting the days until I see you again. Hoping we'll be one again.

Em

To: Emily Amherst
Geoff Morris
Friday, January 27, 2012, 5:19 p.m.

US

You post those pictures on Facebook for anyone to see, but I tell myself you do it for me. You like to tease the stalker, so you wind your hair up and wear it like a crown of strawberry diamonds because you feel me near you, my lips near the back of your neck, on the knobs of your spine, tracing up to your earlobe.

You're not the only one who can tease, Heart.

Great news on the job. Knew you'd land it if you got the chance. I cracked the door—you kicked it in.

Ordinarily, I'd drop everything and come help you set up the new house, but doctor says I gotta keep my space, and he's right. I've really pulled into myself lately, haven't even been talking to Yaz. I wish I could explain why I have to do this alone. I have to face my fears, stare them in the eyes until they blink. I can't do that if someone's holding my hand. Until I tell Death to play in traffic, I'm on my own.

Please don't take it personally when I don't show up with Yaz this evening. I'm not even in LA right now.

You got me thinking. New paper, right? So, I chat with Ninecore's sound engineer and tell him I need a day. He says, "No problem. We gotta lay down Jason and Yaz first anyway. That'll take the day. Back tomorrow?"

"Afternoon or evening, yeah," I tell him. Then, since Jason's not going anywhere, I grab the keys to his new car and tell him to bum rides off Hailey. Man, you see the two of them and you think, are they the next Yaz and Steph? Anyway, I get moving. Six hours later,

I'm back in Ralley, and my stomach's on fire. I'm nervous; I'm angry; I'm a fist without a face. I swallow it all, taste the iron and wonder when the results will come in on the maybe cancer.

Why Ralley? That's where Rotherman Hospital is. I sign myself in to see Barry and realize he's had no other visitors. The doctor hoists an eyebrow when he sees me. He remembers me. "I have to ask why you're here," he says.

I tell him new paper, and he doesn't get it. "I need to put things right," I say. He lets me in.

Barry's as big as ever, a buffalo of a man. When he sees me, he shakes his head. I figure he hates me, wants the handcuffs off so he can finish what he started at Mitch's. Instead, he sits across from me, shoulders slumped, eyes clear, and he says, "You saved my life, man."

He doesn't say, "I hate you," or "You stole my girl."

"How do you figure?" I say.

"I was out of control," he says. "Had my life together, I thought, but the PTSD, the injury, the pain pills, they snuck up on me. Ruined the greatest thing I ever had."

"Em," I say.

He doesn't stop talking. This is therapy for him. I'm the doctor all of a sudden, wanting to ask about his mother.

"You stepped up. You saved Em from me, and saved me from myself."

"Wasn't trying to."

"Doesn't matter. You did. Rotherman's been the best thing to happen to me since Em. They're treating me here, finding a better way to deal with the addictions."

I'm paraphrasing, but you get the idea. We talked for an hour. When I left, he shook my hand. "Take care of her," he says.

I still don't want you seeing him alone. But I see him differently now. I handed him a sheet of paper when I left. "What for?" he asks.

"Up to you," I say. "Write a new story."

He smiles. He gets it.

That's your super power, Heart. The power to make the unforgiveable forgivable.

I figure you're on a hot streak. I'm living on the high of how things went with Barry, and I call my mom. I've kept her number all these years, but never dialed. She answers, but I've got no words. Finally, she says, "Geoff?" There's hope in her voice. I say, "Yes," but that's all I get out. By now, my stomach's twisted, and I start to wretch.

I wanted to ask why she stole my money, potentially my education, my future. You've got a point, but I've been building up resentment for a decade. I can't bury that in an afternoon. What I should have said? "Be patient. Let's talk. How's your health?" But I can't call back, can't make my fingers dial her.

She never calls me back. That tells me what I need to know.

I thought, by now, she'd have seen my face somewhere, heard my music, maybe looked me up. If she had, she'd know, or at least suspect, I had money, and she'd be finding a way to weasel it out of me.

You're sweet to offer to handle my finances. Do this: name yourself my beneficiary, if that comes up. And don't put my mom's name anywhere near it. I'd rather the money rot in a coffin with me than for her to lay her skeletal fingers on it.

I'm done here. I was going to stay the night in a hotel, but I'm over Ralley. Too much history. I'll drive home after I write my next letter.

But this one hasn't been much about us, and it's supposed to be. You write me these long, beautiful letters. They wreck me, Em, to see you desperate for me. You have to know it goes both ways. Not being with you is eating at me too. I wish I could explain better, but now all I can give you is assurance. I'm not running. I'm not hiding anything. You're on my mind a million hours a day, and my heart breaks each second I cause you pain. But if you want me to come back changed, you gotta let me change.

Still no word on the biopsy. I'll let you know when I hear. I have to email my girlfriend. You'll excuse me.

Always,

Geoff

G

To: Emily Amherst
Geoff Morris
Friday, January 27, 2012, 5:31 p.m.

NOTHING

MEMORY FROM PHOENIX: Changed up the play order for the show. We headlined, something I asked Tony not to push for, but it was Ninecore's idea. I'm not comfortable having our name above Whisper or Gainsae or Token, but they wanted to do something different, something memorable. We play our set last, just after Whisper finishes. It was a nice moment. Alison stayed on stage while the rest of the band filed off. I came out and we did "Underbelly" while the roadies broke down Whisper's set up and readied our gear. By the time we were done, we moved straight into "Soul Eater."

We played three extra songs, right? Then, completely spent, we head backstage. They call us back for an encore, of course. We satisfy their demands, but when we go back, we figure the crowd will die out. Alison and I put our feet up. Jason and Nesmeth strip down (God knows why) and play poker with Yaz and Hailey. We're sitting for fifteen minutes, no lie, expecting the crowd to dissipate and quiet down. No such luck. Finally, Alison rubs her temples and says, "I've gotta killer headache. Get out there and shut them up." But it didn't work that way. They're chanting "Skin of My Teeth," a tune she and I put together. It got leaked online somehow, and now it's about as popular as "Underbelly." I tell Alison, "Only way they're shutting up is for both of us to go out." She sighs, and we're off. Nesmeth throws on some pants, and Jason figures his boxers are good enough. Long story longer, they loved it. Get this: After we play, Sterling's backstage, and he's thinking big. Wants Alison and me to put a couple more songs together, then back each other on our singles. That'd give us about six songs. Why? $$$. Ninecore wants to put out an LP. Tony and I look over the contract, and it's legit. Only problem? We'd have to tour to support it. A full year on the road. I tell him I need some time to think on it, but Alison's pen is getting itchy.

What do you think, Heart? You can work on the road. Would you be up for a year-long tour? I can't sign unless I know you'd be with me. I know you're worried about your dad, but the tour wouldn't get started for a while. You'd have some time. Think about it.

Glad you liked the lyrics. In continuing with the "nothing" tradition, here's a story you didn't want, but one that'll help me heal for the telling.

I've got this tattoo on my calf (you know the one), the woman trapped in the teardrop, hands pressed against the water like it's glass. I get compliments and questions on it more than my lyrics. My answer's the same, but never entirely true. Ophelia, trapped in her misery. Our song "Woman in the Water" is about that. They accept it and move on. But it's not Ophelia. It's my mother. It's my tear she's trapped in. She can't escape her misery, and I can't accept mine. We're linked forever in melancholy ink.

Fun trivia: The dragon circling my abs and arms, the one swallowing the mountain of gold? That's my mom, too.

I can't tell you how strange it was to hear her voice again. Bold, hopeful, terrified. She says my name, and I wonder how much she knows. My ulcer? My money? My newfound fame? The Grammy nods? If she knows, why hasn't she called? Why didn't she say anything other than my name? And why couldn't I say anything?

Always,

Geoff

To: Geoff Morris
Emily Amherst
Saturday, January 28, 2012, 7:22 a.m.

US

I'm curled up on my bed, hugging my pillow and wishing it was you. Is it possible to be homesick for a person? Every hour that passes, I fight the depression of this ordeal. My insecurity stabs at me like daggers every night. I've lost about eight pounds. Maybe I'm better for it.

I yearn for you. I hope that sounds poetic. Nothing, however, can match your magic "crown of strawberry diamonds." :) The photos I put on Facebook are for you. Besides you and the paparazzi, no one else is interested.

Funny you were in Ralley. So was I. Frankie helped me load the Yukon with what little I had left after the brawl. Barry smashed up the kitchen table and the couch. They were old when I got them. Not worth the repair. I walked out with a wingback chair, the bed, and some dishes.

Olivia had the place professionally cleaned, but I still found glass in the carpet, shards hiding under the kickboards in the kitchen. I shouldn't have survived. When you see how much blood is still on the carpet, there's only one conclusion: God saved me and gave me to you for safekeeping.

I can't believe you visited Barry. It makes an already good man better and reminds me why I fell in love with you in the first place. Revisiting this relationship from the ground level allowed me to reconnect with the heart of the man, not the star. I like Morris, but I love Geoff.

I'm surprised Barry was repentant and more surprised you were forgiving. I know you wanted to beat him, but look what beating got me. It took real strength for you to visit him. That's the man I see. I'm proud of you, and no worries about me making any further trips to see Barry. I've made my peace, offered the clean sheet of paper, then walked away on a breath of forgiveness. It'll take time for all the fear and bitterness to end. As long as I physically see the result of his rage, it'll sting.

I'm proud of you for calling your mom. No matter how much you resent her, you must still love her. Why else would you have a permanent reminder of her inked all over you? Give her another chance. You don't know how much your mother knows about Sideshow. You're only guessing. If you try again, and find out she's as bad as you say, you can walk away without regret. But you have to know for sure.

I'll travel with you wherever you go. Sign the deal with Alison as long as you promise I'm in the seat beside you.

I take my phone out every hour, think about calling or texting, but then put it back. I keep hoping I'll wake up in the middle of the night, and you'll be sitting next to me, staring, breathing over me, tinkering with my hair, whispering you're home and you're mine.

I won't look for you tonight, but you can't stop me from dreaming.

Only yours.

Em

To: Geoff Morris
Emily Amherst
Saturday, January 28, 2012, 6:30 p.m.

NOTHING

Last night, Yaz busted through the door two hours early. Guess he refused breaks during the recording session. He wanted to surprise Steph, instead he surprised me and Tripp. Steph had gone to the store for chocolate donuts. Said it was a thing between her and Yaz. TMI, you know? Anyway, he starts playing with Tripp for a bit and then looks at me. "You know Geoff's ballistic for you, yeah?"

I nodded.

"Trust him," he said.

Hard as it was to hear, to be reminded you love me from a distance, I took comfort in the fact that he believes in us.

When Steph got home, there was laughing and kissing and grabbing and other stuff. You get the point. I snatched up my purse and slipped out.

Ninecore called this morning. Got me logged into their system. When I got back to LA, I met up with one of their attorneys to sign papers. Still had all my stuff in the back of the Yukon. I knew you said you wanted me to make myself the beneficiary of your estate, but I thought you were blowing steam. He had me fill out insurance forms, co-agreement papers, and something to do with appointed beneficiary to all your past, present and future royalties. I signed signature cards for your banking, and they added me to all those accounts. But the kicker was having to sign your durable and medical power of attorney papers. I got sick. I'd done well not to think about your "maybe cancer." Now, it stared me square in the eyes. I already have to make decisions about Daddy's care. Thinking

I'll have to make the same decisions for you makes my stomach hurt. I'm starting to understand your ulcer in a way I never wanted to.

Promise you'll do everything in your power to get better. Promise no tour, no career, nothing rates above us, Geoff and Emily.

Anyway, Ninecore set me up with a sweet computer and gave me full access to merchandising for all their bands. I manage supplies, warehouse shipping, and ad space. Funny—I'm working so close with Hailey now. A lot of the merch has her stamp on it. I recognize her style. They've got her busy with all sorts of graphic design, not just web work. She creates; I sell.

By the time I finished with Ninecore, I took the rest of the day off to get my stuff into Mrs. Statzer's. She's the one who's renting me the house behind Yaz and Steph. Yaz made a couple calls, and Jason and Nesmeth showed up to help me assemble the bed and put things in order. Get this: Hailey even came by and helped do some cleaning. Maybe Jason's getting to her, but she seemed downright nice.

After lugging all my stuff back down to LA, once the guys had it unloaded, I couldn't get the image of Barry out of my mind. These things were heavy with memory, except the bed. Everything else had to go. So Yaz stuck it in their garage. Steph says she'll do a garage sale with it soon. I told her to keep whatever money she made from it. It's the least I can do for putting up with me for so long.

Daddy's got enough in his accounts for me to buy a few things for the house. I'll pay him back with my second check. The first is going to Mrs. Statzer. I want to spruce up the garage apartment a bit, maybe get a new bed for it, so you have a place to rest for a night or two.

Last night, I dreamed of sunrise on the mountain, an alabaster morning where the sun winks at you over the ridge, then slowly lifts itself to its place of honor. The morning air has a nip and the breeze whispers in your ears, "Come to me. See." I sat on a huge rock and reflected on the hike to this place. Then I woke. It wasn't a complete picture and won't be until you're sitting on the rock with me.

Tonight, I was restless. Still trying to get used to the new home, and I felt lonely after so many nights with Steph and Tripp. I missed our night in Vegas, our night in LA. I went for a walk on the beach. I ducked into this trendy little restaurant on the beach. They sell fish tacos, something I've always wanted to try. I sat at the bar. Seemed the right place for a lonely wanderer. Anyway, I ordered my food, and the barkeep smiled at me, a funny smile, you know, like he knows something. "Are you Emily?" he asked.

The paparazzi have been following me around for almost a week, but I'm not used to being recognized. It felt nice.

He rolled up his sleeve, and he had "Hate Breed" tattooed on his forearm. Can you imagine? He set me up at a quiet table in the back and asked me to sign a napkin. But he wanted me to sign it Emily Morris. I'm not making this up.

So here I am in Mrs. Statzer's house, my house, wishing I was on the mountain instead—wishing you were here, playing your Taylor and humming to me.

I keep staring at my dress, at the golden ticket for the Grammys. I'm counting the hours.

Here's my prayer for the day, "Clarity and peace, God. Discernment with our words. The hurt to be healed and the new to begin."

Dreaming of an alabaster morning with you.

—Em

To: Emily Amherst
Geoff Morris
Saturday, January 28, 2013, 9:12 p.m.

US

How'd we both end up in Ralley and not see each other? Not like it's a big city. It's no LA, no Seattle, no Phoenix.

You didn't ask, but I'll tell you.

Why I love Em: I love you because I've not slept with you. I love you because you said "No," and made me want to honor that. I love you because you've made me into someone better. You've not judged me for my countless failings. You poke and prod like a doctor, asking "does this hurt," and it does, but I know it's for the best. I love you, not because I want to, but because I have to. This is not a decision I've made, but one that's been made for me. And I couldn't be happier.

I'd like to promise you I'll never disappoint you or upset you. I'd like to promise life with me will be a bed of daisies. I'd like to promise you'll always be proud of me. But I can't make those promises, can't make those guarantees. You know me. I've hurt you too many times. I've twisted my words into weapons. I want to change, but Jennifer promised me she'd change. Look how that worked out. Promises like those are precursors to pain. I won't make those promises—I love you too much.

Please don't misunderstand. I can make better promises. I promise to always be with you, to come to your bed each night, to love you faithfully and truly until I die. I will not run from you like I ran from my family, not without cause, but I'd need a similar commitment from you.

This may sound contradictory. How can I promise I won't run

from you when we're in this terrible in-between of space and time right now? Aren't I running from you, insisting on two messages a day? Aren't I holding you at arm's length? As much as you may think I'm running, I'm not. I'm here in LA. I'm never more than a freeway away. If I ran, you'd never find me. Ask my mom.

Speaking of which, I called her again. Took an extra hit of the sludge before I dialed. I made up my mind; I'd lay all my cards on the table. Before I hung up, I'd tell her exactly what I thought of her. And I did. I told her she was a miserable woman who'd never be happy, who sought sorrow like sapphires, treasured turmoil like topaz. I had the whole thing written out (in lyrics, of course), and I laid it on her. Know what she says? "You're right."

We're quiet for a minute, and then she talks again. "Your father died two years ago."

It hits me like a missile, and I can't breathe. I'd suspected, of course, but it still hurts.

She follows that bomb with, "Christmas. Day after, actually. It's been over two years now. I thought you should know. A good son would know something like that."

I hung up on her. Didn't have a chance or the guts to ask her about the money from my uncle.

I stopped by to see Dad in Ridgehaven after I put my tracks down. Spent an hour with him. Wish I could give you good news, but he didn't seem very coherent. The pastor guy was there. Wanted to talk to me about forgiveness of all things. "Got a good handle on it," I tell him. "New paper."

He goes off about taking the clean paper. Like, it's no good if you don't take it. He dropped the J bomb, too. Probably figures, with my long hair and tattoos, I need to hear about Jesus. Why is it the more you look like Jesus, the more Christians think you need him? You'd be proud of me. I was polite.

He asked what I believed in.

Here's what I thought: I believe in pain. I believe we hurt the ones we love no matter how much we try not to. I believe I'm dangerous to myself and to the people around me. I believe I have some work to do, some changes to make. I believe in Em. I believe I can change for her.

"Do you believe in miracles?" he asks.

"Don't push it," I say.

Right now, an alabaster morning with you snuggled under my arm sounds pretty good.

I feel a little like I'm in a cocoon now.

Hope. I believe in that too.

Always.

Geoff

To: Emily Amherst
Geoff Morris
Saturday, January 28, 2012, 9:28 p.m.

NOTHING

While you're buying things for the garage apartment, look into fish tanks. I'm not promising anything, but Cobain could use a little more space. The fish has a place in my heart. Can't wait for you to meet him. You'll dig him too—just don't put him in a taco.

Crazy to hear about you in the restaurant. It's nice to be recognized, but uncomfortable. They want Morris, not Geoff. Hope that doesn't sound egotistical, but there it is.

Put my tracks down today. Had some good licks, some solid riffs. Nothing like Yaz, but I hold the rhythm. Did the first layer of vocals, but had to quit after that. Started spitting and coughing. Haven't had much to eat the last few days. Nothing goes well with blood. But I drink my sludge and take my meds like a good boy and eat whatever I can when I get a chance.

I'm struggling to think of what to say here.

I got a call after I laid down tracks. My biopsy came back.

Good news is it's operable.

Bad news is Doc was right.

Don't freak. Don't panic. This changes nothing. I talked to him about treatment. He's giving me some more pills to swallow for now, but he wants to get inside me and pull the stuff out. Soonest he can do it is Thursday. He thinks I should be fine until then.

More good news: Our date for the Grammys is still on. Two more days, baby.

All my love.

Geoff

To: Geoff Morris
Emily Amherst
Sunday, January 29, 2012, 10:50 a.m.

US

My mind's blank; I'm as incoherent as Daddy. I get how he must feel, a soul imprisoned in a shell of a body, banging on the walls, trying to escape. Shouting, screaming blood curdling screams no one hears.

I'm numb.

I'm surprised you had the doctor call me to talk through the results. It means a lot. Tells me you trust me and that you're terrified still.

He spoke to me for some time, made sure I understood his thinking on the surgery. Says the spot is "encapsulated," so it shouldn't be too hard to get it all. But the ulcers and lesions are pretty bad, especially near the esophagus. He said he'd fix those up when he grabbed the cancer.

I'm trying my best to be positive. We have a diagnosis, a treatment plan, and an agreement it will be taken care of. I have to be there when this goes down. Don't keep me away. I need to be there when you close your eyes and when you open them again, okay?

I never asked why you loved me because I was afraid you wouldn't be able to say or I wouldn't like what you said. But oh, how you spill words onto the page. Perfect words for perfect emotions. They took me to the mountain, lifted me from the rocks, and pulled me toward the alabaster sky.

I found Dad's Bible as I was boxing up stuff in Ralley. He had Isaiah 40:13 written on the inside cover. "They will soar on wings like eagles; they will run and not grow weary, they will walk and not be faint."

For a minute, I thought God borrowed your words. But then I realized it was the other way around. He gave you those words as a gift to me. You and I are brought together, not by chance but by plan, and we'll soar on wings like eagles, never growing weary, never fainting as long as we do it together and with Him. A little churchy for you, but I think you'll get it now.

And I don't need fancy promises from you. Only these: You will always love me, and we will always work through whatever roadblocks we find along the way.

I'm sorry about your father. I hope you're not feeling regret. I know you hadn't seen him in years, but I'm sure it's still tough.

I'd like you to give your mother one more chance, though it doesn't sound much like she deserves it. Let her explain. Let her do it without your temper slashing at her. If she doesn't have a good answer for you, you can move on without regret. If she does, you can open the lines of communication and forgiveness and healing.

I find this odd attachment you've developed with Daddy sweet. It thrills me thinking about the two men I love most being together. And to think you went because you wanted to, not because I dragged you along. I cherish how you call him Dad. It tells me you want to be part of my family. I want to ask what you talk to him about, but I'll let you two have your man talk, your secrets.

I believe in you too.

Every beat is yours.

Em

To: Geoff Morris
Emily Amherst
Sunday, January 29, 2012, 10:55 p.m.

NOTHING

You spoil me. The florist arrived and brought me a small basket of daisies. One can never have too many, IMHO. Not too big, simple. Pretty. Perfect.

Jason, the sweetie, called a security company and had a system installed. Apparently, he had a small mishap in the driveway with a gentleman and his camera. Long story short, the camera lost. :) He stormed into the house, called Tony's secretary, and told her he was giving me a housewarming present. Next thing I know: security system.

He must have talked to Hailey too, because she showed up with a pizza last night. She plopped herself on the couch, put her feet up, slapped the cushion next to her and said, "We gotta talk, Em."

We did, for several hours. The long and short of it is this: She asked for new paper. She gave me a satin-covered black box, gold letters on the top. Inside was the ring Mark gave me when he proposed. Gold rope with a ruby and two small diamonds. She'd kept it this whole time, debating whether to keep it or not. But she said it was time to start over. My forgiveness was more important to her than the ring.

I couldn't keep it. It was the last piece of Mark she had left. I told her to keep the ring. Mark would want her to have it, not me.

I know you're trying to get tracks laid for the record, but the Grammys are Tuesday. Try and rest your throat. Be kind to yourself. I gave Tony some green tea bags to give you. They're soothing. Drink some warm tea. Try to eat. I know cottage cheese is not your favorite, but it's good for you. This will all be over on Thursday, and we can start new in every aspect.

And you can tell Cobain he has a nice 20-gallon tank, complete with foliage, a Sponge Bob Square Pants pineapple house, and three buddies who can't wait to meet him. I feel sure I found the perfect "fancy goldfish lady" for him.

The house is mostly empty still. Haven't been in the mood to shop. Yaz let me go through some of the LPs you keep at their place. Pulled a few out to frame—your Beatles albums and, at Yaz's request, an old Monkees album. Whenever I think I have you figured out, you throw me another curveball.

I did see a chair at Marshals, a double-wide, over-stuffed recliner. It's got a nice ottoman. Wasn't sure if you thought $475 was too much for a chair and another $200 for the ottoman. :) Thoughts?

Before I go. Check out www.ninecore.com/shopbands. I got the site online about six this morning and linked it to the ticket sales page and all seventeen band pages, FB pages, and even Twitter. I sent an email blast to your fan club, and by three p.m. almost everything sold out. I've already re-ordered twice as much merchandise. With that much product, it should take two days to sell out. :)

Hailey had to step up the pace and get additional designs to the printers. Hope Ninecore likes my work. I'll talk to Sterling tomorrow about it.

This house is quiet, but the solitude is refreshing. Restful.

Tomorrow is Monday, and then it's MYDAY. :) Rest well, baby.

Missing you more every minute.

Emily

To: Emily Amherst
Geoff Morris
Monday, January 30, 2012, 12:19 a.m.

US

Funny how things change in a few days. I was ready for bed around nine but hadn't gotten your second message. I ended up waiting around for it, expecting it any minute. Usually, I'm still up at this hour, chatting with Alison about the show, hanging with fans backstage, watching Jason and Nesmeth make fools of themselves. Actually, since Hailey got to him, Jason's been pretty tame. Now, since I'm trying to be good and get my rest and my sleep, midnight seems late to me. Good news is it's Monday now. We see each other tomorrow.

Part of me wants to call Snide Doctor up and tell him how stupid he is to keep us apart like this. Another part says it's given us a chance to fall in love again, to rethink what we want to say before we say it. Strangely, I feel closer to you now than I ever did before. Absence makes the heart grow fonder, sure, but it makes being together so much sweeter.

If you were with me when I got the news, if you saw what it did to me, things would've been weird. I needed to hear it alone, needed to experience it, absorb it, without having to worry about losing my temper.

I took the call in the office at the studio. He said, "Cancer," and my legs went out, and I slipped to the floor. I was a hot mess. Instead of getting angry, instead of blaming, I found myself missing you, wishing you were there. I can't lash out at you anymore, Heart. It hurts too much.

Maybe I'm being overly optimistic, but the changing I needed to do, the cocoon I've built around myself—I'm thinking I'm ready to come out of my isolation.

I get what you say about Dad's Bible. I've heard the verse, something my uncle used to say. I visited Dad again today, and the pastor was there again. No J bomb this time. We talked about you. This new paper thing, this forgiveness—it's changed me. Staring at cancer, thinking what it could do if it doesn't go away, makes me wonder about the next step. What happens after if things don't go well? I don't like thinking about it, Heart, but I have to. Have I already lost my chance? You talk about Jesus, and here I am getting ready to meet him, and I'm not ready. I've blown it already, haven't I? I've done too much for him to forgive.

When I go in for surgery, you'll be there with me. You'll be the last thing I see when I close my eyes and, God willing, the first I see when I open them.

Still working on the Mom thing. Couldn't get up the strength to call her today. Instead, I sent her a message on Facebook. Figure it'd be best to stick to writing. Lessens my chances of lashing out. I asked her a simple question: "Why'd you do it?" I didn't specify "steal my college money" or "leave Dad" or "torment me." I'll let her guilt make the choice.

I miss you, Heart. I plan to keep myself busy today. Hope that time goes quickly.

One more day.

Geoff

G

To: Emily Amherst
Geoff Morris
Monday, January 30, 2012, 12:22 a.m.

NOTHING

I'm impressed. A twenty-gallon tank and friends? Cobain's as excited as a fish can get. We can't name the girl Courtney. How about Blevins? Alison would be honored, I'm sure. Cobain's been in studio with me, watching me work my magic, laying down about twenty tracks per song, harmonizing with myself, improving melody over melody. Feels a little overdone IMHO, but Sterling's pushing for the layered vocal tracks. "Your album has to be as good as your show," he says. "And since they can't see you, your voice has to paint the picture." I spent nearly eight hours in studio today. My throat's raw.

Not sure why you're surprised by the Monkees. They're some of my earliest musical influences. Dad used to listen to them and the Beatles while he drank his way through a case. I listened in my room, away from him and Mom, away from the shouting and slapping. Picked up a guitar fairly early on and plunked out their tunes best I could. Yaz and I will still throw down a little "Last Train to Clarksville" or "Daydream Believer" or "I'm a Believer." Sure, we bring an edge to it, but it helps. Reminds me of simpler times, when music was strong enough to drown out the chronic angers of my house.

I drank the tea you sent. It helps. Gargled with saltwater. Not fun, but keeps the swelling down. Gagged down some cottage cheese for dinner and then visited Dad. All in all, a very rock star evening.

Glad to hear you and Hailey worked things out. I know it was tough. Deep down, she's good. I'm telling you, she and Jason make each other better. Not sure how it works, but it does. I'm glad for it too. Jason needs some stability. Don't get me wrong, every rock band needs a healthy helping of crazy, but Nesmeth's got that covered.

Sterling's been coaching me on interacting with the media and fans so I can remain private but not come across as aloof or arrogant. It's a tough line to walk. He gives me homework—I have to read and respond to ten fan letters a day. Apparently, he tells me, I get hundreds. Yaz gets twice that, but who's counting. These are strangers, Heart. What do I have to say to them? But I take a few breaths, put on my positive face, and do it anyway. And there's something about it, a closeness you don't get onstage, a vulnerability. These people open up and tell you everything. In a sense, it's like reading the voice of my lyrics. Until he mentioned this, I hadn't realized I was getting fan mail. Ninecore pays someone to read and respond to most of them. Standard letters for most, but they hand-pick the ten I respond to.

As for the chair, it sounds great. A little pricey, but you get what you pay for, right? Wonder if it'll fit on the bus? If so, I say live large, snatch it up. Put it on my tab.

I got plans for Tuesday, and you're in them.

All love,

Geoff

To: Geoff Morris
Emily Amherst
Monday, January 30, 2012, 6:45 p.m.

NOTHING

What a day. The garage sale went better than I imagined. It might be because Yaz and Jason and Nesmeth spent the morning walking around shirtless signing all my old furniture. People couldn't pay enough for my old junk. Steph and I took fistfuls of money. Hundreds of people milled up and down the street. Paparazzi were in full force, which was cool because they were buying too.

I tried to put some money back in Yaz and Steph's pockets for their hospitality over the last few weeks, but they wouldn't have it. When I insisted, Yaz called the battered women's shelter. Their manager came down, and Yaz slipped them a fat stack of cash. Thousands of dollars. I shook my head. Why hadn't I thought of that? Now, the money can help other "Emilys."

I took the bit of money they saved for me (and your checkbook) and headed down to Ikea. I didn't go crazy. I'm not a big spender, but I wanted to be comfortable in my new place, and wanted you to be comfortable too, when you're ready to stop by and see me. Picked up a sleeper couch for the garage. Nesmeth grabbed what he called "the essentials": a television stand, some hooks for you to hang your gear, a few pieces of pop art. I half expected someone from HGTV to narrate the shopping experience.

Between the fish tank, couch, the chair and ottoman, and the television Nesmeth insists he's putting in, the garage is a bit crowded, but comfortable. I picked up a few mission tables from an antique store by the ocean and an awesome old pine rocker. Reminds me of my childhood in Tennessee. I filled out my kitchen with utensils and an eclectic mix of dishes from Target.

Jason and Hailey took a few hours out of their day to help me get everything set up. You should have seen the monstrous televisions Nesmeth brought in. I'm not sure what he spent on them, and he won't tell me, but I'm guessing Best Buy could open a new wing with what he spent on these things. Sixty-five inches, LED HD display, SmartTV, integrated Blu-ray, and a couple BOSE sound systems to go with it. "You want Geoff here, you gotta have bait," he says.

Hailey, Steph, and I spent most of the day cleaning up after them. Tripp followed Yaz around, "helping" him find the right cords to plug into the whole set-up. The first thing we watched? *Finding Nemo*. Felt good to sit down and put my feet up finally. Tripp sat on my lap the whole time, eyes wide as saucers.

Yaz's kindness got me thinking this morning. Ninecore's been very good to you, and you're sitting on a pile of cash. I was a little shocked when I checked your account. Even after you bought the Yukon, you still have six figures floating around and almost no expenses. You may want to consider charity, Dimples. Maybe help the battered women's shelter? I know you have the heart for it. You bought me a train ticket when you had no money. You've been covering Dad's bills (every time I ask about it at the hospital, they say it's been taken care of by an "anonymous donor"). Besides, whatever you give can be written off in taxes. It's a win-win. But it needs to be your decision. You already saved my life twice. Imagine how many more you can save.

Yaz and Nesmeth put up a volleyball net in their front yard. Don't know where they find the energy after the day we've had, but they're out there playing. Jason and Hailey too. Even Steph's in on the action. Wish I could play, but can't with the shoulders. I'm sitting with Tripp, watching the media and fans huddle around. Yaz calls them over. It's a pick-up game. Paparazzi take turns playing and snapping pictures. Yaz makes it very clear to them: hang out, have a good time, snap some pictures, but leave when he says, and never hound Steph or me again. They seem agreeable.

This is my family, now, Dimples. They're all here, batting a stupid white ball over a net, laughing and smiling, playing volleyball shirtless in the dead of winter. Only one missing is you.

Can't wait until tomorrow.

Em

To: Geoff Morris
Emily Amherst
Monday, January 30, 2012, 8:33 p.m.

US

I'm sitting on the new couch. The chain on the overhead fan clicks in rhythm with each rotation. Candles are lit around the room, and I'm balled up, holding your shirt. Burying my face in it and breathing deep. It's as close as I can get to you, your scent, the sweet cologne lingering on the material.

I'm re-reading your letters, trying to figure out how you string words together to make such perfect sentences. They drive me insane with longing—send electricity through my limbs.

"Part of me wants to call Snide Doctor up and tell him how stupid he is to keep us apart like this. Another part says it's given us a chance to fall in love again."

Took the words out of my mouth. You leave me speechless and breathless. You say you lash out in fear, but I say fear's not a mountain anymore. It's a trail by a stream we walk together. We walk on the stones now, instead of being crushed by them.

When I went shopping today, I thought very little about what I wanted. Every time I considered buying a couch, a chair, a set of dishes, even something as simple as a can opener, I asked "What would Geoff want? What's best for us?"

We'll travel together. I can't wait. But there will be times when we won't, times like now, when I sit alone and long for your slender fingers to wrap around mine, moments when all I have to cling to are your words. Spin me some words, Dimples. Make them burn in my heart.

In a month, you've completely turned my life inside out. Three months ago, I didn't believe in love at first sight. But then I was blind to what real love was. You waltzed into my life, found things in me no one's ever seen, ran your fingers over them like guitar strings, played them, and turned me into a song. That's why we work: You're the musician; I'm the instrument. Neither is whole without the other.

Every time you visit Daddy, he seems better. So do you. Healing happens in those quiet moments you spend with him in the hospital. Thank you, Dimples, for your selflessness.

I still worry it won't be enough to save him, though. His heart's getting weaker. He can hardly swallow on his own. When I visit, he seems farther away, and nothing I say can bring him back. My words aren't as strong as yours, I guess.

He'll be gone soon, and I'll need you when he leaves.

When he does, I know exactly where he'll go. And no one, including you, is too far out of the reach of Jesus. You said once that you didn't think Jesus would listen to you, but I'm proof that he has. We're proof. We're an answer to a prayer you never realized you prayed.

I keep dragging out my dress for tomorrow. I borrowed Steph's steamer and dropped the wrinkles from the train. I dress and undress and dress again, inspecting myself in the mirror, fiddling with my hair. I want tomorrow to be perfect, but perfection's always out of reach.

I hope I can sleep tonight, but I doubt I'll be able to. I've waited for this moment. Too many sleepless nights, restless days. But they end soon, when I feel your eyes walk up my body and meet mine. Tomorrow, my waiting ends.

Wholly yours.

Emily

From the Journal of: Geoff Morris

Tuesday, January 31, 2012, 7:19 a.m.

I get to Yaz's earlier than any man should be awake, but there he is, answering the door in pajama pants. His eyes are blurry and stubble shadows the tattoos on his head. "I hate mornings," he says.

"Me too."

He lets me in, and I smell coffee and eggs. My stomach immediately clenches, and I push down the nausea. Steph's in the kitchen, finishing up breakfast for me and Em. She's got a daisy on a tray—eggs, toast, coffee for Em, cottage cheese and strawberries for me. I give her a kiss on the cheek, and she grins. "Good to have you back."

"Like I never left," I say. I take the tray to Em's, and Steph unlocks the door.

I walk up the stairs and hear Em's voice. "Hello?" She's scared.

"Easy, Heart," I sing.

"Oh my gosh. Geoff?"

I'm outside her door. "You decent?"

"I'm not up yet. I'm still in my pajamas, no make-up. I haven't even brushed my teeth."

"Perfect," I say and open the door.

Her face is bright red. She's got the covers up to her neck. "I'm not presentable."

"I disagree." I pull the covers back and sit next to her, put the tray on her lap.

"What's all this?" She smiles.

"You get the good stuff; I get the nasty curdled milk."

She laughs. "It's not that bad."

"The strawberries are nice." I kiss her forehead and put my arm around her.

"I've dreamed about this," she says.

"A little better than letters?"

"Much."

I kiss her softly, and she snuggles into me as she eats. I hold her like that, eating my cottage cheese, even though it irritates my stomach.

"I was supposed to make myself beautiful before you saw me again."

"You did an excellent job," I say. I trace the scar on her face with my finger. Kiss her again. "This is how I wanted to see you, the real Em, before you got yourself 'Grammy'd' up."

She smiles again, her lips pulling thin. "You could have called."

"Where's the fun in that?"

We make small talk for a bit, cuddle, and eat. I want to pull her on top of me, to feel her weight on my body, but we've waited this long, and I worry, if I did, she wouldn't resist. I wouldn't resist. Instead, I kiss her forehead, hold her with all my strength.

"Spend the day with me?" she says. "The whole day?"

"You gotta believe I want nothing more," I say. "I have to be in studio at ten. Sound check and practice. Yaz has plans for our set."

She kisses me again, presses herself against me. "You can be late."

I want to be late. I want to be very late, but my stomach's fisting. The smell of eggs wrenches my esophagus. I gently pull away from her. She frowns. "What?"

I kiss her again. "We've waited this long, Heart. Let's not give in so easy."

She covers her face. "That's not what I was getting at. I just want to be with you."

I swallow water and wash down my pills. "I'm yours until 9:40."

I say. "And at six, you get Grammy Geoff."

She stretches and yawns. "Sounds great. Plans until then?"

"Don't know about you, but I could use a shower."

Emily Amherst's Journal

Tuesday, January 31, 2012, 8:10 a.m.

Geoff doesn't look good. His eyes are dark, his cheeks sunken. He's thinner, and I wonder how much he's had to eat over the last two weeks. Is the cancer that bad already, or has the agony of separation done this to him? Either way, I'm worried. He gets off the bed and slips into the shower. I lie down on the couch, listen to him sing, try to make out what song it is over the water.

Finished with the shower, he walks over to the dresser in the robe I bought him to pick out his clothes for the day.

"Feel better?" I ask.

He pulls me close and runs his fingers through my hair. He doesn't answer.

The clock ticks down to 9:30, and I watch as he sorts through his clothes. The robe hangs off his thin shoulders. His abs used to ripple, but they've thinned. I try not to worry about it. That's what tomorrow's for. Today's for enjoyment.

"How's this?" He pulls out a tank shirt and jeans.

"For the Grammys?" I laugh. "That's so you."

"Kind of what I was going for."

After he dresses, he pulls me into his arms. I kiss him hard and long, hold him close to me. "It's perfect." We hold hands, run our fingers together, explore the physicality we've missed the last week. We whisper the few words we find.

The alarm beeps, and my door opens. Yaz calls from downstairs, "Morris, let's ride, man."

Geoff kisses my head. "Be ready by four. I'll send a car. You good until then, Heart?"

I nod.

He gently kisses me and takes a little extra time to stare into my eyes.

"Love you, baby," I say.

"You better." He winks and stomps down the stairs. The door closes and the latch clicks. I sit and cry. Something is wrong, and it's not between us.

The day slips past, and I dress. The gown Geoff picked out fits perfectly, and I wonder how he managed. White chiffon with a pale-yellow bodice, no sleeves but enough back to cover the scars. "You were trying to make me feel better," I say as I spin, watching my reflection in the mirror.

My stomach knots, and for an instant, I think I understand how Geoff feels. Is it nerves or the nagging feeling he's not well? Lord, get us through this, and Thursday we'll be at the hospital. He promised.

There's a knock on the door, and when I open it, Sterling extends his arm. He's wearing a tux. "There's Ninecore's merchandising manager extraordinaire. May I show you to the car?"

"Aren't you the handsome one? One minute. I need my purse."

My oversized purse sits on the desk next to a manila folder with Geoff's important papers. I shouldn't need them, but something inside me insists I do. Must be my outfitter's instinct. I don't get these hunches often, but when I do, I listen. I slip the envelope into the purse and take Sterling's arm.

"Quite the purse," he says. "Must've been made in Texas. They do everything big down there."

I grin. "Geoff picked it out. Ordered it online. Said it was the only one that matched the dress. Besides, I don't think it looked as big on a computer screen."

"A man of particular taste," Sterling says. "Wouldn't have signed him otherwise."

The car Geoff sent is a limo, long and black and beautiful. Inside, Tony sits next to Steph. Tony wears a pressed tux and sports a clean shave for the night. "So people don't think I'm a musician," he says.

Steph laughs and smooths her dress. She's giddy the whole ride over. In the long line of limos outside Staples Center, she snaps pictures on her phone, texts Yaz, and updates Facebook and Twitter by the minute.

I'm too overwhelmed to worry about any of that. The lights, the limos, the cameras and media, the screaming fans, it all presses in on me until I can't breathe. For years, I've watched stars walk the red carpet, but television doesn't do it justice.

The night's streaked with long lines of lights. The air buzzes. Energy hums like swarms of bees. Flowers spring up from concrete.

Only Sterling seems unimpressed. He's been here before. Another night of business as usual for him. "I got your tickets, ladies. Here are your passes. You'll need these to get backstage with the boys. Keep them in your purse, if you have room." He grins at me.

Cameras flash like fireworks as we pull into the drive under. Sterling continues. "You look beautiful, ladies. Smile, wave, and don't say anything. Media will try all kinds of stunts to get you to pay attention. They've done their homework. They'll try to shock you. Focus on your men. Let them lead. I've coached them, and they know what to do. Nervous?"

I nod. "A little."

"Don't be. It's a first date, that's all."

Steph puts her arm around me and pulls me close. "Smile," she says. She holds her phone at arm's length and snaps some pictures. "Facebook!" she sings.

Her giddiness diffuses my nerves, and I finally feel ready to step out. The crowd roars as we step onto the carpet, but it's not for us. The cameras point to the opposite end of the carpet where Yaz and

Geoff wait for us.

Fans shriek for them, hold their hands out, pads of paper to sign. Yaz and Geoff oblige, sign and smile like they've been doing it for years. They talk with the fans, learn names, nod, throw rock fists and grins. They've chosen tuxes with tails, but neither wears a shirt. Instead, their bare chests peek out from under their coats.

They walk side by side down the carpet in their spit-shined shoes. Steph gives a playful cat roar. "Look at our men."

Geoff smiles at me, his beautiful teeth polished and bright. My heart soars. "Got you something," he says, and pulls a dainty chain from his pocket. On it, a small diamond heart hangs. "May I?" He reaches around my neck and latches the chain. "A heart for my Heart. Ready to meet the world, baby?"

"No," I say.

"Too bad." He pulls me down the carpet between the gauntlet of media and paparazzi. "We've dreamed of this moment for weeks. Let's enjoy it." He folds his fingers through mine and leads me. This is the dream every girl wishes for, a fairytale moment when the royal carpet is extended and onlookers hang on your every move.

"I need you," I say.

He stops and gives me his full attention. "I need you too."

A reporter whistles at Geoff, and he turns. "Five Grammy nominations. How's that feel?"

Despite his calm demeanor, his kiddish grin, I see his wariness, his fatigue. He's overwhelmed by the cameras, the people calling his name. He holds on to me, draws on my strength, my patience.

He smiles at the reporter. "Feels surreal."

Another reporter cuts over, a camera in Geoff's face. Two more are snapping my dress. "Who's the beauty, Morris?"

Geoff kisses my forehead. "This is Emily, my Heart." He wraps his arm around me tight and moves us through the crowd of reporters.

"How about a last name?"

"You'll dig it up soon enough," he says. "Everyone loves a little mystery."

His hand shakes. Is he angry? Nervous? Sick? He leans over, makes a show of whispering something romantic in my ear. Instead, he says, "Way too many people here."

I smile like he's said something dirty, smack his chest playfully. He's struggling, needs me, so I help best I can. This isn't about me meeting the world; it's about him surviving it.

The reporters eat up our "flirtatious" conversation as we press forward toward the entrance.

"You okay?" he asks.

"It's a bit much, isn't it?"

"You're doing great."

"You too, Dimples." I lean in, play the part of the flirt. I whisper in his ear, "It's a different kind of show, sweetie, but it's still a show. You know how to act; you know what to do. It's in you. And when it's done, there's us. Right?"

Geoff coughs. "We do what we have to." He coughs again. His hand squeezes mine.

I can't see for the flood of flashes. Fans scream Geoff's name, and press against the lines of security. He signs a few autographs. One girl grabs his neck and holds tight. I see his knees give and know he's weak. A security officer peels the girl loose, and Geoff waves. He blows it off, but he's shaky.

I know something's wrong. "Baby?"

He glances around. He knows I'm on to him.

"I need to sit," he says. We make our way up the carpet to a concrete bench, and Geoff sits. Security brings him a bottle of water, and he plays off the opportunity to sign autographs. He's good at his job. No one is the wiser. He scribbles his name on a napkin, cocks his head toward me, and gently nudges me with his shoulder. He's playful and happy, but hurting. "I've been dreaming again," he says. His voice is rough, and I wonder how hard he's practiced for tonight. "All my dreams begin and end with you."

We stand, and he wraps his arm around my waist.

Yaz and Steph move down the carpet, signing autographs, answering questions, enjoying the moment. Jason and Hailey walk arm-in-arm. He points and waves like a politician. Nesmeth moves slower than anyone, talking with each fan, leering over every woman. Tony has to move him along, break off conversations and quick kisses.

I can't get over the chaos among the fans, and I think for the first time, Geoff sees the impact. "This is crazy," he says.

Sterling leads the four of us to our seats inside the arena, third row from the front and four seats in. Jason and Nesmeth are behind us. Sting and his wife sit in front of us. Geoff's right; this whole thing is surreal, especially when he leans over and shakes Sting's hand. "You know him?" I ask.

"We talked a bit today," he says, as if he'd been chatting with the hot dog vendor down the road.

Dave Navarro and Dave Grohl make a point to stop by and congratulate Geoff on the album. I'm a little awestruck, as much by the stars as Geoff's place with them. Patrick Stump kisses my hand and tells Geoff, "Nice landing."

The crowd inside the arena shouts and chants "Sideshow." Geoff turns, looks up to the nosebleed section, and raises his rock fist. I'm nervous there are so many fans on the lower level. Even with tight security, it's scary.

I hold tight to my purse.

The lights go down, the music starts, and Geoff squeezes my hand. "You getting this? You feeling it? Grammys, Heart. It doesn't get bigger." He's like a kid at Christmas, and I'm happy to be a part of his dream come true.

I burst into laughter. "More than amazing. You deserve it, baby. No one's worked harder."

He squeezes my hand. "Enjoy this, Heart. It's for you as much as it is for me."

From the Journal of: Geoff Morris

Tuesday, January 31, 2012, 9:12 p.m.

Over half the night is gone. We've sat through performances ranging from pop to R&B to country. They hand out awards, and it occurs to me we might win. There's a chance I'll have to give a speech tonight. I hadn't bothered preparing anything. Somehow, even with the nominations, we felt like an afterthought. These other artists have been getting good press, great reviews, the entire year. We've had a month of relative success.

Em squeezes my hand, and I see Tony waving at me. Showtime. I stand, brush down my tux. Em strokes my cheek and smiles. I head backstage to change. My legs shake a bit as I walk, but I will them straight, strong. I swallow some more water and shed my tux. I'm glad to be out of it, glad to be back in my jeans, something a little more comfortable. I drop a thick chain around my neck with a heart like Em's.

Yaz hangs his guitar around his neck, double checks the tuning. We've got roadies for that now, but he doesn't trust them. He's a musical genius with a perfect ear. If I'm a little off, Yaz is the first one in my face.

Nesmeth jumps up and down, gets his blood flowing. Jason spins sticks, taps them on his thigh. The producer wants me on stage first, wants me to lay down the rhythm and have Yaz come in with the hook. But we've never played by producers' rules. I nod at Jason. "How many measures you want?"

"Give me eight," he says. "Got some licks I want to put down."

"Nesmeth, you take eight. Yaz, take four."

They nod, and I wonder if my legs will hold out that long.

We get the cue, and Jason heads out on stage. The producer shrugs. Eight measures later, Nesmeth lays down the fatty bass line. The crowd's in a frenzy. By the time Yaz comes out, it's hard to hear the music over the roar. I swallow some water, cough, and spit before I head out.

The light hits me like flames. It's hot on my face, and I'm instantly dizzy. I can't see the crowd; everything's stars and space. My ulcer flares and my legs slack, but I sing anyway. I've done this too many times. It's automatic. I reach for where the crowd should be, but don't feel anything. I'm starting to worry. It's like my church is burning before my eyes. Fear becomes real, and I grab the mic hard.

We have time for one song, but we were going to blend it into a second, have Dave Grohl come out and back me on "Soul Eater." I'm not sure I can even make it through "Hate Breed."

Yaz grabs my elbow. "You good?"

"I can't stand," I say. "Can't see."

My stomach fists; my entire body clenches. I need to throw up, but I won't, not here on stage. I try to stand, to walk offstage, but my legs aren't moving.

Stars and space.

I hear my name. The music, my music, my soul, devolves into discord and darkness.

Oh, God. Not now. Not here. Not like this.

"Geoff!"

I struggle to my knees. My stomach's on fire. I cough and spit. It's wet, and the sharp smell of iron nauseates me more. Someone pulls at my arms. I roll over on my back.

"Geoff!"

I reach a hand up. "Heart?"

Emily Amherst's Journal

Tuesday, January 31, 2012, 9:30 p.m.

I'm sitting on the edge of my seat, hung on the band's showmanship. My fingers clutch the chair in front of me, and my knees bounce. Geoff moves across the stage, but I can see his feet drag. The lights drain the color from his face.

Steph slips her arm under mine and grabs my hand. "I've never heard them this amazing. They're flawless."

Geoff's voice rasps, but it fits the song. Maybe the fans don't notice, but I do. Yaz breaks into his interlude, and Geoff's leg buckles like he's missed a stair. I stand up, gasp. Steph gets it now.

I drop the chain of my purse over my head and let the bag hang against my hip.

Geoff steps. His other leg folds, and he grabs the mic stand. He looks drunk, but I know better. Yaz steps up. Geoff claws at him, spins, falls.

Nesmeth steps in front of him, takes the lead.

Yaz isn't playing. Steph's on her feet. He looks for me, sets his guitar down.

I'm in the aisle, running. Tony and Sterling reach for me, but I squirm out of their hands and rush the stage. "Em, wait," they say.

Behind Nesmeth, Geoff finds his knees, bends over and spits blood. There's more than there should be, too much. Security lunges for me, but I twist out of their grip. Something rips. "I'm his girlfriend," I say, and show my pass, but by now, chaos has erupted. People flood the stage. Producers and musicians and fans. Security has their hands full sorting out the mess. Steph is beside me, holding up her pass and screaming, "Let us through!"

Sterling cuts his way through the masses to Geoff, pulls us along with him.

By now, there are paramedics on the scene. They're always close for big events like this. Security tries to clear space for them, but we, the crowd, we're not moving. Geoff lays on the floor, surrounded by the band, by Alison and Hailey, me and Steph, Sterling, and Tony. We're all here, all terrified, but none more so than me.

"He just fell," Yaz says. He puts a hand on my shoulder. "Just collapsed."

It's hard to see through my tears. I'm pleading, whispering, "God no, please. Please let him be okay."

Blood streaks Geoff's lips, his cheeks. His eyes are bloodshot, and his face is completely colorless.

I kiss his head, put my hand on his cheek. He's cold, and I can't find his pulse.

A paramedic slips an IV into the crook of his arm. He hands the bag to Yaz. "Hold this up." Yaz does. Another paramedic grabs a cold compress and puts it behind Geoff's head. "You awake?" he asks Geoff.

Geoff's eyes are open, but he's not talking. His voice is gone. My heart hollows. There's a hole inside me, an abyss that threatens to swallow me. I lean into him, hold his hand, shake like a child.

He blinks twice, looks distant. He reaches a hand to my cheek. He doesn't see the chaos around him, only me. "Heart?" he says.

Blood lines his fingers, smudges my face. I swallow back the tears. "Baby, I'm here."

The paramedic looks to me. "Any idea what we're dealing with here? Drugs?"

I can't speak. Instead, Yaz says, "Stomach cancer."

How can Yaz be so calm, so in control? My world is blowing up in front of my eyes, and Yaz's voice is a rock.

They put him on a gurney. One puts his fingers on Geoff's neck. "Pulse is gone."

My heart stops.

A paramedic calls for a helicopter. The other grabs paddles from a suitcase. "Clear." He presses the paddles to Geoff's bare chest. His back arches, but his eyes don't move. He makes no sound.

My stomach burns. I grab Geoff's arm. "Don't you dare leave me. Don't you dare, Geoff."

"Let them work," Steph says. She stands behind me, tries to pull me up.

"Is he?" Tony asks, but he can't finish the sentence. None of us can.

The paramedic hits him with the paddles again, then lowers a bag over Geoff's mouth and nose. He squeezes.

"Come on, Geoff," Steph whispers.

"Got something," the paramedic says. "Pulse is back."

"He's going to make it, right?" Jason asks.

"This is our fault," Nesmeth says. "We shouldn't have played Phoenix."

"Open your eyes, baby," I say. "Open them for me."

I hear the helicopter outside, and the paramedics lift Geoff to a gurney. I walk beside him, but Yaz grabs my elbow. "You can't go in the chopper."

"I'm not leaving him."

"Trust me," he says.

"Trust?" I shout. "He's dying, and you want me to trust you?"

Cameras flash as security presses the media back. Geoff's wheeled out the back, and Yaz won't let me pass. Steph takes me in her arms, and I break. I hold onto her, hoping my legs will stop shaking, hoping my tears will clear.

"Come on," Tony says. "I got us a car. Em, you have to come.

You've got the power of attorney."

"What?"

Sterling ushers us toward the back where a limo waits, doors open. "The paperwork Geoff signed. You have to make medical choices for him."

"No. I don't want to. Not like this."

"I'll help," Steph says. "We're here with you, Em. We'll do this together."

Outside, the media's a hot mess with blinking cameras and squawking mics. "What are your scars? Did Morris do that?"

It takes me a minute to figure out how they know about my scars, but then I realize the back of my dress ripped in the melee when Geoff fell. I can't process their questions; my mind and heart aren't here, but with Geoff.

I'm dizzy with the flashes. My stomach knots. Sterling pushes me gently. He puts his hands in front of the cameras. "Not now."

Tony sheds his tux jacket and drapes it over my back. "We'll have a statement when we know more. For now, please honor Morris's privacy."

"What was he taking?" a reporter asks.

I haven't seen Yaz move so quick since Barry. He snatches the man's camera and smashes it on the ground. He grabs the man by the throat and lifts him an inch off the ground. "Shut up!"

Terror fills Steph's eyes as she touches his shoulder. "Let him go, babe. Geoff's more important."

He listens to her, and the man he grabbed slinks back into the crowd.

Sterling helps me into the limo, and shock sets in, a panic in the shape of numbness. My tears have run dry. I've got none left. Somewhere between dry sobs, Sterling pulls a bottle of water from a cooler and pours it over my hands. He washes Geoff's blood from my fingers, from my cheek. I'm too frozen to move, to cry.

"He's dying," I whisper.

Yaz breaks. His chest heaves, and he sobs in heavy, gasping breaths.

"Don't let him die," Steph whispers. "Please, God."

To: Geoff Morris
Emily Amherst
Wednesday, February 1, 2012, 1:23 a.m.

I'm scared to death. We're worried about you, the way you collapsed. The doctors won't talk to us, won't let anyone see you, not even me. I showed them the power of attorney papers, but they didn't care.

Everyone's here. The guys, Sterling, Tony. Yaz had the doctors check Steph's arm. She was having trouble moving it. We got pretty messed-up in the excitement at the Grammys. When you went down, we rushed the stage, and security tried to stop us. I came out of it okay, but I think Steph's arm may be broken.

The guys are pacing the hallway. Nesmeth's got his hands in his pockets, head bowed. Jason calls Hailey every few minutes to tell her there's no news. Yaz is holding it together barely, but I can tell he's hurting. He's as scared as me. He keeps muttering, "He's my brother."

Sterling's freaked because I have blood on my clothes—your handprint in red on my beautiful white Grammy dress. Not much of a daisy anymore. Sterling keeps telling me to go home and change, but I'm not leaving until I hear something. Besides, the blood on my dress is the only part of you I have now.

It's hard waiting for news. Every time a doctor comes out, I ask about you. They say it's too early, but it's been hours.

I want to cry. I want to punch somebody. Can't decide which would make me feel better. Maybe both.

I still can't believe you had me sign all those papers, the power of attorney and beneficiary notice. Did you know this would happen?

Yaz and I take turns hovering around the doors to the OR.

When I got here, I told them about Dr. Remington diagnosing the cancer and referring you to Dr. Howall. Yaz said he heard a doctor say something about getting Howall down here ASAP.

It's early Monday morning, and you're wheeled into surgery a day before you're scheduled. It's like you planned this. Always the performer, aren't you? Everything's on your terms.

This has been the most horrific night of my life. You looked so sick. And then you fell, and I ran to you, and that stupid security guard grabbed me and ripped the perfect dress you picked out for me.

The news is all over the story. Longest commercial break in Grammy history, babe. Even dying, you still set records. I've been watching replays of your collapse all night. It's like a car chase. I know how it ends, and it hurts every time I see it, but I can't look away.

I'll write more later, baby. Doctor's coming.

Em

To: Geoff Morris
Emily Amherst
Wednesday, February 1, 2012, 5:30 a.m.

Dr. Remington showed up in the OR. He spent a lot of time with Howall and the other doctors. He came to me about 3:30 a.m. They got the bleeding stopped but not until after you'd lost two pints of blood. They're both shocked you made it as long as you did. The damage was far worse than they anticipated. Anyone else would have been laid up weeks ago, but you'd been pushing yourself like no one they've ever known.

They're moving ahead with the surgery they'd planned. No sense in waiting once they had you stabilized. Dr. Remington listed you in critical condition, and they've sedated you fully. No plans to bring you out for several days. If he's able to repair this tear, he wants you completely down. I'm not sure if I'm more worried about how long he wants you to rest or the doubt in his voice when he spoke of repairing the tear.

Good news is he got all the cancer. Even took a couple of lymph nodes to be sure the cancer hadn't spread.

He said three months' rest, no exceptions. No travel, no performing. I asked about studio work, and he said guitar and limited vocal. Nothing strenuous—and only for an hour or two each day. Your voice has been damaged, but you already know that. If you push yourself too hard, you'll lose it completely.

Dr. Remington says he likes to be optimistic, but the surgery is risky. He asked if I wanted to have him do it. Said there was a chance you may not make it. I had the same feeling when I signed the DNR for Daddy.

What would you want me to do? You could die if I make the

wrong choice. I listened to Remington talk about the odds, the aftermath, recovery time. I never wanted your life in my hands, only your hands in my life. This isn't a decision anyone should have to make, not for their father and not for their boyfriend. But I believe in you. You survived on your own from sixteen on. You're the strongest man I know. Who else could keep up the pace you have with the damage you've got inside?

You'd want me to say yes. You'd want to get better as fast as possible, no matter the risk. I understand you now. You can't lie down while life keeps moving forward. You don't slow down, not for me, not for cancer. You say you want to settle down, but you want to live life at light speed and pull me along with you.

You promised me US. You wouldn't wait for that either. Despite the risks, I said yes.

Here I am, baby, waiting, pacing, broken. My name was the last thing you uttered before you lost consciousness, and I have to believe it will be the first you speak when you wake.

While you sleep, dream about Willow Creek. Remember the Scripture in Daddy's Bible and how you'll be renewed. I'm clinging to my faith right now and praying to not grow faint or weary.

Geoff Morris, don't you dare die. I'll be the heart that beats for you.

All my love.

Emily

To: Geoff Morris
Emily Amherst
Wednesday, February 1, 2012, 6:20 p.m.

I haven't eaten since yesterday. Nesmeth brought me a cup of hot tea, but it was tough to finish. I think he still feels guilty for pushing you to play San Diego and Phoenix, so he's trying to make amends by taking care of me as much as I'll let him.

Steph ended up with a dislocated shoulder. Yaz fumes about it. She says it's better than getting trampled. It could have been worse, but I've seen Yaz when he's angry and scared. He nearly choked a reporter to death on the way to the limo. I'm telling you, Geoff, when you two get going, you can be terrifying. I think it's that passion your fans feel. Good to know you're on our side.

Before you got hurt, I knew your friends had good hearts. You wouldn't be so close if they didn't, but even Tony and Sterling are stepping up. Tony shared Steph's cab to make sure she got home okay and got the baby back from Mary. Sterling told me not to worry about work for now. Said he'd find someone else to fill in for a few days, but I want to work. Since I can't be with you every minute, I have to fill my hours somehow.

You went to surgery about 5:45 this morning, and the doctor came out at 4:20 this afternoon—almost eleven hours, baby. Dr. Remington said it was nasty. He patched the tear with some synthetic stuff, but there was more than one tear. He also looked at your esophagus. There was some scarring there and at the base of your throat. He scraped that, so you'll have a killer sore throat for a while, but it'll heal, and you'll be back to singing. The whole thing took so long, you needed two more pints of blood.

The doctor finally let me see you for a few minutes. You were sleeping. When I walked into the ICU, I wanted to pass out. There're tubes and cords, lines and bags snaking around you like Medusa's head. Your face is swollen and your eyes are taped shut. There's a mask over your nose, a tube down your throat, one monitor beeps with your heart, another hisses air into your lungs, and there's nothing, absolutely nothing I can do.

In case you couldn't hear me, I whispered "I love you, Dimples" in your ear. Please breathe on your own, Geoff. Please don't die. Hold on to us. I am.

The nurses only let me stay with you ten minutes. And they said I could only visit every two hours. I understand why, but that's not enough. Why are we always torn apart?

After they ran me out, I stood at the glass window watching your chest rise and fall, wishing I could breathe for you.

Yaz has been in to see you too. He wasn't happy about the ten-minute rule either, but at least he didn't choke any nurses. :)

This wasn't our dream, Geoff. You weren't supposed to get sick. We were supposed to be happy. I've been in enough hospitals, seen enough death to last a lifetime. I can't watch you die.

Sterling came in a couple hours ago. Brought me the envelopes from the Grammys. You won three. I know you hoped for all five, but three is an incredible accomplishment. You and Alison won for best duet. The other two are for album of the year and song of the year.

Sterling says Sideshow is the first band to win Grammys for a self-produced record. He put the statues in the garage apartment. Hailey's staying at Mrs. Statzer's and feeding Cobain and the other fish for you. It's nice to know she's there, watching out for us. I hate to admit it, but I'm glad you forced the issue with her. We'll never see eye to eye, but for now, we're at least on common ground.

I think she volunteered to watch the house so she didn't have to stay here at the hospital. It's too much for her, after watching Mark wither away. This time, there will be a happy ending.

I thought Yaz would be excited about the Grammys, but he hardly looked at the envelopes. He stares in at you and says, "Look what they cost." Steph calls him every hour or so to check on him, but I've never seen anyone so sad. If anyone understands how terrified I am, it's Yaz.

Your fans are piled outside. The hospital had to hire additional security, and the executives are insisting Dr. Remington and Ninecore make an official statement. Sterling said the doctor would address your health, and he'd address Ninecore's plans for studio work and spring tours.

He wants to talk about me too. Not sure why. I know you'd say no. You're crazy about keeping me under wraps, but they have pictures of my back. Sterling says it needs to be addressed, so people don't start to accuse you of battery. Damage control is a necessary evil of the business. They've set the announcements for tomorrow when Dr. Remington can better assess your condition.

Alison's here. She's decided to stay in LA until she knows if you'll be okay. She called her husband and talked to her daughter to let them know. Then, she brought me a ham and cheese sandwich. I love that girl.

Watching and waiting.

Em

To: Geoff Morris
Emily Amherst
Thursday, February 2, 2012, 10:45 a.m.

It was a long night. Up and down every two hours until the midnight nursing shift finally conceded and asked me to stay with you. When I touch your hand, your vitals go up. I spent the last half of the night with my head on your hand.

There's no movement. Your muscles are quiet. I've never seen you still. Even when you sleep, your finger taps a beat. You've gone through another bag of blood, but the nurse said that was normal.

Hailey came by sometime early this morning. She couldn't sleep at the house, so she texted me. I asked her if she'd bring my quilt off the foot of your bed, the one I had on Daddy last week. She did. We stood in the hall and talked for some time.

The website has been flooded with requests for the heart necklace you gave me. Hailey wants to add it to the mix of items to sell, even wants a shirt with a heart crying blood. I told her that was a bit much. She said the fans want our romance on their chest. I don't know. I'm not big on it. I was surprised when the paramedic gave me the chain from around your neck. It had a heart like mine. I cried. Anyway, I don't have the final say, but from the requests on the site demanding the necklace, sales could be incredible.

Hailey brought me a change of clothes. I'd been in this torn dress and Sterling's jacket for two days, so it feels good to change. The hospital staff allowed me to use their doctor's suite to shower and clean up. I can't tell you how happy I was to brush my teeth.

Sterling wants me to attend the announcement about you, I guess, to let the public know about what we've kept so private. I pray he'll use the same discretion he used when he signed you.

The nursing home called. Daddy's slipping. I've got to go there later today. This is killing me. I have to choose between the two of you. Daddy is dying, you're barely hanging on, and I'm stuck in the middle holding both of you, trying to pull you both back upright.

Sleep well, baby.

Em

Emily Amherst's Journal

Thursday, February 2, 2012, 11:30 a.m.

I'm standing next to Dr. Remington and Sterling. The hospital's set up a small platform in front of the building. I see what Geoff sees when he's on stage. The crowd is huge.

Yaz uses those long legs to step up on the platform next to me. "It'll be fine." He kisses my hand.

I smile, but don't feel any better. Nesmeth and Jason join us. They're huddled around me, brothers protecting a little sister from schoolyard bullies. Geoff would be proud. These men are my family now, our family.

Dr. Remington steps to the mic. "I'm Dr. Remington, personal physician for Geoff Morris. Morris began seeing me a number of weeks ago. And while I can't divulge great detail, I can say Morris suffers from a bleeding ulcer. I can confirm this directly relates to the incident Tuesday night. I want to make this point very clear. I've read speculation Mr. Morris was on some sort of drugs, or that he was drunk. Neither case is true. Mr. Morris is not currently, nor have I ever known him to, using illegal drugs. In the course of treatment over the last few days, I can state with accuracy and confidence that neither drugs nor alcohol played a part in what transpired Tuesday, nor have they contributed to his failing health.

"When he was brought in last night, he had significant blood loss due to internal bleeding. We immediately gave him more blood, and performed several surgical procedures to correct the problems. We were able to address his condition successfully, and Mr. Morris is now in ICU in critical but stable condition. We're optimistic Mr. Morris will make a full recovery, though the process of healing will take a matter of months."

My knees slacken, start to give. Yaz and Nesmeth grab my elbows to support me. Maybe it's exhaustion, fear, or both. I can hardly stand. "I got you," Yaz says.

Sterling steps to the mic. "Good morning, I'm Sterling Amundsten of Ninecore Records. Ninecore is a tight family. Sideshow hasn't been with us long, but they've worked their way into our hearts. We're honored and thrilled to have them on our label and as friends.

"In regard to the Overkill tour, tickets are on hold until Morris is back on his feet. Those who have pre-ordered tickets will be fully reimbursed if they wish, or they can exchange their tickets for any other concert featuring Ninecore artists. We take care of our family and our fans.

"Currently the tour, slated to begin in March, will be postponed until late May. Continue to visit our site for updates. Sideshow will move into the studio to produce the album you're demanding, and it'll be ready by the Overkill tour date.

"A few other points need to be made. Cedar Sinai is an amazing facility, and we're grateful for all they've done to accommodate us. However, we ask that you clear the premises so the hospital physicians and staff can care for the hundreds of patients entrusted to them. Ninecore has made arrangements for Whisper and Token to present a mini-concert tonight at Beach Front Park, free of charge, to honor Morris. We encourage you to attend. We'll offer updates on Morris through the evening, and in this way, we can honor Sideshow and Morris in a productive way.

"Lastly, I'd like to address some of the questions I've heard regarding Morris' girlfriend, Emily Amherst. I understand you want to speak directly to her, but I don't think it's in her best interest right now. She's been gracious enough to speak with me and has given me permission to speak on her behalf.

"We do this, in part, in the hopes that you'll respect her privacy. Morris is a private man and wanted to keep his relationship with her quiet to protect her from the media."

Yaz holds me harder. I don't want to hear what he has to say, but I'm glad I don't have to say it.

He clears his throat and speaks again. "By now, you've seen the pictures of her back taken in the skirmish last night. Many of you have speculated her wounds and scarring were something Morris had done to her. I can say with full authority this isn't the case. The scarring is a result of domestic violence. Her previous boyfriend, a user of both alcohol and drugs, attacked her. When she confided this to Morris, he immediately removed her from the situation to protect her. Their relationship grew from that time forward."

Yaz puts his arm around me.

Sterling continues. "We'll keep you posted as news develops. Now we ask that you go home. Allow the hospital to do its job uninterrupted. Thanks."

Jason jumps off the platform and lifts me down. Sterling, Yaz, and Dr. Remington are behind us, ushering us forward as the media snaps pictures and shouts questions. Yaz keeps me tight to him.

We're in the hospital less than a minute when my phone buzzes in my pocket. It's the nursing home. "Not now," I say.

Yaz answers the phone for me, talks for a minute. Finally, he says, "Em, you need to get down there." I sink to the floor. It's started.

Sideshow, Off and On

by Martin Stamos

Los Angeles Times

Friday, February 3, 2012

Beach Front Park—Ninecore Records artists Whisper and Token presented an open-air concert to honor Geoff Morris last night at Beach Front Park.

Officials at the park estimated the crowd was over 10,000.

Morris, hospitalized at Cedar Sinai after his collapse on stage at the Grammys, is listed in critical to fair condition.

Hospital doctors say Morris is progressing nicely. "He's young, in good shape, and fairly health conscious. We anticipate a quick and complete recovery," stated Dr. Louis Remington, Morris's physician.

After being airlifted to Cedar Sinai, Morris underwent surgery. Authorities state Morris suffered a huge blood loss. Doctors have used this as an opportunity to remind the community of the need for blood. Alison Blevins spoke about it as Whisper performed, as did Jerry Erickson of Token. Mobile blood banks were set up in the parking lot, and fans lined up outside to listen and donate.

Sideshow heads into the studio today to begin laying tracks for their new album. When asked how the band will produce an album without its front man, lead guitarist Yaz responded. "There's more to an album than vocals. We'll do all we can do without Geoff, and when he's better, he'll top it off."

To: Geoff Morris
Emily Amherst
Saturday, February 4, 2012, 10:20 a.m.

This last week has been more than I can handle. I'm pushing through on autopilot, but I feel like a pot dropped on a tile floor.

I got a call right after the news conference. I didn't get there in time. Daddy died without me. He slipped away quietly, the nurses said, minutes before I got there. I sat by his bed for a few hours. They gave me time, didn't rush the process of moving Daddy. Steph and Hailey came. Not sure I could have done it alone. They gave me the strength to get up again.

His will designated cremation. It killed me. I crumbled when they brought me the urn. I brought him up to Willow Creek. It's cold, but warming. The sun has melted most of the snow from the storm a few weeks ago. I wore my coat, and my breath still came out in smoke, but the sun was warm on my cheeks. Looks like winter's giving us a break.

I made my way to Moses Rock. Tough climb. Steep and overgrown. Had to grab saplings to pull myself up the incline. I shimmied up the old downed tree north of the path. It runs straight up to the boulder, jutting out from the mountain. It was beautiful. Quiet. The birds rustled, built nests, sang to each other. Made me miss your voice. The stream bubbled and ran carefree, bouncy, like you.

I'm sorry I had to leave. Alison promised she'd stay with you, and, of course, the guys have been at the hospital around the clock. But it's me who should be there, and I have to bury Daddy. I was starting to think life might work out, and then everything dumps down on me, and I'm not sure my legs are strong enough to stand.

"*But those who hope in the Lord will renew their strength. They will soar on wings like eagles; they will run and not grow weary, they will walk and not faint.*"

I've never needed God more than I need him now. I've never been more fatigued and exhausted and terrified and sick.

I'll come back soon, as soon as I take care of Daddy. I sent you daisies in case you woke before I got back. If I can't be there, at least you'll have something to remind you of me.

We've walked separate paths this month, and they were trails we needed to blaze. Now, the only path I want is the one that leads to your door.

I got a text from Alison. She said this woman showed up at the hospital claiming to be Karen Morris. She texted me her picture. She looks just like you. It has to be her. I'm hoping she's there for new paper. Might be good for you both.

I'll be there soon. I have to find the heart to let Daddy go.

Wake up soon. "You're a daisy if you do."

Only yours,

Em

To: Geoff Morris
Emily Amherst
Saturday, February 4, 2012, 8:26 p.m.

I got back to the hospital earlier than I expected. Thing is, I don't remember walking off the mountain or driving here. I remember rain starting, and I couldn't make myself open the canister with Daddy's remains. But with the rain comes the wind, and so I finally opened the urn. I held it over my head, turned the opening into the wind, then closed my eyes.

The wind rushed into the canister, whipped and tugged until I nearly dropped it. Years' worth of anger boiled out of me. I've never been one to get angry until you came along. It's a new emotion for me. But I stood there on Moses Rock, screaming, finally understanding your scream in the Yukon. Then I tossed Daddy's urn into the river below.

I knew life with you wouldn't be an easy road. The lifestyle, the media, the lies and demands of the business. But almost losing you like this wasn't part of the deal. I knew Daddy would die. I was prepared, not ready, but prepared.

But you have to get this, Geoff: Without you, I'm alone. I have no other family. Mom and Daddy are gone. Mother was an only child, and Daddy's sister died years ago. I'm an only child. You're the only thing I have.

You're my protector. I knew that from the start. You're possessive, jealous, but it's because you refuse to lose what you love. You understand how valuable they are because you didn't have much growing up. But, in the back of my mind, I still thought you'd flaunt me like you flaunt your songs. You haven't. You've kept me under your arm and pushed the world away. I understand that now.

We've fought this month. Had some pretty good arguments, partly because of our stubbornness and selfishness, but mostly because we speak the same words in different languages. Facebook has no inflection, no emotion. Words are easy to read, to hide behind, to misunderstand. But it gave us an outlet for vulnerability. Easier to type the words than to say them.

But our words are too valuable to keep on Facebook. From now on, we speak them.

Yaz hasn't left this whole time. And when I look around this darkened waiting room, he's balled up in the chair next to me.

When you get out of this mess, and I get you home to the garage apartment, I'm going to trust you'll do what's necessary to protect your health and your life, to protect us.

Karen came by the hospital again. Tony ran a background check to be sure she was your mom, but I knew the minute I saw her. Same eyes, same smile. I introduced myself to her, and she clasped my hands in hers and said nothing. I'm not sure she could. Her expression said it all. And I'll not ask. This, too, is your path to travel. You made the first move—she made the second. Now you have to find middle ground. You may not be able to repair your relationship, but forgiveness can't be given conditionally.

When I was a kid sitting in Sunday school, I never imagined my teacher's metaphor of new paper would change so many lives. I latched onto it as a do-over.

We've given each other new sheets, and now we write a new story.

They'll bring you out of the sedation slowly. We're all praying you'll wake up soon. I'm waiting here for you. Praying you'll come back. Don't leave me alone.

With all my heart.

Emily

From the Journal of: Geoff Morris

Sunday, February 5, 2012, 9:19 a.m.

Eyelids are heavy. It takes crazy energy to lift them, but I'm determined.

Lights stretch out like cotton. Fog hangs in the corners of the room. I try to put sensations together, try to make sense of where I am. Is this death? Doesn't seem much like heaven. Em says there's no pain in heaven, and I'm all kinds of messed up. Nerves are on fire. Everything feels swollen.

Not making it into heaven doesn't surprise me. I suppose this is the other place, then.

My eyes decide to work again, and I find I'm in a white room, machines beeping, floating voices, the smell of disinfectant.

I move my fingers, and beneath them, something smooth. Sheets.

My mouth's dry, my throat raging with pain.

I'm alive, then. A hospital. Where's Em?

I try to speak, but my jaw's locked. I struggle, work the muscles in my neck enough to turn my head toward the door.

Of course, a hospital.

I'm hot. The room's a microwave. I may burst into flames. "Nurse," I whisper. My throat lights on fire.

A girl in pink scrubs walks in. "You're awake now? Great. I'll let the doctor know." She's gone before I can say anything, and I'm alone again.

I figure someone should be here. Heart, at least. Maybe Yaz. They busy? Or they can't come in? If they're not here, I must be pretty bad. The cancer?

A man walks in, all olive skin and black hair, long, down to his shoulders. He's the Indian Fabio, this guy. Dr. Remington. I remember him. My mind's working again. Information's clicking.

"Mr. Morris. Glad to see you awake. How do you feel?"

"Hot," I say.

"I'll have the nurse take your temperature. You may have a slight fever. Not uncommon when you've been through what you've been through. Do you remember much?"

"Where's Heart?"

He scowls. "Same place it always is. Your heart was fine, Mr. Morris. It was your stomach that needed surgery."

"Where's Em?" I say.

He nods in understanding. If this guy's this dense, I need a new doctor. "I'll send her in. There are rules for visiting the ICU. One person at a time, no more than ten minutes."

"Move me out of ICU," I say. My voice, though burning, remembers how to talk. It's not about to stop.

"Let's check your temperature and give you time to wake up a little more fully."

"Send her in." I say. "She can fill me in on whatever you have to say."

He folds his arms. "Very well." He walks out. A few minutes later, Em walks in. She's smiling, but tears line her eyes.

"Heart," I say, and reach up to her cheek. My arm's about eighty pounds, but I reach up all the same.

She takes my hand and puts it on her cheek, then kisses my fingers. "You scared me so bad."

"Sorry," I say.

She laughs and sits next to me. "How long have you been awake?"

"Minutes. Weeks. Years. Don't know. Time's blurry."

"I can imagine." She kisses my hand again, then my forehead.

"How bad am I?"

"Well, I'd say you're pretty good for having nearly died in front of thousands of people."

"That bad?"

She fills me in on the night of the Grammys. Tells me about being airlifted, the emergency surgery, the four pints of blood. The cancer's gone. She says. "Your ulcer ruptured. You nearly bled to death."

I close my eyes, suddenly tired. "These things happen," I say.

"They're not supposed to."

Her touch feels good on my hand, and though I want to sleep, I want to stay awake for her.

A nurse comes in, waves some sort of magic wand over my forehead and declares I have a slight fever. She pulls my covers down a bit and walks out.

"Your mom's here," Em says.

My eyes open. "What?"

"Drove down from Ralley a couple days ago. Tony didn't want to let her in, but she's your mom. She had ID, proof, everything. We didn't have much say in the matter."

"I woke up and thought I was in hell. Then you came in and I thought it was heaven. Now, it's starting to sound like hell again."

"Give her a chance," Em says. "New paper. And this isn't heaven or hell."

"Probably wants to ask for money."

"Stop it."

"I'm tired," I tell her.

"You want me to go?"

"No. Stay with me. Need another nap."

"Make sure this one isn't as long."

When I wake up again, Yaz is there in all his tattooed glory.

"Hey," he says.

"How long you been here?"

"Since Sunday," he says.

"For real? Why?"

"Didn't want to miss you waking up."

"Em would have called."

"I had to keep your mom away."

I grin. "You use your karate on her?"

He stands in the corner near the window, leans against the wall, and folds his arms. "No. Hospital has rules about that kind of thing. Why? You want me to?"

"We'll give her a pass this time," I say. I'm feeling a little stronger, a little cooler. I pull my covers back up. "No television in here," I say. "What am I supposed to do to pass the time?"

"Make up lyrics for the new album. Something about ulcers and helicopters."

"Not happening," I say.

He crosses the room, sits next to me. "Had me scared out of my mind, man."

"Thanks," I tell him. "For everything at the Grammys. You get yourself into trouble choking that reporter?"

He laughs. "Can't believe Em told you. Turns out the paper he works for issued us a formal apology."

"They say anything about moving me out of here?"

"Tomorrow morning, if all goes well," he says. "Hailey's flirting with Dr. Remington, seeing if he'll move up the transfer to a step-down unit a bit sooner."

"At least she's using her powers for good. How's Jason feel about it?"

"It was his idea."

I laugh, and my stomach clenches. I wince and groan.

"Sorry, man."

"Laughter's supposed to heal. Don't worry about it."

Dr. Remington comes in to check on me again, and I'm nicer this time. "Maybe we can move you tonight," he says. "Your fever broke, and your vitals look good. How do you feel?"

"Better," I say. "Sore, but good."

He smiles, jots something in my chart, walks out.

Yaz runs his hands over his scalp. I've never seen him with so much hair. Must not have had a chance to shave recently. "Go home," I tell him. "You saw me wake up. I'll be here a few days. Get some rest."

"Steph would like that," he says.

"I bet she would."

"Want me to send your mom in or tell her you're sleeping?"

I sigh. "Send her in. Might as well get it over with."

He pats my shoulder. "Rest up, man. Get better. We have tracks to put down."

"I'll get on it tomorrow," I say.

He laughs and walks out.

My mom comes in minutes later. Aside from a little gray hair, she looks exactly like she did when I left ten years ago. She stares at me for a minute, clutches her purse like it's going to open on its own.

Em would want me to say something nice, would want me to give her new paper, but I'm not feeling particularly chatty or cheery. Instead, since I've got nothing to say to her, I say nothing at all.

She comes closer, gestures toward the chair. "May I?"

"Free country."

She rolls her eyes, bends over, and kisses my forehead. Her lips are cold, and it's awkward. I wish she hadn't done it, but she can't take it back. She sets her purse between her feet, takes my hand in hers, pretends to be a good mother, pretends to be worried.

"Why are you here?" I ask.

She sighs. "I guess I deserve that."

"Seriously," I say. "Ten years, you never bother to look me up. I fall down and you come running? You want to put a band-aid on my knee after all these years?" I taste venom in my words, but I'm too tired to turn it off.

"Please don't antagonize me. I had to take a week off work to come and see you. It wasn't easy, you know."

"I'm sorry my nearly dying has inconvenienced your work schedule. Maybe you should have stayed in Ralley. If you're looking for love, I'm fresh out."

"I can't expect you to love me again," she says, her hands still holding mine. She squeezes her feet together on her purse. She's done this all her life, and it surprises me I'd forgotten her nervous tendencies. "At least, not in the same way."

"Listen," I say, wishing I had water to drink, to moisten my dry mouth. "You saw me on television, figured I had money, right? Probably want to make sure you're in my will? Hoping I'd die?"

She takes her hands away, puts them in her lap. "Geoff Morris, stop it."

"You stole thousands of dollars from me, Mom. You ran Dad out of our lives, let me live on the street for two years. What am I supposed to think?"

"I didn't steal your college fund," she says. Her nervousness is gone, and she's in full Mom-mode, doling out misery like it's fries in a fast food joint.

"Then where'd it go?"

"I borrowed it," she said. "I had to get us set up. Your father wasn't safe. We needed a place to stay."

"Dad was a drunk, but he wasn't dangerous."

She gets quiet for a minute, stares at her hands. She opens her mouth, ready to say something, to find some way to stab me, but she says nothing. Her mouth hangs open for a minute before she snaps it shut. She picks up her purse and walks toward the hall. "I'll come back when you're in a better mood."

It hurts, but I speak louder. "As long as you're here, I won't be."

To: Geoff Morris
Emily Amherst
Sunday, February 5, 2012, 5:35 p.m.

I've loved your eyes since I saw them at the train station, but I don't think I understood exactly how beautiful they were, exactly how deeply green, until you opened them today. God has answered my prayers.

You've been a little cranky, but you've earned cranky for a bit. But this isn't a free pass for continued crankiness. :)

I know you hurt. Dr. Remington said you'd be sore for a couple of weeks. Says you need to be quiet so your voice heals and you can blow fans outta the water again.

The doctor's rules are set. Take it easy to allow your stomach to heal. Acting like a manic for a while can cost you your life. No sliding across the stage, jumping like a madman or screaming (i.e., the Yukon a couple weeks ago). Dr. says you'll heal fine if you behave. I trust you'll follow his orders.

He also said when you came in, you were dehydrated and showing signs of malnutrition. We're guessing you gave up eating when it became too painful. Good news is, it shouldn't hurt to eat anymore, if you eat right. I'm a decent cook. Once you're home, I'll fix you right up.

Poor Yaz finally went home. He and I have been here since Sunday. He stayed when I left to go to Daddy. You were sleeping when I lost Daddy. I haven't had time to mourn, and at this point, I'm not sure I can. It's weird. I should be sobbing, but instead, I'm rejoicing. Dad is gone—at peace—and you're "renewed." The loss of one, the rebirth of another.

Since I can only visit for short amounts of time, we can still

Facebook. Funny to have to message you when you're down the hall, but even in the step-down unit, Dr. Remington demands you're as quiet as possible.

I sneak down the hall every now and then and peek in the window of your room. I need to see you're awake. You're still groggy, still sleep a lot, but that's okay. I'd say you're about five years behind on sleep. :) Time to play catch up.

How about we dream together?

Since Nesmeth bought you that new iPad, I'm hoping you've read the emails I've written while you were away. I'm banking you have—at least for this dream.

Here's the dream. I'm Emily Morris, not Emily Amherst. We've got a wonderful marriage. You bought the little house and garage apartment from Mrs. Statzer because you know I'd never be comfortable in something huge. We've turned the garage apartment into a studio.

We made an awesome kitchen with room to cook perfect meals and space to feed the band. You let me paint the living room yellow, which was a stretch for you, but when I told you it reminded me of daisies, you reluctantly agreed. I promised it wouldn't be girly. (You know I'm not a girly girl).

I made it rustic with remnants of Willow Creek. You insisted on adding a large bathroom with a hot tub. Anyway, I've fixed you this wonderful meal of homemade baked chicken. And we eat on the deck. A nice breeze blows, and you clasp your bear-sized hand around my face, pull me to you, and kiss me. Your kiss is as amazing two years later as it was the first time you touched your lips to mine. I press my face against your ear and whisper, "Geoff, if you had a son what would you name him?"

You laugh and say something silly like Rosco. Then I say, what would you name a daughter? You say Taylor, like the guitar, like

Swift. You've always loved that name.

I say, "At least Taylor is a normal name. I could live with that. I think our little girl would like that name."

It takes a minute for you to figure out the game, but when you do, you get excited. A baby girl for you to love. Could you possibly share your love between two women?

Our daughter grows into a beautiful teenager, and we do our best to be good parents. But we're not perfect. We make decisions our Taylor misconstrues. None of them made to hurt her, only to help her. Still, she's a teenager. She only sees what her youthful, selfish eyes want to see. And though we've made mistakes, when we come to her as an adult to try and explain, she pushes us away. Our hearts tear, we're broken, and we wonder if we'll ever have another chance to share in our baby girl's life. We know why we made the decisions we made, but she won't allow us to speak. We step back and sacrifice so she can find her own way. It's a gamble but one we have to take.

How do you feel about that dream? Sad? Disturbed? Angry? Maybe you're still looking at your mom through the eyes of an angry youth.

Give her another chance to explain? If the explanation doesn't satisfy, fine. But she deserves it. If you could've seen her when she came out of your room, you'd understand. I don't know what you said to her, but she was crushed. I've never seen anyone so broken.

Please don't be mad at me for pushing this, for stepping in your "mess." I want you to heal, inside and out. The doctor fixed the scarring in your stomach and throat, but what about the emotional scars, the stripes on your soul? Only forgiveness can fix those.

If you're mad at me, imagine the hot tub. :)

Forever your Heart.

Emily

The Heart of the Sideshow

Melody Rolfs, *StoneRock* staff writer

Monday, February 6, 2012

Ninecore Records is used to doing things differently, to taking risks on unknowns. The company has had mixed results with their different approach to business, from the successful rehabilitation of Token front man Jerry Erickson, to the meteoric flameout of the now defunct punk-core band Thirstmonger. But even they are reeling after the last month.

Ninecore took another risk, this time on an ultra-talented but unproven and unsigned Southern California garage band, Sideshow. In the following weeks, the band went from a relative unknown to the hottest name in hard rock. The band's wild popularity reached a fever pitch when front man, Geoff Morris, collapsed on the stage at the Grammys.

From the first strum of their guitars, mystery has surrounded Sideshow, and the band appears to like it that way. On several occasions, Ninecore has denied reporters the opportunity to interview members of the band. They've limited the backstage access most record companies grant the media. While they've maintained a level of privacy for their other bands (three years ago, reports of Whisper singer Alison Blevin's pregnancy surfaced shortly after she had her daughter), they've gone beyond even their conservative measures with Sideshow. Many guess the secrets around the band are part of a PR ploy—a calculated effort to add mystique and mystery to an otherwise dark and talented band. Others assume there's a more nefarious reason—a twisted history the public isn't ready for.

Though Ninecore granted me exclusive access to their bands backstage on the Apocalypse Tour, even I had limited access to whom I could interview and what I asked. Each interview was preceded by a preliminary briefing by Ninecore representative, Sterling Amundsten.

I expected things to fizzle quickly, but have found there's more to Sideshow than haunting lyrics, chilling minor chords, and intoxicating angst. There's a new standard rising from this group of hometown boys, an expectation that music not only speak to people, but change them as well. Ironic for a band popularized by its hit "Hate Breed" to talk about the healing power of music, its ability to empower a disenfranchised generation with a voice calling, "We are not who you think we are." But this is exactly what they're doing.

In light of recent events, Ninecore's hand has been forced. The outcry from the media and fans for answers can't be ignored. True to form, Ninecore remains tight-lipped. They have, however, allowed me to tell the story they've fought so hard to keep out of public light. I expected a dark history of drug abuse, of alcoholism, maybe of molestation or embezzlement. Instead, I found a heart.

Emily Amherst, Geoff Morris' girlfriend, whom he calls "Heart," has been the best kept secret in music history, and now she speaks out.

SR: Thanks for sitting down with me for a few questions. I realize how hard this must be for you.

EA: I've never been one for the limelight. That's Geoff's thing.

SR: You know I have to ask. Why hasn't Morris talked about you?

EA: (She sighs and hesitates) Geoff's always been private. He works hard to draw a line between his work and his personal life.
SR: (I grin) Nice sidestep. Let me rephrase. He calls you Heart. Reason?
EA: He does. Geoff has a reason for everything. He's not one to take relationships lightly, and he told me from the beginning, he loved my heart. He says when he's away on tour, his heart's home with me.
SR: It's that simple?
EA: That simple.
SR: There's so much to ask and so little time. Let's back up. What can you tell me about Morris' collapse on stage?
EA: Not much, but Geoff wants to clear the record and make sure people understand it wasn't related to drugs or alcohol. He'd been dealing with a bleeding ulcer for several months. He was under treatment.
SR: An ulcer can make you collapse like that?
EA: It ruptured. He lost a lot of blood very quickly.
SR: We've heard rumors he has cancer. Can you verify?
EA: (she pauses) Not anymore.
SR: But he did?
EA: A very small tumor in his stomach, mostly from complications of his ulcer. But they were able to remove it when they brought him in after the Grammys. He's healing beautifully and eager to get back to work.
SR: I'd like to talk about the pictures of your back, if that's okay. Are you able to talk about it?
EA: I'd rather not, but I know I have to at some point,

so I might as well tell you.

SR: I appreciate your candor. I'll try to be sensitive. The scars seem pretty deep and pretty extensive. How bad are they exactly?

EA: (sighs, looks down at her hands. Her voice is soft, but determined) The scars run all over my back, up my neck, and some on my face. The ones on my face aren't as bad. They're healing, but the back is still sore, still tender.

SR: The Internet's on fire with rumors Morris did this to you. Can you speak to those rumors?

EA: It's hard not to take the rumors personally. I'm sure if Geoff heard them, he'd be pretty angry. But, I suppose, in the absence of information, people always assume the worst. Geoff had nothing to do with it.

SR: Amundsten said it was from a previous boyfriend?

EA: My last boyfriend was an ex-marine. He served two tours in Afghanistan. When he came home, he was different. He suffered from PTSD and fought hard to beat it. But, as is often the case, he decided to try to beat it with alcohol and drugs. The combination wasn't good, and he snapped. I was the target of the rage. The scarring (she pauses here and looks again at her hand, running her fingers over her yellow nail polish) came from a glass coffee table. He picked me up and threw me into it. (She pauses, quiet). He left me alive, but banged up. Once I told Geoff about it, he immediately got me out of the situation.

SR: You knew Geoff before this happened?

EA: Yes. We were old high school friends. Went to

UCLA together. We weren't close then, but we'd started talking again on Facebook when we heard a mutual friend was ill.

SR: Is it possible your boyfriend was jealous of you talking to Morris?

EA: It's possible, but you have to remember, this was before Sideshow signed with Ninecore. My ex-boyfriend and Geoff were friends in school. He needed help, and didn't get it in time.

SR: So Morris became your knight in shining armor?

EA: Yes.

SR: And Morris knew all this? He wanted to protect your privacy? Keep you out of the media eye so you didn't have to explain the scarring?

EA: Exactly. But I'm glad to finally talk about it, to get it off my chest. And I'm glad I can clear Geoff's name. I'm a little disappointed people would immediately assume he'd done it, and that I'd stayed with him after he had. They must think very little of us. One of the things I love about Geoff is he doesn't drink. He doesn't use drugs. And he'd never lay a hand on me.

SR: How can you say that when you know he's violent? He attacked someone in the crowd at one of his shows. The video's viral.

EA: That's the only time I've seen him do anything like it, and he wasn't attacking me, he was protecting me. My ex came to the show looking for me. I thought he'd be civil. I thought he'd be sober. I was wrong. He punched my lawyer and then came after me. Geoff wasn't in a blind rage; he was putting on his armor again. Can I ask you a question?

SR: Shoot.

EA: In your years of covering bands, have you ever met a group of guys more dedicated to each other and the ones they love than Sideshow? Have you ever seen their kind of loyalty and kindness? Have you ever seen anyone change their fans the way Sideshow has?

SR: I haven't.

EA: They may sing about anger and pain, but they also champion hope and healing. Want to know why they caught fire so fast? People are hurting. They feel Geoff's anger, but sense his kindness. They understand his pain, but they also latch on to his hope. That's what makes Sideshow so special. Their music heals.

When she leaves the room, I'm left with my notes and a weight in my heart. It's not hard to see what Morris is attracted to. Aside from being beautiful, Emily is strong, determined, and gentle. When Morris calls her his "heart," I have to believe he recognizes those qualities in her. In my short time with her, I start to realize she's the heart of Sideshow.

From the Journal of: Geoff Morris

Monday, February 6, 2012, 9:19 a.m.

The step-down unit's much nicer than the ICU. At least here I have a television, though I haven't turned it on since they brought me in late last night. I've been sleeping, thinking, catching up on Em's messages. She brought me a Bible. I've been reading it. Didn't know where to start, so I just open to random passages and read. Not much makes sense, but Em's good about breaking it down for me. Keeps telling me to start in John and go from there.

I don't know much about the Bible, but here's what makes sense to me: I should be dead. I was reckless, and somehow, I've got another shot. Not sure I deserve one, but here it is. I resolve to make the most of it.

Nesmeth was smart enough to load up the iPad before giving it to me. It's got all our songs on it, and the entire Ninecore catalog of artists. It's enough to keep me busy and my mind off the incessant beeping and clamoring of nurses. Helps me ignore the needles they stick in me every few hours. "Just taking a little for lab work," they say. I figure they've taken so much blood, they might as well bring in a bucket instead of the stupid glass vials.

My mom comes in, her arms already folded and sits down. I'm surprised she came back after what I said, but she must have more misery to hand out. She stares at me for a bit. She's waiting for me to say something, for me to put the iPad down. She'll stare at me until I'm uncomfortable enough to break the silence. This is how she's always worked. In a decade, she hasn't changed her tactics, her subtle power plays.

I'm not a child anymore. I won't give her that satisfaction. If this is a game she wants to play, I'll show her I can win.

I glance up at her, raise an eyebrow.

She frowns.

The machines beep. Nurses walk by in the hall.

I pull a bird back in a slingshot and send it rocketing toward green pigs.

"I wasn't there when your father died," she says.

I want to say, "I win," but don't. I'm better than that. "You came down here hoping I wouldn't make it? You wanted to be here when I died so you could off shift your guilt? Sorry I couldn't die for you. Guess living has inconvenienced you again."

"You're as insufferable as your father," she says. "I know you hate me for leaving him. I wasn't the perfect mother, but I wanted what was best for you."

"Not having a dad, that was best for me? Stealing my college fund was best for me? You're going to have to help me follow your logic."

She stands up and paces, and it hits me—I get it from her. The posture, the head tilted toward the floor, the hand on the back of the neck, the other hand on the opposite shoulder. She's me before a show, the nerves, the excitement, the roiling stomach.

"If I talk, will you listen?" she asks.

"Not going anywhere."

"Take your headphones out, Geoff. You're not listening if those things are in. I swear, for going on about how grown up you are, you still act like a child."

"It's not enough for me to be in a hospital? You have to make me a little more miserable, don't you? You make me sicker than the runny eggs they serve for breakfast."

"That's enough!" She claps her hands together like I'm a dog that's wet the floor. "I'm trying to talk to you. How can I apologize if you won't listen?"

I take my headphones out. "Say again?"

"I'm sorry, Geoff. This is what I'm trying to say. Now, can I please apologize? I promise, if you still hate me, I'll go. But for the love of God, let me talk and listen to what I have to say."

A nurse comes in. She looks worried, like she ate the eggs. "Everything okay in here?"

"Splendid," I say.

The nurse moves out, her eyes on Mom.

Mom sits down again and folds her arms. "When I left your father, I made a decision not to say anything bad about him to you. I knew how much you loved him, and I knew the divorce crushed you. And I know when your uncle died, you felt lost. But I didn't want you to know how bad your father was. You needed a hero, and as drunk as he was, your father was all you had to look up to. I made up my mind not to talk bad about him. But there was very little good to say for him. The best thing he ever did was making you. And even with that, I did most of the work."

"Let's not talk about that," I say. "I'm sick enough as it is."

"You know what I mean." She brushes my hair out of my face. "It may be hard for you to believe, but I love you. I wanted to take care of you, give you everything you wanted. We needed the money to get on our feet, to support us until I got a job. I had to go back to school. I borrowed the money. It was a loan."

"A loan? You have to pay loans back. With interest."

"I did," she says.

"Yeah? So, where's all this money? I figure by now, after ten years of compound interest, it'd be somewhere around $150,000."

"I calculated at seven percent. $157,000 in your name at my bank in a protected account. Even I can't withdraw from it."

I blink.

"When you ran away, I had no idea where to find you."

"How hard did you try?" I ask. "You know I finished school at Ralley High. You know I went to UCLA on scholarships. You could have called."

"I did," she says. "You never answered. And after you graduated UCLA, I never heard from you. You dropped off the map. Until recently."

"You're serious about the money?" I say.

She pulls her purse from between her feet and digs through until she finds a card. "Here's the bank information. I know you don't really need the money anymore, now that you're making so much from the band. But I wanted you to know."

I stare at the card. "$157,000?"

"A small price to pay for your forgiveness," she says. Her hand runs down my arm to my fingers. "You need to clip your nails," she says.

"You used to do that for me," I say.

She smiles. "Every week until you were eight. I tried to get you to do it yourself. You never wanted to."

I shrug. "Mondays, right? I looked forward to it."

"You'd watch these shows on television. They had some cartoon on around seven. You'd watch and laugh so hard, I nearly pulled your nails off several times."

"You used to yell at me," I say.

"I didn't want to hurt you."

I close my eyes. "How did Dad die?"

She's quiet for a minute. "I don't want to say anything bad about him."

"I need to know."

"Cirrhosis. Drank himself into the grave. You don't drink, do you?" she asks.

"Haven't touched alcohol in years."

"Drugs?"

"Whatever the doctors are giving me. Nothing illegal."

"How do you do it?" she asks. "I thought everything in rock and roll was drugs and alcohol and sex."

"Most of it is," I say. "Yaz settled down pretty early, and I settled down with him. I did the drinking thing, the drug thing in college. Experiments, really, parties and all. Then we graduated, and I didn't have many friends. Just Mark. He kept a level head. Found Jesus and all that. Kept me honest. When he moved to Seattle, I found Yaz—greatest guitarist on the planet. Married and even-keeled. They're my conscience. Besides, I never had the money for drugs."

She smiles. "So now that you do?"

"Heart would kill me," I say.

"She's a sweet girl." She puts her purse between her feet. She's planning on staying a while. For once, I don't want to rush her out. "You have plans with her?"

I shrug. "She's coming with me on tour," I say.

"Marriage?"

"Eventually," I say. "When we have time."

"You never have time," she says. "You have to make it."

I open my eyes and stare at her. She's a different woman.

"Didn't she used to date Mark?"

I nod.

"How is he?" she asks.

I sigh. "Died. A month ago. He got sick. That's when I contacted Em."

"Dead?" she asks. "How? He was so young."

"Some crazy neurological disease. Can't even pronounce it."

She holds my hand, runs her fingers over my nails. "How's Hailey?"

"Holding up. She's got herself a job at Ninecore and rides with us when we play. She and Jason have something going."

"Your drummer, right?"

"You've been reading the papers?"

She grins. "Have to pass the time somehow. I've been here for a few days."

"About that," I say. "Don't you live in Ralley? What do you do there that you can take so many days off?"

"I'm an architect. Started my own company. We're still small, but we do okay for ourselves."

I think of Em's messages. New sheets, dreams, the mountain. "You draft homes?"

"Partly. We do commercial buildings, too."

I turn the iPad off. "You want my forgiveness? You want to earn my trust?"

"Wouldn't have come here if I didn't."

I hold her hand. It's warmer than I remember, and I take a breath. I'm about to do something very romantic or very stupid. "Do me a favor?"

"Anything."

Emily Amherst's Journal

Monday, February 6, 2012, 12:00 p.m.

As I'm walking in to see Geoff, Karen comes out smiling. I'm stunned.

She hugs me. "Thank you, Emily." She moves on, her lips still tugged up into a grin.

Jason raises an eyebrow, and Nesmeth shrugs. Maybe Geoff's given her a new sheet. I want to ask, but I won't. He'll tell me if he wants me to know. This is the hard part of learning to trust.

He looks tired when I come in, but not angry, not irritated. I figure that's a victory. He's playing on his iPad, probably reading my messages. "Hey, Heart. How's my girl?" His smile looks lazy, but I know he's drained.

He still has a power over me. Weak as it is, his smile sends a rush of relief through me, and for the first time in weeks, I feel like things will be okay. "You sound hoarse," he says.

"I'm good." I touch his hand, and he pulls me toward him.

He's not nearly as strong as I remember, but any exertion means he's feeling better. He kisses my head, stares at my shirt. "You haven't changed since yesterday?"

"I told you I wouldn't leave."

"I'm fine, Heart. Go home. Shower. Eat. I'm not going anywhere."

"Are you saying I smell?"

He winks. "If the stink fits."

I laugh. "You're not exactly a bowl of lemons yourself."

He runs his fingers through my hair. "You're tired. You need sleep. You need to eat. You need to shower."

"Are you trying to get rid of me?"

"I'm trying to make sure I don't have to visit you in the hospital once I'm out. Take care of yourself. How can you take care of me if you're so tired and smelly?"

I smack his chest. "Enough with the smelly jokes. I'm getting a little offended."

He kisses my hand. "You need to laugh too."

My eyes burn, and I wonder if I'll cry. With so little sleep, my emotions are frayed.

"You can come back later tonight, if you want. For now, let me take care of you. I had something put together for you at the house."

Even from a hospital bed, he's in control, and I love it.

I kiss his forehead and promise I'll be back by eight. "Read my letters?"

"I will," he says.

I'm a little sad he hasn't read them already, but remind myself he's been busy recuperating, visiting, sleeping. I can't expect him to wake up and immediately read five days' worth of messages.

Nesmeth drives me home. It's a quiet drive. We're both too exhausted to speak. He stays long enough to see me get inside, and then heads back to the hospital.

"Hello?" Hailey calls from upstairs.

"It's me," I say.

"Don't come up here yet," she says.

I shake my head. If she's up there with Jason, I'll have to bleach the sheets. "Why not?"

"I'm not ready."

"For what? Geoff sent me home to shower and sleep."

"Got the message," she said. "Okay, I'm done. Come on up."

I take the stairs slowly, wondering exactly when my legs became so heavy. "What in the world are you doing up here, girl?"

I open the door to the room, and Hailey's grinning wide. On the bed, there's a pair of designer skinny jeans and a yellow chiffon shirt. "Is that my dress?" I ask.

"It was." She nods to the sewing machine. "Geoff's idea. He felt bad you wouldn't get a chance to wear it again, so he turned me loose with it. What do you think?"

I pick the shirt up, marvel at the flawless stitching, but more so, at Hailey's eye for design, and her heart to do something like this for me, even if Geoff put her up to it. "It's beautiful," I say.

"He wanted you to have something special to wear tomorrow."

"Why? What's tomorrow?"

"He didn't tell you?"

"He's coming home, isn't he?" I ask.

She grins again. "I'll let you shower."

From the Journal of: Geoff Morris

Tuesday, February 7, 2012, 10:19 a.m.

It feels good to be out of the gown, and while black sweat pants and a plain white T-shirt don't exactly scream "rock star," it's the most comfortable thing I can wear. I sit in the wheelchair and Em pushes. "How many are there?" I ask.

"No more than a million," Yaz says.

Em smacks his arm. "Stop it. Don't scare him. There's maybe twenty. You're not as big a deal anymore since Ninecore shipped Jerry Erickson back to rehab."

She looks great in her shirt. Hailey did an incredible job on it. She took in the back a bit. It's a tight fit, accentuates her curves. "Sad about Jerry," I say. "We had some laughs."

Outside, the reporters line the sidewalk. Doctor Remington, walking on my other side, keeps his head down. He's quiet, not answering questions.

Yaz stares the reporters down, and they're careful not to crowd me. But they call from a few feet away while they snap pictures. "How's it feel to be out of the hospital?"

"Good," I say.

"Want to elaborate?" the camera asks.

"Nope."

"What are you plans now?" another asks.

"A bath and a nap."

"When will you be back in the studio?"

"When I'm better."

Em laughs at my responses. She leans over, whispers in my ear. "You know, if you gave them more than one word answers, they'd probably ask fewer questions."

She kisses my ear, and excitement and pain surge through my gut. I grin. "That'll make a great photo."

"I don't care," she says. "Let them put it on the front page."

Yaz makes a fist and his knuckles crack. Doctor Remington answers a few questions about my condition while Em and Yaz get me in the passenger seat of the Yukon. I've got to step up, and the exertion tires me. I feel like I've lost whatever muscle I'd put on in the last year. I lean the seat back and close my eyes. The camera flashes are giving me a headache.

Em pulls out of the lot and steers toward the house.

"You're not planning any coming-home parties or anything stupid like that, are you?" I ask Yaz.

"Steph wanted to," he says. "I roared her down."

Em laughs. "It was the other way around."

"Don't ruin my rep," Yaz says.

I laugh, and fire erupts along my stitches. Still, it feels good. Sunlight, fresh air—feels good.

When we get to Mrs. Statzer's house, Yaz helps me to the garage. Em opens the door, and I limp through. She's had it painted. Not sure when she had time to do that, but I like her choice of furniture. The bed's simple, but comfortable. Shelves line the west wall, and my Grammys welcome me home with golden stares. Already, they're dusty.

I sigh and sit on the couch.

Cobain swims with his friends in the new tank on top of a cherry wood dresser. Yaz kicks a stool over to me, and I put my feet up. Emily sits next to me. I slide my arm around her and grimace. "I was hoping to feel better for my homecoming," I say.

"You're here," she says. "That's all that matters.

My fingers trace her smooth skin from shoulder to elbow. "You did good," I say. "Apartment looks great."

Yaz winks. "I'm going to let you two settle in." He lets himself out, and before the door has finished closing, Em's kissing me.

I kiss her back hard, but the pain's too much, and I pull away. "I gotta lie down," I say.

She helps me to the bed. "You read my letters?"

I roll on my side. "I did."

"And?"

I'm quiet for a minute, searching for the words to say what my heart feels. "I never got to say good-bye."

She puts a hand on my shoulder. "I think he knew," she says.

"When I'm better," I say, "we're going up to Willow Creek."

Her hand loosens on my shoulder. I wonder if I've upset her. I can hear her breathing irregular, her chest searching for control over her lungs.

I take her hand, pull it over my ribs and under my arm. I put her hand gently on my stitches. "They opened me up. Shuffled my organs like a deck of cards. Cut a part of me out. When I woke up and read your letter, I felt like it all happened again."

She presses her face into my back. Her tears dampen the back of my shirt.

"I want it all to be over," she says. "No more drama. No more sick dads and estranged mothers and backstabbing friends and death and disease and surgeries and cars breaking down."

"It's over," I say. "All of it."

She takes a deep breath. "Then what's left?"

I say, "We are."

Epilogue

Of all the things I remember,
And all the things I forget,
I wish I could bury the memory,
And live with the rest.
—Geoff Morris and Alison Blevins, *Underbelly*

MESSAGE FROM GEOFF MORRIS
Tuesday, May 8, 2012, 12:32 p.m.

Barry,

It's weird to write to you, man. Not sure what to say. Congratulations on your release. Glad you're doing better.

I know this is awkward, so I'll get to the point. You know where I stand. I still hate you for what you did to Em. Not sure I'll ever be able to truly forgive you, but Em rides me about it. She's on me, telling me I need to give you new paper. And she's right.

Not sure if you've been following music news, but I had a bit of a scare while you were in Rotherman. Ruptured ulcer. Nasty stuff. I won't bore you with details. Here's the point: I got better—until I saw the bill.

Lucky for me, the band's hitting on all cylinders. We finished our new album which releases in a couple of months. We're still living large on the money we made from the Apocalypse Tour and our album sales and whatever we make from merch. Long story short, I can afford the bill.

But how many people can't? Em's dad passed. You should know that. He got sick and all the money he'd saved his entire life was eaten away with the care he needed at the end. How many people don't have money saved up for that kind of stuff?

I got to thinking about charity causes. Ninecore's on me about selecting a charity to support, but I can't choose. I had this idea. I ran it past Em and my mom and Hailey and Ninecore. Everyone's on board with this. We're going in together to start an NPO called "Music Heals." We'll pay medical bills for those who can't afford it. We'll raise money on tours, sell shirts, organize blood drives, you get the idea.

Here's where you come in. Em told me about the message you sent her. I'm not thrilled with it, but I get you're broke. We were friends once, man. I miss those days. I wish we could erase what's happened between us, but I can't. What I can do is offer you new paper.

I recognize PTSD is a disorder. But you've cleaned yourself up, and I respect that. If you're okay with it, Music Heals wants to take care of the bills from Rotherman. I know your VA stuff will pay some of it. We'll pick up what it doesn't, maybe get you a bit of cash to help you get set up again.

Wishing you the best,

Geoff

From the Journal of: Geoff Morris

Wednesday, May 23, 2012, 2:18 p.m.

Willow Creek's a whole different place in the spring. Dark clouds crowd the horizon. Sunlight punches through, but the mist coagulates into a simple rain. The stream swells, overruns its banks. Fish team in the water. The ground's covered in pine needles and patches of grass. The hike to the cabin's easier, too. Em holds my hand. "Slow down," she says.

"I've been slow for months. I'm ready to move."

"My legs aren't as long as yours. Not all of us are half stork."

I laugh. "Keep up, Heart." I pull her along, and her chest heaves from breathing. She's wearing her "Music Heals" shirt, the one Hailey designed. I've seen them around. I figure, if Hailey wants to use the heart crying blood, it should be for a good cause. I had her add in a treble clef and a few quarter notes to round out the design. These shirts sell for $30 on Ninecore's site, fifty percent of the profits going to the company Em helped me found. They're one of the top sellers.

It looks good on her, tight, flattering. Her hair's grown back, and she wears it long, down to her shoulders. "What's the big rush?" she asks.

"I want to say good-bye. And I want to see the cabin."

"Is it running from us?"

"No."

"Then slow down." She pulls me back to her, latches on to my neck, and kisses me hard. "Getting there's half the fun."

I pick her up and carry her. "This is what you wanted all along, isn't it?"

"Can't say I planned it, but I'm not going to turn it down."

She's light. Either I'm back to full strength, or she's lost weight, or both. "How'd we miss each other for so many years? How'd we not get together in high school or college?"

"We're together now," she says.

I smile and move forward up the hill until she tells me to stop. "This is the spot," she says.

I see the log she talked about in her letters. Below, the stream presses on, moving like it's late for the Grammys. I take a deep breath, turn around, survey the land. "This is it?"

She nods. "You need a minute alone?"

"No," I say. "I don't really know what to say."

"How about good-bye?"

"Too easy, and not enough." I think for a minute, take Em's hand, and say, "You weren't my only father, but you were the best one I knew."

Em squeezes my hand. The rain presses our clothes to our skin, drips from my hair.

"Miss you, Dad."

Em holds my arm, rests her head on my shoulder, then her breath catches.

"What?" I say. "A rainbow?"

"Better."

"Double rainbow?"

She laughs and smacks my arm. "The cabin." She points.

I look further up the hill. "Not too shabby. I had some friends fix it up."

"Fix it up?" Em breathes and takes off in a run. "It's amazing."

I catch up and lead her to the cabin. It's twice the size of the one she spent a week in. "I had them keep the original wood. They found similar timber for the expansion. Doesn't match exactly, but it's close. Furniture's all new, too."

Her hand's over her mouth as we move closer. "How'd you do this?"

I grin. "I'm a mysterious man, Heart." I put my arm around her, open the door. Daisy-print drapes cover the windows. The polished wood furniture matches the pine flooring. A television sits atop a pine stand. "Turns out my mom's an architect."

She runs her hand over the granite countertop. "She designed this?"

"She had help," I say, following behind her. The surprise on her face is intoxicating.

"This is too much," she says. "It must have cost a fortune."

I shrug. "I figured it was this or a couple kilos for some of my buddies."

She smacks me. "Don't even joke like that," she says. "How'd you get the money for this? I would have seen the money coming out of the account."

"My mom had an account set up for me with my college-fund money. I had Tony put some of my earnings in that account so I could surprise you."

"But this isn't ours. We never owned it."

"You do now," I say, and hand her the key.

Tears squeeze out of the corners of her eyes.

"Don't get too caught up in it now. We've got a tour to go on. Besides, this is our vacation home. We'll live in the Foothills when we're not on the road."

"We don't have a house in the Foothills," she says quietly.

"It'll be done by the time we're back from tour. It'll have a yellow living room like you wanted."

"I need to sit down," she says.

I help her to the couch, and she gawks at the cabin. "It's perfect,

Geoff. But we can't live together. Not until we're married."

"About that," I say, digging in my pocket. I take out the black box and kneel in front of her.

"No," she whispers. "Don't. Not if you don't mean it."

"Heart," I say, "I've never meant anything more than I mean this." I open the box.

Her hand shakes when she reaches for the ring.

I pull it back. "Don't," I say. "Not if you don't mean it."

She snatches the ring fast and slips it on her finger. She squeals and grabs my neck. She crawls onto my lap and buries her head into my neck.

I see our life together—life in the small cabin, church on Sundays wherever we may be. We'll travel the world, and always find home in each other's arms.

Her goodness, her heart, spreads across the sky for miles, always falling, always moving with the wind. With her in my arms, we are everywhere and nowhere, freezing and unfreezing, an unending cycle of love. Here, now, carried on the breeze, I hear and understand Heart's song.

About the Authors

In addition to being a loving father and husband, Aaron Gansky is an award-winning novelist, teacher, and podcast host. In 2009, he earned his MFA in Fiction at the prestigious Antioch University of Los Angeles, one of the top five low-residency writing schools in the nation. His first novel, *The Bargain* (2013, Lighthouse Publishing of the Carolinas) was a finalist for the Selah Award for debut novel. Two years later, *The Book of Things to Come* (2015, Brimstone Fiction), the first book in his *Hand of Adonai* YA fantasy series, won the Selah Award for YA fiction. The second book in the series, *The Blood Sword* (2016, Brimstone Fiction) also was a finalist for the Selah Award. His novel *Who is Harrison Sawyer* (2016, Lighthouse Publishing of the Carolinas) has met with critical acclaim. He has written two books on the craft of fiction: *Firsts in Fiction: First Lines* and *Write to Be Heard* (with Diane Sherlock). He also hosts a bi-weekly podcast on the craft of writing fiction, co-hosted by his father, author and novelist Alton Gansky.

Kaye Morrison is the pen name for best-selling author Cindy K. Sproles. She met Aaron Gansky in 2008 at a writer's conference where the two became fast friends. Cindy credits Gansky for helping her land her agent and launch her writing career. Sproles is married to her "prince," Tim, and they have four adult sons. She serves as the managing editor for Straight Street Books and SonRise Devotionals, imprints of Lighthouse Publishing of the Carolinas, and is the cofounder of Christian Devotions Ministries. Cindy is the author of two novels, *Mercy's Rain (Selah Finalist)* and *Liar's Winter*, both from *Kregel Publications*. She has coauthored one devotional, *He Said, She Said*, with ministry partner and friend, Eddie Jones, and a second devotional on her own, *New Sheets–Thirty Days to Refine You into the Woman You Can Be (Selah Finalist) (Lighthouse Publishing of the Carolinas)*. Cindy is included in the compilations *Spoken Moments*, *Christmas Moments*, and *Divine Moments books (Grace Publishing)*. She is a writing mentor and a life coach. Sproles has enjoyed the writing experience with Gansky, often saying, "It's quirky and fun, yet somewhat odd, to write a romance with someone the same age as your children. Aaron has become our fifth son."

Suggested Soundtrack

Thanks for reading Heart's Song. It was a fun book to put together with Kaye. We hope you loved the story. If you're a fan of good music, and you're wondering what types of bands influenced Sideshow, just know the primary influence was Gainsae, the band I was in for a number of years. Sadly, our music isn't available to the public. But there're plenty of great bands you can listen to when you're thinking of Geoff and Emily.

The first group of bands are secular, and many of them have songs with explicit lyrics. If you prefer a cleaner listen, check out the list of Christian bands below who still bring the heavy "Sideshow" sound with appropriate lyrics.

For the secular listener:

- Breaking Benjamin
- Brand New (their album Daisy was a huge influence on how I imagined Sideshow and Geoff).
- The Myriad
- A Perfect Circle
- Muse
- Nirvana
- Soundgarden
- Velvet Revolver

For the Christian listener:

- Chevelle
- Stavesacre
- Project 86

- Fold Zandura
- Skillet
- Pillar
- Decyfer Down

Enjoy!

29706228R00208

Made in the USA
San Bernardino, CA
18 March 2019